MIDLIFE NEWS

DRUID HEIR BOOK 3

N. Z. NASSER

HANORA SKY PRESS

Midlife News: Druid Heir Book 3
Copyright © N. Z. Nasser 2021
Published by Hanora Sky Press

eBook ISBN 978-1-915151-05-6
Paperback ISBN 978-1-915151-06-3

THE PLAYERS

Alisha Verma - Druid Heir
Ezra Neuhoff - Alisha's half-werewolf, half-wizard mentor
Echo - Alisha's leopard sidekick
Marina Ambrose - Alisha's best friend
Joshi Verma - Alisha's father
Sahil Verma - Alisha's brother
Alma - Joshi's neighbour
Orpheus Might - Vampire, Minister for History and the Today
Margola Silver - Selkie, Minister for Information
Gaia - Goddess of the Earth
Joe Dumfrey - Alisha's boss at the community centre
Fei Yen and Faeza - hu hsien, shapeshifting foxes
Pert, Mirabel, Nagma, Santiago, Marek and Farzad - Alisha's
night class students
Robert Jameson - Detective, Shadow Squad
Phinnaeous Shine - Shapeshifter, Prime Sorcerer
Gunnolf Zev - Werewolf, Minister for Justice
Maximillian, Dominic, Deirdra, Ruud, Rashida - Gunnolf's pack
Rayna Willowsun - Druid, Minister for Education,
Headmistress of Wildwoods School of the Wondrous
Lavinia Drach - Witch, Minister for Defence

Helio Woodwink - Fairy, Bestiary Minister
Erelim - Angel, Minister for Diplomacy
Cillian O'Meara - Leprechaun, Minister for Finance
Calypso Archer - The Custodian of the Celestial Library
Tielbu - a dragon
Flinar - a dark elf
The Ravenmaster

1

———

I trembled on the main rope bridge at Wildwoods in my silk gown. Goosebumps raced up my skin, not from the cool London night but from terror. I didn't want to leave the comfort of the towering oaks and fir trees. Not when the movers and shakers of the Otherworld waited for me inside the vaulted cabin.

Ezra tipped my chin up and scanned my glum face. He wore a tuxedo and looked like he'd walked off the pages of a romance novel. "It's a medal ceremony, not a funeral. Try and enjoy this. Your friends and family will be in there—"

"Yeah, and about a million other peculiars. Some with claws and fangs."

"Come now." He pulled me against his hard chest. "It's not that bad."

I liked being the centre of his world. Being the centre of attention in the Otherworld made me sick with nerves.

Echo nudged his head in between us. Leopards didn't like playing second fiddle to wolves. He'd been hunting in the rain, and his fur left a damp patch in the crotch area of my dress. "Alisha is right to be nervous. They will look at her like vultures eyeing up a piece of meat. Still, your grandmother

I

learned how to enjoy fame, and you will learn too. Fame is a route to accomplishing great things. Indeed, the lyrics of the song by the same are so apt that I have decided to adopt it as my personal anthem."

"Maybe you're right." I took a ragged breath and raised my hand to dry the damp patch. Being a druid with wind powers had its perks.

"You are lucky to have an adviser such as me," purred Echo. "Is it a good time to remind you to stock up on our freezer supply of sirloin steaks?"

"Don't push it. On paper, you're a Bengal cat. Shall we?" I hooked my hand through Ezra's arm, feeling like a jittery bride. The rope bridge was a physical impossibility in heels. Any woman worth her salt knew slippers were infinitely preferable.

We stepped towards the vaulted cabin, Echo padding at my side. The heavy arched door creaked open, though no hand touched it. Inside, a thousand lit pillar candles floated in the air, and a throng of peculiars—vampires, werewolves, druids, fairies, angels and elves—draped in finery stared at us before erupting into cheers.

The crowd parted as Phinnaeous Shine approached, resplendent in his flowing Wildwoods robes. His lips curved into a smile, but his eyes were cold. He still considered me an outsider, even after I'd passed my magical trial. Even after I'd animated a dragon and thwarted the will of rogue gods. Maybe he liked to keep women small. I'd heard the rumours about the succubi who worked in his home. My intuition told me he was one of those men who constantly worried about the size of his dangly bits or his wand. His posturing didn't bother me. I'd long since given up begging anyone to like me.

I kept my voice cool as the cheers subsided. "Good evening, Prime Sorcerer."

His silver-streaked afro gave him a distinguished look, together with pearly white teeth too perfect to be his. "Alisha

Verma, granddaughter of Rajika, when we met mere months ago, who knew you would be honoured in this way by the magical community?"

"She is of good stock," Echo purred as if I was in a breeding programme. His golden coat glimmered in the candlelight, and his chest puffed up with pride. Little wonder. He had pledged himself to my family line, and it wasn't every day a Verma received a medal of honour from Wildwoods School of the Wondrous. I wouldn't put it past him to burst into song in the middle of the ceremony. Maybe some Lionel Richie or Kool & The Gang.

"A rare talent," said Ezra, turning hooded grey eyes on me —bedroom eyes.

A shiver ran down my spine. "When the Information Minister rang to tell me, I had to ask her to repeat herself. I haven't won anything since coming third in the egg-and-spoon race at primary school. An evening in my honour really wasn't necessary."

"But it really was," said the Prime Sorcerer, dark eyes gleaming. "Nights like these hold many secrets. Your exploits have captured the imagination of humdrums across this city. A medal ceremony is as good a place as any for friends and foes to find common ground."

The crowd was growing impatient for a closer look at me. I could feel the hairs standing on end at my nape and in the shifting and pressing of the masses. Which foes was he talking about? Lavinia, who blamed me for derailing her attempt to crush the dark elves? Helio, the bestiary minister, who had longed for control over my dragon Tielbu? Or Gunnolf, Ezra's alpha, who complained I didn't know my place and I was a bad influence on Ezra?

"Follow me. It is time to lay the gold around your neck." Phinnaeous Shine's lips pressed together. He swivelled on his block heel, heading for the stage where the senate awaited:

nine peculiars of immense power and privilege, each with their own agendas.

Ezra gently uncurled my fingers from his hand. "You look beautiful. Go ahead. You have to do this bit alone."

"Everyone's watching," I hissed.

"It is better to be in the spotlight than in the gutter," said Echo.

Ezra put a hand on the small of my back and urged me forward. "Now go on."

I climbed the steps to the stage, quivering with nerves, and willed myself to see the audience naked as a distraction but found myself unnerved by the anatomy of magical beings. A spluttering sound came from the on-stage senate members. Judging by his mottled face, Orpheus the vampire had done his pesky mindreading trick again.

I frowned at him. *Stay out of my head.*

At the podium, Prime Sorcerer leaned into the microphone. His velvety voice boomed through the vaulted cabin. "We are here today to honour Alisha Verma, druid, dragon-raiser, god-challenger. There are those of you who argue that Alisha Verma broke one of the cardinal rules of the Otherworld by meddling with the gods. You would be right."

My legs turned to jelly.

Would I be arrested instead of honoured?

Would Justice Minister Gunnolf's pack drag me to the Court of Wolves in my dress?

The Prime Sorcerer milked the moment, relishing the murmurs from the crowd. My best friend Marina caught my eye and signalled to the fire exit. As if we could hightail it like Thelma and Louise. Dad's brow furrowed in worry. Echo tail swished back and forth, suddenly on the alert. Only Ezra stood relaxed, hands in his pocket, his expression not betraying any anxiety. He knew well how the Prime Sorcerer, true to his shapeshifting nature, liked us all to be putty in his hands.

Phinnaeous Shine rocked on his heels at the podium like a pastor finding his rhythm. "You could say that Alisha Verma is a maverick. You could say that she is a thorn in our sides. You could say that disobeying the rules of the Magical Constitution is a way to get yourself killed. But there is another reason why the senate decided to award the Wildwoods medal of honour to her." He paused. "She is an example to us all that an old dog can learn new tricks."

Charming.

At the rear of the stage, Orpheus rolled his eyes like he knew how tempted I was to send an *accidental* burst of wind to knock the Prime Sorcerer off his feet.

"Let Alisha Verma be the reason that ostracised peculiars submit themselves to the Wildwoods trial," said the Prime Sorcerer. "Let her be a reason why peculiars attempt ambitious feats." His eyes twinkled. "Although, please do yourself a favour and seek out the guidance of the appropriate senator."

The crowd laughed, clearly enjoying this public slap and tickle.

The most powerful peculiar in the Otherworld waved his hand with a flourish. "Alisha, please step forward."

I approached the podium, every nerve in my body tingling. Fireflies danced in an arch around us, a glittery cheerleading squad all their own, utterly at odds with my instinct to fight or flee. I forced the corners of my mouth to turn upwards like a constipated Cinderella.

The Prime Sorcerer plucked a firefly from the arch and smothered it in his fist. He opened his hand with a glint in his eye, revealing a medal threaded with a navy blue ribbon and stamped with the Wildwoods crest before placing it around my neck. "Alisha Verma, I award you the Wildwoods medal of honour. May you walk in the footsteps of the greatest peculiars through the ages."

The medal was heavy around my neck. I shook his hand,

not keen on the thought of harking back to the past. If my divorce had taught me one thing, it was to look forward. And to always beware of a man who refused to use a washing machine.

Deafening cheers filled the vaulted cabin up to the rafters, a surge of sound that made the flames from the floating candles dance above our heads. Dad, Marina, Ezra and Echo glowed with pride. I wished we'd made it far enough to embrace our identity as a magical family while Mum had been alive. Of course, my werepigeon brother wouldn't have been seen dead at an event to celebrate me.

The Prime Sorcerer murmured in my ear as cameras flashed. "Your grandmother, too, was sometimes too big for her boots. Maybe you'll learn now to fall in line. You are truly one of us now."

Sweet. He still thought of me as a little fish. I might have landed in a pool of sharks, but I was a badass in my own right. I could rescue myself from any situation, couldn't I? "Oh, I don't know, Prime Sorcerer. I think I was a humdrum for too long to fall in line completely. I enjoy my freedom of spirit too much. In fact, my favourite people are cut from the same mould."

He flushed at the intended insult.

The ability to deliver a polite burn was satisfying and so very British.

Orpheus stepped forward, his eyes lingering on the neckline of my dress where the medal had found a home. "I'll escort the wayward child down from the stage, Prime Sorcerer."

Pale, piano-player's hands cupped my elbow.

Gratitude flared in my belly. Orpheus and I weren't exactly friends, but he'd come through for me before. I also was pretty sure his adventure with my dragon had inspired him after a blip with depression. A dragon adventure was bound to give anyone a bounce in their step, even a vampire who had become bored with life.

"Congratulations, Alisha. From your internal monologue, I can tell that—like me—you don't enjoy the limelight." Orpheus's stern lips twitched. "Although, never fear. It's quite remarkable how quickly you are able to alienate people. You must teach me that trick."

I grinned. The cameras flashed as we walked down the steps in sync with one another. At the bottom of the stairs, Ezra bristled, although I had no idea why. Orpheus floated off into the crowd, too introverted to stay by my side as well-wishers swarmed me. I made a beeline for Dad and Marina, but I didn't manage to reach them. Grasping hands, shouts of congratulations, mobile phones held aloft in film mode, kisses pressed to my cheek, snatched conversations. Only Ezra and Echo managed to remain beside me, creating space for me with their bodies.

"Alisha, Alisha," called a sultry voice. "Just a few words for *The Otherworld News*?"

Ezra, in full bodyguard mode, groaned.

I looked over my shoulder and spotted Margola Silver, Minister for Information, clutching a dictaphone with a camera assistant in tow. A channel opened amongst the throng for them to catch up with me. I pushed on, anxious for air.

"Alisha! Our readers would love to get under your skin."

Well, that wasn't creepy. I swatted away a hairy hand from my medal. Ezra couldn't teleport in Wildwoods, but what I wouldn't have given to have my elf friend Flinar conjure up some of his black hole magic right now.

"As your adviser, I must tell you that it would be wise to give an interview. Control the narrative, as it were," Echo purred.

I gave an exasperated sigh. "You're not my adviser, Echo."

He growled. "Be like that."

"Okay, okay." I plastered a benign smile on my face and swivelled around to face her. Ezra had told me during a drinking game that Margola Silver was a selkie—a being capable of changing from a seal to a human by shedding their skin—but I wouldn't have known it to look at her. "Of course, Minister. I'm happy to answer a few questions."

Margola Silver had pale skin, flame-coloured hair and brown eyes framed with cat-eye glasses. She was perhaps thirty-five, but age was nothing but a number in the Otherworld. Her hourglass figure and pointy bosoms poured into an unforgiving satin dress the colour of the ocean reminded me of the golden age of Hollywood. The sort of woman that made both genders stare. Hell, you would have had to have been a lamppost not to fancy her. We hadn't had dealings before, but she had cast a yes vote for me after the trial. The Minister for Information was known for publishing the Otherworld newspaper, but as her formal title suggested, she had a murkier side. She was a whizz with computers and coding, and her role included surveillance of social media and private messages.

I would rather have told Vladimir Putin my secrets than her.

Margola's brown eyes danced with excitement. She held a manicured finger to her lips. "Shh. That's it. Quieten down everybody, or we'll not hear what the woman of the hour has to say."

Just like that, the writhing mass of bodies around us stopped being quite so grasping and stilled in anticipation. The cameraman with her, who on closer inspection appeared to be a fallen angel, shone a blinding light in our faces.

"She's tired. Five questions only," Ezra growled.

Margola flashed him a sultry smile. "I think the lady is perfectly capable of speaking for herself."

Ezra stiffened, Echo preened like a peacock, and I

clenched my arse cheeks together in case I let off a rogue anxiety fart at the worst possible moment.

"Tell our readership, Alisha. Who are you?" said Margola.

"I'm just a new peculiar finding my way," I said. "Pretty unexceptional apart from that."

Margola cocked her head. "To the contrary, in your recent past, your marriage combusted, your mother was murdered, and you animated a dragon. Not to mention befriending the dark elves, drinking tea with the goddess Gaia, visiting the Celestial Library, and somehow escaping with your life after you tussled with two gods." Her scathing laughter tinkled through the air. "I think we all want to be as unexceptional as you."

Ezra raised an eyebrow. "Are you going to ask a question?"

Margola swung to face the camera. *The Otherworld News* video segments had proven to be very popular in the past. "The wolf is very protective of the druid, although they have only known each other for a hot minute. But, dear viewers, I wasn't the only one to witness the chemistry between Alisha Verma and Orpheus Might tonight. The wolf could be in for a cold shower yet."

"What the hell?" said Ezra angrily.

Echo purred. "She is baiting you."

He wasn't wrong. The thought of Orpheus and Ezra fighting over me was quite frankly ridiculous. I reached for Ezra's hand to assure him who I wanted.

Margola thrust the dictaphone under my nose again. "Why did your marriage fail?"

I drew in a deep breath. There was no way I was airing my dirty linen in public. "No comment."

"Can you tell us about the circumstances surrounding your mother's death?"

"It's all in the police report."

Margola gave a disappointed sigh. "In the history of the

Otherworld, it has only happened once before that the senate vote following the magical trial of an initiate has split down the middle. Why do you think you inspired such division?"

The crowd buzzed with curiosity.

I would've liked to have known the answer myself. I could only guess that my late admission to the Otherworld meant I wasn't made in the same mould as others. I'd raised my head above the parapet once too often when I should have fallen in line. "You'd have to ask them. I guess I'm not everyone's cup of tea."

"That's very diplomatic of you," said Margola. "But you're not always a peace-lover, are you, Alisha? I'm sure many of us are wondering why you sided with the dark elves, even though infamous prisoner Meriel Naehorn killed your grandmother?"

That smarted. "I think you are confusing being peace-loving with standing up for what's right, Minister. How can one elf's crimes lead us to tarnish a whole community? Do I hate bees because one once stung me? Do I hate all men because my ex-husband was an arsehole?"

Margola looked into the camera and raised a sceptical eyebrow, and the murmurs of the crowd suggested she wasn't the only one. "If you say so." Her eyes sparked with mischief. "What do you say, Alisha Verma, to those who think you have been hyped up? That you are no better than the rest of us? That the medal of honour you received is more to do with who your grandmother was than who you are?"

Ezra scowled, his fingers clenching mine. "Time to wrap it up."

My stomach churned. "I can't influence what others think of me. I can only be myself."

She tossed her mane of red hair, shimmying closer. "I suspect you barely understand your powers. In fact, many would say that what you have achieved so far has been sheer blind luck."

My mouth went dry as the camera zoomed in on my face.

Echo let out a growl. "Blind luck? This is a Verma you are talking about. Let it be on record that you are all invited to a performance of Alisha's animation powers. She will animate the creature of your choice, picked by any peculiar in attendance. You will see. She is one of the most talented peculiars of the era."

Margola's pink-coated lips curved into a smile. "Perfect. There's nothing quite like a magic show. That will set to rest whether what we witnessed during your magical trial was a one-off or something more." She turned to the camera. "You heard it here first. Margola Silver, reporting for *The Otherworld News*."

The camera stopped recording, and the crowd around us dispersed, like Margola had singlehandedly pierced the bubble of illusion that I was anything special. I didn't know whether to be cheesed off or relieved.

I turned to the leopard. "What did you do?"

"A showboating druid isn't going to solve anything," said Ezra.

Echo's emerald eyes narrowed. "You have to give the crowd what they want, Alisha, or they will eat you alive."

2

———————

Ezra teleported us to the pack farmhouse in a swirl of monochrome and stolen breath. "Listen, hellfire. The pack are a solid bunch, but they're not always welcoming to strangers. Introducing you to them might not be plain sailing."

I shrugged, looking around in awe. "What families are easy? I think I can handle a bit of aggro."

The farmhouse stood on the outskirts of Windsor, surrounded by woods. It suited the wolves to live away from the city. Here, they responded to the call of the moon without provoking the suspicions of neighbours in packed London streets. The house itself was a sprawling building with white cladding, bordered by bright orange dahlias in the summer sun.

I tucked my arm into Ezra's. "It's beautiful. It's a shame your parents aren't buried here."

His Adam's apple bobbed in his throat. Even after all this time, it was hard for him to talk about them. "I begged for them to be here. Lavinia bartered for their bodies to lie in the witch cemetery. It was part of her deal with Gunnolf. That way, he got to raise me with the wolves. Lavinia got to keep my parents' bodies. In the end, all that matters is that they are together."

I chewed my lip. "Do you think Lavinia wanted your dad's body to find out the secret to teleporting?"

He frowned. "It's crossed my mind, but she's better than that. And he was family. She wouldn't desecrate his body. Power and family have always meant the world to her. But family a little bit more."

I wasn't so sure, but it wasn't my place to shatter his illusions about his aunt. I didn't trust Lavinia anymore—no doubt, she'd finish me off, given half the chance—but Ezra had to make up his own mind. Lavinia wasn't all bad, either. She had introduced me to the Wildwoods reading nook after all, and I'd never seen an older woman perform such incredible aerial acrobatics.

"Are you ready to meet the pack?" A vein throbbed in his neck like he was nervous too. "There are about fifteen minutes to show you around before the pack meeting."

Gunnolf had summoned Ezra back to the farmhouse to deal with pack business. I hadn't wanted to intrude, but Ezra figured bringing me along was perfect. I'd get to meet the pack, but I wouldn't be subjected to a lengthy grilling with a pack meeting scheduled. We'd keep it short and sweet. It had sounded like a decent plan, but now I wasn't so sure. For the second time that week, I wished I wasn't being paraded around. It would have been easier if I had Marina's extroverted nature or Echo's self-confidence, but I could only be myself.

My stomach fizzed with nerves. "Ready as I'll ever be."

He gripped my hand as we walked across the lawn and over the creaking deck. Judging by the state of it, the wolves weren't into DIY. The front door swung open.

Creatures with terrifying teeth and hulking strength didn't need locks.

A roomy kitchen was situated at the front of the house,

with a large picture window over the sink with a view of the woods. The kitchen was hardly a chef's dream. It smelt of overripe onions and sweat. Muddy pawprints marred the stone floor. Empty beer bottles stood on a wooden counter crying out for a coat of varnish. An old Aga burned in the corner, stacked next to a grubby fridge.

But it was the wolves that made my breath catch in my throat.

They sat around a long table in their human form and assessed us for a long moment as if nothing happened in this place without the alpha's say-so.

"At last, the errant wolf brings his girlfriend home to meet the pack," said Gunnolf, Ezra's paternal uncle and Minister for Justice.

"Who are you calling errant? My mission tally matches yours. There's a reason I'm your beta." Ezra smiled and pulled me forward with a flourish. "I want you to meet my girlfriend, Alisha Verma."

Gunnolf, a grizzled bear of a man with worker's hands and a smattering of white hair peppering his hairline, glowered. Many peculiars disapproved of relationships outside their own kind, and Gunnolf was a case in point.

He pinned Ezra down with a stare. His broad chest and coiled energy signalled he'd be a formidable wolf. "A beta should know better than to dip his wand in outside waters."

Ezra dipped his head to break eye contact while the rest of the pack shifted uncomfortably. "We've had this conversation."

Black eyes like flint. "So you know where I stand."

Ezra ignored him and pushed on regardless. "Alisha, you know the minister. Let me introduce you to the rest of the pack. Ruud's over there in the green T-shirt, Dominic's the bruiser next to him and Maximillian's the youngest of us all."

"We saw the latest broadcast from *The Otherworld News*." Maximillian's lip curled. "What did you do to get underneath

Margola's skin? We were expecting a puff piece after your medal. Not a grilling. Time of the month, maybe."

The brunette next to him elbowed him in the ribs.

I shrugged. "I didn't take it personally. Drama sells, I guess."

Ezra continued. "Deirdra's the one with the sharp elbows. She and Max are together. And Rashida, well…"

"Hello, my love." A copper-haired, flat-arsed werewolf sashayed over to us, taking her sweet time, and held out a delicate hand for me to shake. Then she pressed a kiss against Ezra's cheek, leaving a smudge of coral lipstick there. She tossed her fiery hair. "Have you been taking the druid to our old haunts?"

"I'm pretty sure a teleporting wolf has the pick from the globe," said Gunnolf.

I raised an eyebrow. Ezra could have warned me about her. She might as well have lifted a leg to mark her territory.

I'd only been inside for two minutes, and my female intuition told me the farmhouse was like a bed-hopping university dormitory. If I'd taken a match to the sexual chemistry between the wolves, the place would have gone up in flames.

Ezra ushered me over to the table and pulled out a seat for me next to Ruud. "Can I get anyone a coffee?"

Ruud gave me a sheepish smile.

I flashed him a smile in return. A silent welcome was better than a frosty one.

"Actually, now we're all here, we should press on," said Gunnolf.

Ezra glanced at him in surprise. "If you insist. Alisha can wait in my bedroom while we deal with the pack business."

Gunnolf pushed back his chair and prowled the room. "Sit down, nephew. Let the girl stay. I'd tell her to leave, but this will be common knowledge in the Otherworld by evening anyway."

Ezra took a seat sandwiched between Rashida and me. "Why are we here?"

In a heartbeat, Rashida draped herself all over him.

My side-eye left her in no doubt that her behaviour was unsisterly. She was welcome to make a tit of herself, though. I knew who Ezra was coming home with. He'd made it clear in bed last night.

"We're no closer to knowing the identity of the two dead wolves on pack land," said Gunnolf. "This morning, I found a third body less than a few hundred metres from where we're sitting. Killed the same way."

"Dammit." Ezra pushed the fawning Rashida away.

I gave her a winner's smile to rattle her.

"Three's a pattern, Gunnolf. What are we going to do about it?" said Ezra.

No one else had the balls to speak up. I understood why he was the beta of the pack.

"Until we find the culprit, no wolf in this pack runs alone," said Gunnolf.

The pack exchanged glum looks, but the alpha laid down the law. This family wasn't like my own, flawed as we were. Here, they just obeyed.

I cared about Ezra and wanted to understand his family. What had led to Gunnolf becoming alpha? Was it age, strength, alliances, wisdom or fate? Was Gunnolf a patriarch or a mini dictator? Ezra trusted him, so they had to be more to him than a grumpy old wolf.

"Dominic, will you do the honours?" said Gunnolf.

According to Ezra, Dominic was the strongest of the pack in both human and wolf form, a possible rival for beta. He stood up from the table in a display of bulging muscles and thumped Ezra's shoulder as he passed. A moment later, he returned with a wolf carcass slung over his shoulder. He flung it onto the kitchen table without ceremony, an unholy foul-smelling mess of blood, flesh and guts that somebody had once loved.

The pack didn't flinch.

I ignored Ezra's worried glance. Pathos sent a lump of tears to my throat, but I refused to show weakness. Not here, amongst seasoned predators. I'd killed before, of course, but a vampire didn't really count, given they were technically not alive. At least, that's what I told myself.

Ezra stood to take a closer look. "These were clean killings. Executions. We can send a team out to follow the scent, but we all know what happened last time. The best noses here failed to find the scent of a perpetrator."

I turned my eyes away from the poor wolf's limp body, raised my hand like a schoolgirl then dropped it. "Maybe Echo can help follow the scent. My friend Marina is a vet. She could do an autopsy."

Gunnolf's voice rumbled like distant thunder. "It's bad enough that you're here, druid. I don't need your silly suggestions. Leave your leopard protector and empath weirdo out of this. This isn't amateur hour."

He had called me *girl* and *silly* and had voted against me at my magical trial. I was tempted to launch a tornado at his arse. When someone showed their true colours, I'd learned to believe them the first time. Still, I wasn't a fool. Ezra was on my side, but I was surrounded by predators. I kept very quiet, channelling a silent assassin with her finger on the trigger.

Ezra kept his tone even. "She's my guest, Gunnolf."

The alpha scowled.

Ruud broke the awkward silence. He was the friendliest of the pack, the one who played mediator when there was a fight. "Let's stay on task. What if this is a real threat to us? We are only seven. It feels like there's a fight coming. Maybe it's a good time to swell the pack. There's plenty of options knocking at our door."

Gunnolf glared at me. "That's the druid's fault. Her exploits have brought more peculiars than ever out into the open. Old ones, who have been hiding for decades. Unskilled ones, who wouldn't know their tail from their snout. Young upstarts, with more brawn than brains, who have no sense of order and rules. We can do without them."

At the far end of the table, Deirdra, a brunette dressed head to toe in denim, shook her head. "I don't know, Gunnolf. More numbers might not be a bad idea. This is looking pretty hairy."

I could see her point. It wasn't every day that a family had a dead wolf on the kitchen table. I gagged. Hopefully, someone would give it a scrub with some anti-bacterial spray before serving their Sunday roast.

Gunnolf growled, moving behind her in a flash, intent sizzling in his predator's eyes. "Are you questioning my authority?"

Deirdra cowered. "I'm with you a hundred per cent. You know that."

"We shouldn't accept any riffraff into our pack, but we should keep an open mind if the right wolves come along," said Ezra.

"That's not your call. It's mine." Gunnolf pointed a thick finger at the dead wolf. "And right now, we should concentrate on the fight someone has brought to our doorstep. Make the change, wolves. Use your god-given noses to find the culprit of this heinous crime."

The pack reacted to his invitation like Pavlov's Dogs. Chairs fell against the stone floor, and they stripped out of their clothes, some discarding the clothing with abandon, others like Ruud choosing to neatly fold theirs in piles.

Only Ezra stopped to glance at me, yearning in the depths of his grey eyes.

I gave a small nick of my head. No way I was standing in between a wolf and his needs.

He discarded his clothes like the others, and then the bone breaking began, an eerie, inhuman sound that made me shudder. They turned into their wolves, panting and groaning as they did, but Ezra was silent as he endured the change, even as his bones stretched and his claws emerged. When he was his other self, he padded over to me, his charm necklace still around his neck, and put his wet nose in my palm. Then he turned, raised his copper-grey head and gave a mournful howl, and the pack responded, mimicking his cry.

I pressed myself up against the fridge, out of harm's way, and matched each person to their wolf. Burly Dominic had become an enormous tawny wolf. Maximillian was medium size, silver-white in colour, with piercing blue eyes. Deirdra's copper brown fur was the same shade as Ezra's, but she was smaller, with less lustrous fur. She was perhaps the runt of the litter, judging by her skittish eyes. Ruud was the smallest, a grey beast with rough fur and a white muzzle. It was Rashida who was the beauty, a red wolf with a snow-tipped tail. Not that I was going to be complimenting her anytime soon.

The pack sniffed the body of the dead wolf laid out on the table, pawing at him. Then Ezra raced out of the front door towards the woods with Dominic on his heels so fast they were a blur. The rest of the pack followed close behind—Maximillian followed by Rashida, Ruud, then Deirdra—howling with joy.

"Well, I hope you find the murderer."

Gunnolf smiled. "Clean up while you wait, will you?"

What a jerk. He didn't deserve an answer. As a teacher, I had plenty of practice doling out scathing looks.

I met his gaze and held it, gasping as he, too, transformed before my eyes.

He wanted me to be scared, but if things turned nasty, if all else failed and even Ezra turned against me, I could still save myself. I had my wits, I had the winds, I had a dragon and I even had a rooster. I would be fine.

His transformation wasn't painless. I could tell by how his arrogance dimmed, and he entered survival mode, rocked by the churning and breaking of his own body. The twisting of limbs and growing of thick silken black fur. Until all that was left was a beast who smelled of fire and earth, and the man had entirely gone.

Gunnolf leapt towards me, six-foot long and the stuff of nightmares: teeth and claws and so very strong.

I raised my hands in fright but also power. My hands tingled. *Just you try it,* I thought.

He spun around, seeming younger as a wolf than as a man, and bounded across the creaking deck to join his pack in the woods.

3

My job as an English night class teacher at the local community centre wasn't glamorous, but I loved it. Especially as a counterweight to the unpredictability of the Otherworld. Teaching was all about routine and building blocks. I knew my students' strengths and fears. Often, I even knew their personal lives. We were a close-knit family, which was why it surprised me when my manager Joe Dumfrey popped his bald head around the classroom door with some news.

"Joe, I didn't expect to see you here tonight," I said. He was a creature of habit. Usually, he would have been down the road devouring a dinner of cod, chips and mushy peas at the local café.

He bustled in, beaming from ear to ear. "Marilyn's pottery class is usually the centre's most popular class. That flyer of hers featuring Patrick Swayze and Demi Moore is savvy marketing. But you've managed to outdo her. You did get my email?"

I frowned. "I must have missed it. How many am I expecting tonight?"

Joe flashed me a nicotine-stained smile. If cholesterol didn't kill him, his dental bills would. "Twenty-seven."

"Jesus, Joe. That's short notice."

Worry lines marred his forehead. "You know our funding is tied to uptake."

I glanced at the wall clock. I didn't even have enough time to make a mad dash to the photocopier to prepare more materials. I sighed. I'd have to wing it. "Of course. I'll make it work."

He relaxed. "Oh, that's marvellous. Thanks for being such a good sport."

Five minutes later, my regular students filed in, jostled amongst faces I knew but couldn't place. The new students rushed to occupy the seats in the front rows, muscling out my regular students with sharp elbows, all politeness forgotten.

"There are plenty of seats, everyone. No need to fight over them."

My pleas fell on deaf ears. The family resemblance in the front row could not be denied: four slight bodies in heavy coats, with button noses and blond hair. In the second row, a group of raucous boys in their late teens clearly had no interest in learning. Behind them sat three men in dark clothes who would look more at home in midnight gambling dens than in my fluorescent classroom, judging by the pallor of their skin.

A buck-toothed boy of about sixteen years old wove through the desks and pushed a notebook under my nose. "Can I have an autograph?"

I frowned. "No, you can't. What's your name?"

His voice was like the tides, quiet and strong, with brown eyes as wide as saucers. "Pert Pailach."

"Take a seat, Pert." I turned my attention to the class. "Good evening, class. Welcome to English 101."

"Good evening, Ms Verma," chanted the class in eerie unison.

"We have lots of new students tonight. I assume you all came prepared with pen and paper?" I held up a blank sheet of paper. "Please tear out a sheet from your writing pads and fold it in half lengthways like this." I demonstrated. "Write your name in large lettering and prop it up on your desk so we can learn each other's names."

There was a flurry of activity as some newer students shared their equipment. I wrote my own name on the blackboard in capital letters, and as I turned back to face my students, a blonde girl in the front row whipped her hand back from my unzipped handbag. I always kept my handbag shut. A blush crept up her face as I stared at her, the gold tip of my lipstick clear to see in her palm.

I let it slide for a moment, not wanting to call her out in front of everyone. Humiliating her wouldn't help. I could deal with her thievery at the end of the lesson.

I gave a welcoming smile. "This isn't a normal class. We're here for learning, fun and support. We don't follow a strict curriculum, but you will find your English skills grow week by week. Here, you can expect to learn conversational and written skills in the English language, a smattering of culture and literature, and a few kickboxing skills if time allows. My night class is a special place, full of special people…" I grimaced, raising my voice a notch. "What are you doing? Put those away."

The raucous boys in the second row turned their backs on me. Phones aloft in selfie mode, they photographed themselves in the foreground doing the sign of the horns with me in the background.

"That is very rude," said Faeza, a long-term student and now friend. Not so long ago, I discovered she and her wife, Fei Yen, were shapeshifting foxes called *hu hsien*. They had facilitated my passage to the Celestial Library through their tarot deck and had saved my life at least twice.

"Sorry," said one of the boys, though he didn't sound sorry at all.

I gave a brisk nod of acknowledgement. At least there wasn't any chance of them posting to social media right now. "No phone use in the classroom. That includes you over there. Are you secretly filming this lesson?"

My senses were spinning like a weathervane in a storm. I didn't feel in control of my own classroom. I cursed Joe under my breath.

The door flew open, and in tumbled Mirabel. Mirabel, the fairy I had once rescued from a group of bullying werewolves at Wildwoods. Who had been in a tank with Kraglek, the octopus.

"Hi, Ms Verma." She gave me a cheery wave and bounded over to a spare seat.

My mouth fell open. "Mirabel? What are you doing here?"

"I applied online for a place in your night class," she said. "Sorry, I'm late."

The room spun, and I swept my eyes across the bodies crammed into it. There was no way my new influx of students could be from the Otherworld. That made no sense. Why would they even bother?

Pert put up his hand.

I forced myself to focus. "Yes, Pert."

"What's your favourite animal, Miss? My dad said it was a rooster, but I said it must be a leopard. But my gran said it must be a drago—"

The truth dawned on me.

My stomach heaved as I rushed to interrupt him. "A dragonfly? Yes, that's an option."

He opened his mouth again.

I raised my hand to stop him. My eyes darted to the three pale men, whose stillness set my teeth on edge. They couldn't be vampires, could they? Could the ephemeral family be hiding fairy wings underneath the jackets they had kept on in the summer heat? One of the raucous boys launched himself across his friend's desk, giving me a glimpse of a hairy expanse of back. My heart hammered in my throat—definitely a werewolf.

A shiver crawled up my spine.

This was a recipe for disaster. This class was supposed to be for humdrums learning English as a second language. Not for interlopers from the Otherworld. What the hell did they think they were doing there? I'd already fallen foul of the Magical Constitution once too often. How on earth was I supposed to get through the next hour without my humdrum students stumbling across the existence of peculiars?

I waggled my eyebrows at Fei Yen and Faeza. As long-term students of my class and members of the Otherworld, I'd need their help to get through the night.

They waggled their eyebrows back as if it was some kind of greeting.

I tried again, and Fei Yen added a thumbs-up to the eyebrow wagging. Clearly, they still deserved their place in the class.

I'd have to think of something else. The new students gawped at me like I was an exotic zoo animal. I was going to give Joe an earful about springing last-minute surprises on me.

I kept a close eye on the vampires, knowing full well that not all of them were as reliable in a room full of fresh meat as Orpheus. "With so many new students, the first thing we are going to do is a baseline assessment."

Nagma, a Bangladeshi woman in her mid-sixties, raised her hand. "Baseball is bad. It is not easy to play in a Punjabi suit."

I shook my head. "We're not playing baseball, Nagma. We're going to do a test to make sure our new students are in the right place."

"But we always play a game to start the new term," said Santiago, one of my Portuguese students.

"Not today," I said in a singsong voice, turning to the blackboard. "All you need is a pen and a piece of paper. That's it. Nothing to worry about. I'll write them up on the blackboard." I wrote five questions: *Write a sentence introducing yourself to a stranger. What are your favourite hobbies? Give directions from here to the bus station. Describe your ideal holiday. Tell me about your family.* I finished scribbling on the board and dusted the chalk off my hands before sitting at my desk. "You have ten minutes. Try for two sentences per question. Each question is worth two marks. One mark for vocabulary and one mark for grammar." I looked at my watch. "Write your name and desk number on your test. Then you may begin."

The vampires didn't even pick up a pen. The arseholes.

I gave a bright smile. "No test. No class."

They relented, scribbling so fast my eyes couldn't keep up with the progress of their pens across the pages before putting down their biros with an air of insolence.

The clock ticked on, and my sense of peril grew. Waves of nausea rose in my stomach.

"Okay. Pens down," I said when ten minutes had passed.

Students groaned. Papers rustled. A werewolf opened a copy of *The Otherworld News* with my face on the front.

I strode over to him and snatched it away with a glare before stuffing it in my handbag for Dad, who was sure to get a thrill out of seeing me in print. I had to get the Otherworld interlopers out of my class.

Fei Yen and Faeza gawped, finally wise to what was going on.

I collected the papers, hoping they had walked into the trap I had set. "I have to be honest. I wasn't expecting such a full class tonight. And I'm not sure all of you are here for the right reasons."

"I am," said Marek.

"I am," said Santiago.

"I am also," said Farzad.

"Well, of course, *you* are. I'm talking about the three of you there taking selfies. And you there, who secretly filmed me under the desk. And you, who stole my Lancôme lipstick from my bag. That's a cardinal offence, by the way. Fei Yen and Faeza, will you do the honours, delete the footage and retrieve my belongings?"

Faeza nodded. "With pleasure, Ms Verma."

Chinese culture valued respect, and my fox friends were very good at calling me Ms Verma in a classroom situation.

"Even though some of you have come here without the intention to learn, I am willing to give you the benefit of the doubt." I dug in my handbag for a packet of Hobnobs. "You can share these and talk quietly amongst yourselves while I mark these tests."

Suitably chastised, the students helped themselves to the biscuits. Even the vampires nibbled sheepishly while awaiting their fate. I rushed through the tests, not expecting perfection from my own students. After all, that was why there were in my class.

I handed the tests back with a circled number in the top right-hand corner. "If you scored six out of ten or under, please line up to the left of my desk. If you scored seven and above, please stand to the right of my desk."

One by one, the students separated into two lines. To the left stood my regular students, looking glum at their low scores. On the right-hand side, with the highest scores in the class, the peculiars queued up. I wondered how I had missed their true natures when they first walked in. The more I looked, the more obvious it seemed they were of the Otherworld.

But what I didn't know was why they had infiltrated my class.

To be honest, it didn't matter. I just needed them out of there.

I took a deep breath. "Those of you on my left, well done on your scores. They are an excellent start to the term. Let's get the blood pumping through our bodies by doing a kickboxing sequence in the car park before returning for the second half of the lesson. You've earned it. Off you go. I'll be out in a second."

My regular students whooped and congratulated each other before filing out of the class. Only Fei Yen and Faeza hovered, knowing what dangers lurked in that classroom. Knowing I might need them.

I stood up, planting my feet in an A-frame, not so much an instinctive power move as understanding that Otherworld grievances often ended in a physical altercation. I wanted to be ready just in case. "Those of you on the right, pack up your things and go home. You have no need for these classes. Teaching you would be a waste of my time and yours."

"Ah, that's not fair," said Pert, clenching his fists. "You can't turn us away."

Mirabel teared up. "I'm sorry. We shouldn't have come. I was so excited about spending time with you."

"Orpheus will hear of this," said the tallest vampire.

I rolled my eyes. "Orpheus has no say in this place."

The petite blonde fairy's hands fluttered in distress. "But we've paid good money for this."

"You'll get your money back." Refunds wouldn't be good for Joe's blood pressure. He was going to be livid.

The wolves surged forward, their pack mentality turning them into bullies.

"Yeah, well, Margola Silver thinks you're a fraud anyway. You're just worried you're going to cock up the demonstration of your powers. We were going to put money on you pulling it off, but not now," said one.

"Yeah, I bet you couldn't even defend yourself against us

if we tried one on you," said the delightful one with the hairy back, even in human form.

Quick as a flash, Fei Yen and Faeza darted to my side and unbuttoned their blouses at the neck in case they had to shift. They might have looked like old women but were as fierce as they came. I wouldn't have bet against two wily old foxes. They were all the stronger for how often people underestimated them.

Just like they underestimated me.

"Leave before I make you regret it." My voice was like the quiet before a storm.

My hands tingled with energy. I could unleash a wind and sweep unsavoury types out of the community centre without breaking a sweat. I raised my hands and directed a strong wind at the fire exit. I could challenge my powers with more precision now. Just my peripheral vision was enough to accomplish a feat that only a month ago would have taken immense concentration.

The fire exit swung open.

The Otherworld interlopers gawped at me.

"It was a poor choice coming here tonight. My humdrum life is my own, and you put the Otherworld at risk by presenting yourselves so openly. Go home."

They left, fury in the straight backs of the vampires and the laced growls of the wolves. The fairies, Pert and Mirabel, were more sanguine.

I grabbed Mirabel as she left. "I'll make time for you whenever you want at Wildwoods, Mirabel."

She perked up. "Can you teach a class there?"

I sighed. "Maybe one day when I know enough."

I shut the fire exit behind them and turned to Fei Yen and Faeza. "Well, that was hairy. Who knew that fame would have such unexpected consequences? Thanks for having my back, ladies. If Shanghai Moon"— they ran a tea and occult shop around the corner from my flat— "ever fails to bring in the money, you could have a lucrative bodyguard business instead."

Fei Yen nodded. Her silken black hair shone under the fluorescent lighting and caught the shadows under her eyes. "Well played, Alisha. You are right to keep your two worlds separate. That could have gone very wrong. But I fear the danger has not passed. Our tarot reading this morning gave us great cause for worry."

Faeza gulped. "It told of mixed messages and the crossing of thresholds."

"And it gets worse. We saw another bad omen." Fei Yen shuddered. "A raven in the tea leaves."

"A raven?" I frowned. "Whatever does that mean?"

The foxes spoke as one, as if they were heralding a great misfortune. "A terror is headed our way."

4

____

A downside to living with a magical leopard was Echo's skills in gaining access to my bedroom even when I'd shut the door. After years of parading as a Bengal cat, all pretences had fallen away. Once, he had scratched my door for attention in the early hours or miaowed plaintively at my door until he pierced through the curtain of my sleep. Now, he had no qualms about launching eighty kilos of kitty bulk against my door. He'd destroyed the lock and hinges, obviously. The door might as well have been a swing door, which was why I woke to his upper body crushing my chest and his fishy breath in my face.

A growl rumbled down my ear canal. "Wake up, sleepyhead."

I pushed him off the bed and was rewarded with some goop on my hands. Who knew what he'd been hunting. "Bad kitty, you've ruined my sheets again."

Echo sighed. "Imagine focusing on laundry when your alarm clock is a majestic creature such as me. I have an odd tale to tell you, Alisha. There is no one else I share my life with. I thought you might be interested. Especially after all my years of imposed silence when I had to pretend to be a Bengal cat. It was torture, I tell you."

I propped myself up against my pillow and pushed the strands of hair out of my face. "You have Marina."

"The empath already senses how I feel. She doesn't need me to tell her. Her skill is growing. It's very frustrating."

Living with Echo was like having a toddler, except with sharper teeth. He demanded food, burst into random songs, urinated with abandon and needed a lot of hugs. Plus, he had the odd hissy fit. I patted the bed next to me. The sheets needed a wash so he could do his worst on them, and he obviously needed some attention. "Go on then. Fill me in. What could have upset you so early in the morning?"

He jumped up next to me and nuzzled close. "I was hunting down a kill early this morning. I'd tasted the flesh once, but the little lost French bulldog had more spirit than I thought. I let him think he could get away, just to add a little fun into the game, and was about to pounce when I got distracted."

I tried not to notice the mud and blood on the duvet and traced the rosettes on his golden coat, a trick that instantly relaxed him. "Well, what distracted you?"

"Early morning is a very good time to hunt. At that hour, people in this country are usually glued to the television, gulping down chocolate cereal or staring at their teeny tiny phone screens. But, on this sleepy street in the middle of Clapham, in the middle of my hunt, neighbours began spilling onto the streets in twos and threes, shouting at one another like they'd lost all sense of decorum. And in the midst of that, the bulldog escaped, leaving me with only a tantalising taste of his meat on my tongue."

I rolled out of bed and sipped water from the glass on my bedside table. "Maybe you were in a rough part of town. Neighbours war all the time. They'd fight over spilt milk if they could, or a bin left out a day too long."

Echo stretched out. His eyes were the shade of a misty forest. "Perhaps. But then, why did I see that same scene on countless streets on my way back here? People at cross purposes, raising their voices, more discord than after the pubs shut on a Saturday night?"

Prey didn't usually escape Echo. It had obviously knocked his confidence, and he was weaving tall tales to explain why the little bulldog had gotten the better of him. I didn't rub his nose in it by spelling it out.

"Well, I'm sure they'll all be back to being friends in no time, whatever's at the bottom of it." I pinged Dad a text to give him a heads-up that I was coming over. Now the mourning period for Mum was over, Dad had been trying to keep busy and kept getting into scrapes. "I'm popping over to Dad's this morning. Would you like to come? He was very upset about what happened at the half pipe the other day."

A few weeks ago, he decided the best way to keep the local youth out of trouble was some intergenerational bonding. So, he joined them for a skateboarding session. Despite turning up with all the gear—a new skateboard, a helmet, and knee and elbow pads—he still managed to get a concussion. On top of that, some kid had pulled a knife on him and called him an old man, which he was very upset about.

Echo's tail swished. "That's South London for you. Although happily, it has plenty of pussies and poodles to make up for it."

"So, are you coming?"

"If you don't mind, I'd rather not be crammed into a cat carrier and ride the bus with you. I've done my fair share of babysitting you and Sahil when you were young. Babysitting magic grandpa is your duty, not mine." He raised his head from the duvet. "Unless Joshi wants me to put on a concert for him? I've been learning 'California Dreamin' by The Mamas and Papas. I do all the parts myself."

I put on my best poker face. "Maybe next time."

Nobody needed to hear Echo decimating that classic.

AN HOUR LATER, I rode the bus to Tooting Bec Common, ignoring an angry spat on the top deck. I felt safer travelling nowadays, even with my headphones in. My druid skills meant I was a match for most assailants. I hopped off the bus at my destination, my head swimming with worries about Dad. When once it had been Mum letting herself into my flat to stack my fridge with batch-cooking, the tables had turned. With Mum gone, Dad needed me to check in on him.

At first, the shock of losing the love of his life stopped him from painting. Next, he had only painted Mum. Then, he'd gone into helicopter parent mode, forbidding me from claiming my place in the Otherworld because he was scared of losing me. All understandable emotions, of course. I'd been rudely awakened to the fact that grief is a rollercoaster. Psychologists warned of five stages–denial, anger, bargaining, depression and acceptance—but Dad's grieving didn't seem to be following any pattern. His stages didn't match mine, either. My periods of longing and loneliness. My need for duvet days and mountains of chocolate. The physical ache to hear her voice and touch her face. Dad's grief was as unpredictable as a hand grenade.

He hadn't answered my text message, but I was always welcome here. My parents had an open-door policy, and I loved them for it. I walked up the drive, mentally checking off my to-do list, and rang the bell. When there was no answer, I checked for twitchy curtains and went around the side. A pop of wind from my hands sent me soaring over the side gate like a javelin. I grinned, enjoying the surge of power, then grabbed the key from under the geranium planter and let myself into the house.

"Dad?"

Giggles came from inside the belly of the house. The sort of uninhibited giggle that reminded me of smoking pot with Marina.

Definitely not the sort of giggle that came from my grieving dad.

I followed the sound, cocking my ears, my curiosity piqued. The garlanded photograph of Mum at the shrine looked on, her expression sanguine.

Dad didn't court company. Mum had been the social one. Without her, he would have lived as a hermit with just us and his paintings for company. How I had begged him to leave the isolation of their empty house. To find some mates and go to the pub or make the weekly bingo a thing or get a cat. A real one, this time. Not a pretender. It sounded like he may have taken my advice and found a friend.

I popped my head around the door of his studio, and my mouth fell open.

Dad held a palette of paints in his hands. He stood at his easel, dressed in a Superman outfit, complete with tights and a cape. His brown eyes twinkled, and his cheeks glowed with happiness. At the other side of the easel, his semi-naked neighbour Alma posed, wrapped only in a cotton sheet, shoulders and cleavage bare, with her mouse-brown hair newly curled and one foot pointed like a ballerina's.

I flushed. "Oh, oh. I'm so sorry. I'll come back later."

Alma had seen me grow up. I knew her as someone scrupulous about taking her bins in and a dedicated member of Neighbourhood Watch. After Mum died, she'd been a shoulder for Dad to lean on.

It seemed she'd taken a leap forward in my dad's estimations.

Dad looked around in surprise, like a teenager caught in the act. "Alisha!"

"Hello." Alma giggled and adjusted the fall of the

bedsheet. Dear god. From bringer of lasagne to occasional caregiver to Botticelli's Venus in just a few weeks.

I stifled my laughter. "You didn't reply to my text. I thought it was still okay to come around."

"I thought your text was very rude, so I decided not to answer it." Dad swished his cape. "We've been at this since the early hours to catch the dawn light falling across Alma's skin. I found this get-up in a charity shop. Alma was nervous, and wearing something silly put her at ease. She's doing very well, aren't you, Alma?"

Alma, worried she would compromise her portrait, barely moved her lips. "I hope so, dear."

Dad gave her a fond smile. He turned to me in a flash of Lycra, his eyes wary. "Want to see the painting?"

A quick glimpse at the canvas showed a study in curves, curls and an arched foot. I cringed. An erotic painting if I'd ever seen one. "Maybe when you're finished."

Perhaps it was a professional painting commission, but my gut told me it was the start of something new. Luckily, Echo wasn't with me, or he would have started crooning Barry White. I averted my glance from the canvas, and my heartbeat sped up.

Ravens. Ravens everywhere. Black paint on canvas. Dark slashes of black feathers, thick throats and beady eyes.

My brow furrowed. Hadn't the foxes mentioned ravens too? "What's with all the gloomy birds? There are ravens everywhere. I should bake them in a pie like in the nursery rhyme."

"I think you'll find it was blackbirds in the nursery rhyme, not ravens," said Alma helpfully.

Dad shrugged. "They just came to me. You know what I'm like, love. An obsessive. I get something in my head, and I have to work it out on the canvas like a kink."

Fair enough. It was just a coincidence. A moment of

fascination for a painter in love with the living form. Human or otherwise.

Alma's face creased with worry. "Your dad does have a lot of kinks."

Dad gave a sheepish grin, but when he turned to me, his expression cooled again. "Shall we have a word outside?"

I nodded, wondering what I'd done wrong. "It was lovely to…see you, Alma."

"I'll see you out." Somehow Dad's cape got tangled with the legs of his easel, and he lurched forward.

Alma put her hands out to steady him. Her sheet dropped, giving him—and me—an eyeful of her in all her glory.

"Ay, caramba." Dad righted himself and rewrapped Alma in the sheet, burrito style.

A red flush, hot with embarrassment, swept across her face.

I scurried out of the room faster than you could say *chimichanga*, pretending I'd not seen a thing. Although I was definitely going to share a blow-by-blow account with Marina and Sahil.

Dad chased after me, his superhero cape flapping behind him. "Sorry about that, love. I miss your mother, I do, but Alma's giving me a new lease on life. It's nice to have company my own age. So I was surprised at the contents of your message. I thought you'd understand."

I frowned. "What are you talking about? What message?"

He sniffed. "The one at nine a.m. this morning when you told me that I was focused on myself and didn't care about you."

"Dad, I didn't send you that." My eyes darted around the hallway for his phone. "There must be some misunderstanding. Show me your phone."

"Don't get impatient with me or try to wriggle out of it. I suppose I should be glad you shared your feelings with me."

I missed Mum too. I didn't want another woman taking her place, but tragedies happened. "I swear I didn't text you. You've done nothing wrong, Dad. You deserve every happiness. And I *much* prefer this to you trying your hand at skateboarding."

The loves of our lives were knitted together like patchwork quilts. Mum might have had the greatest share, but if Alma could bring Dad happiness, I was grateful to her.

Tears ran down his face and mingled with his wiry white moustache. He hugged me in a burst of affection. "It's such a relief to hear you say that. Let's move on, shall we?"

I clung to his Lycra-clad body.

He dropped his voice to a whisper. Alma didn't have the foggiest about the Otherworld. "There was such a throng of people at Wildwoods that I didn't get a chance to tell you how proud I was to see you receive the medal. You're just like your grandmother. If only she and your mother had been here to see it."

I smiled. "Thanks, Dad. Although I'm not sure how I feel about all the extra attention."

He beamed. "It just gives you more of a chance to shine."

"I don't know about that. Did you see the Margola Silver interview online? She seems to have it in for me."

He scowled. "Underestimate that selkie at your peril. Selkies are slippery beasts. She may not be the most powerful minister, but she is the most resourceful one. Her information technology skills are legendary, but I've seen her work with much less. A rumour. A chain letter. A leaflet bomb. All with a smile that would melt butter."

"She sounds delightful. Well, I'd better impress her at the performance of my animation skills."

He nodded thoughtfully. "In that case, it's time to give you something." He scampered over to the sideboard in the hallway to open a drawer. "Here you go, darling. You'll need this for the performance of your animation powers. It was your grandmother's once."

I accepted the book, a thick artist's block in a soft leather cover with hand-stitched binding. "You kept it all this time?"

"Of course I did. Your grandmother was here one minute and gone the next. But the things I'd created for her, I couldn't throw them away. Just remember, once you animate them, the page disintegrates. But there can be no giving of life without responsibility. My mother took that duty very seriously. The creature's purpose is tied to your wishes. You must find a way for them to be useful, happy, or free. Oh, and I've included as many creatures as I could think of, given that stupid cat of yours decided the crowd could choose which one you animate."

I opened it with care, marvelling at the artistry. There were beavers, swordfish, giant squid and soaring vultures.

He smoothed down his costume, paying particular attention to the Superman emblem. His swirly chest hair poked out of the top. "Anyway, love, I'll see you at the performance. I should really get back to Alma. I wouldn't want her to get cold feet about finishing the portrait." He hesitated. "Are you sure you're okay about it?"

"I'm happy for you."

Dad beamed. "Send your brother a message, will you? Just so he knows you're thinking of him. I know you don't believe it, but he really does long for your approval."

5

————————

Marina and I arranged to go underwear shopping. I would've loved to have taken after Mum's French nature, who revelled in her sexuality even though she was almost a pensioner. But instead, my Indian side won out. I was a prude. The sort of woman who disliked getting undressed in open changing rooms and would much rather change in a smelly loo.

That was why I needed Marina. This was a woman who could wear PVC leather out with aplomb, turn heads and revel in the attention. She was the perfect person to coax me out of the rut I had been in during my marriage to Alex. Adjusting to being Ezra's girlfriend after years of being a wife meant I wanted to spice things up. I was just too afraid to do it without Marina holding my hand. She was my sister in all but name: my sounding board, my cheerleader, my therapist and my favourite person to try new things with. Her free spirit was the perfect foil for my more reserved nature.

We walked into town, perplexed by the pockets of discord we stumbled across but too busy nattering to give it much thought.

"So let me get this right. Robert Jameson is ignoring your messages? But that man is crazy about you."

Marina toyed with the end of her rainbow-coloured plait. "I know. It's weird, right? I mean, it's usually me who does the dumping. But it's not just that. The last time we were together was good. Like really good. All night long good. Tingling sensations in my toes good. And now radio silence. I can't believe he's ghosting me."

The high street was a hive of activity, as if shoppers were on edge. There was more hooting of car horns on the streets, more rows at the supermarket checkout till, and an increase of police and ambulance sirens. Two grown men came to fisticuffs in the street—men who should have known better. Upstanding men, in corduroy trousers and polo shirts, throwing punches that were slow and clumsy but which stemmed from real anger. They were stone-cold sober yet vexed enough to end up brawling in the gutter.

People could be shits sometimes. Nothing anyone could do about it. Cities like London, especially, could be hotpots of anxiety and stress.

But it was happening elsewhere too. At least, that was what the rumours said. My postman was always a reliable source of juicy rumours. He'd reported all sorts from up north, the Midlands and even as far as the Scottish Highlands. The BBC reported it too. Discord in streets up and down the country. Misunderstandings between politicians who had once backed the same causes. As if the country was gearing up for a civil war. As if we'd turned into a Jerry Springer show overnight.

We ducked into Marks and Spencer's.

"We're not spending all our time talking about Robert. We're here for you." Marina launched herself into the underwear section with the gusto of a kid eating ice cream. "I can't believe you're getting hung up on the fact your control pants could be a turn-off for Ezra. Bridget Jones would weep."

I bit my lip. "I've forgotten what it's like to date. To be in a new relationship. You and Robert were together for five minutes before you were swinging from the chandeliers."

"Stop bringing up that jerk. Seriously though, Alisha, Ezra isn't going to care what you wear in bed as long as he has his hands on you."

I gave a shy smile. "But some nice underwear will help. Maybe even a thong."

Marina winced. "Only girls in their twenties wear thongs. Grown women know that a thong creeping up your crack is a health hazard. Big knickers can be sexy. Marilyn Monroe wore big knickers. Even *Vogue* thinks big knickers are in. I hate to break it to you, but you could have worn nipple tassels, and Alex would have carried on staring at his gaming screen. But those wolf eyes of Ezra's tell me he doesn't need the bells and whistles. He's already hooked."

"I guess so." I headed for the muted colours, casting a sceptical look over the very small underwear, and showed her a black balcony bra with good coverage. "How about this one?"

She put down a set of frilly knickers in the style of a 1950s pin-up and rolled her eyes. "You have a dozen bras like that. Live a little." She grinned. "If I'm here helping you seduce Ezra, the least you can do is spill the beans. Or are you going to make me beg for all the glorious details? Does he live up to the promise? All that tousled hair, hard muscle, and pent-up energy have to translate to something special under the sheets."

I gave her a teasing look. "It does, actually."

Marina punched the air. "I knew the wolf man would deliver. Hell, after all of Alex's robotic foreplay, you deserved a win in the bedroom." She rummaged through a rack of racy bras and thrust one at me, all pink lace and stiff under-wiring.

"Urrgh, no." I handed it back. "We've not exactly sealed the deal, if you know what I mean. We keep getting disturbed. Then Ezra decided we should find somewhere special to pop that cherry."

"Sounds like excuses to me. You need twenty minutes, not a lifetime." She shook her head ruefully. "The man can literally teleport to the perfect place for you to have a rumble in the jungle. What's holding you back?"

I sighed. "My own head. Starting over at midlife isn't the same as dating when you're a fresh young thing."

"Alisha, it's better. So much better. All the time you were married to Alex, how many relationships did you see me start and end? There was Susie and Abdul and Elsie. She was a hottie. And now Robert. And each time, I get closer to my dream companion." She picked a tangerine cotton bra with zip detail and matching knickers from a rail. "How about this? I saw something similar on Instagram. It's all the rage."

A group of girls had come in off the street, raucous and looking for trouble. I gave them a wide berth and refused Marina's choice of undies. Ideally, I was after something bigger than a handkerchief but smaller than a bodystocking. "How much time do you spend aimlessly scrolling on that app? All those perfect posey pics and the filters that give women a complex."

She grinned and put the hanger back. "Speak for yourself. Instagram is life. How am I going to feed my addiction to tattoo art and home interiors? Although I've been getting images of dog meat festivals in China, which have been really upsetting. The algorithms must be up the duff." She grabbed a lacy cream teddy and held it up to the light. "What do you think?"

I gave her a thumbs-up. It was beautiful, offsetting her rainbow hair and buxom curves. Jessica Rabbit, eat your heart out. "Is that how you're going to get Robert's attention."

Her blue eyes sparkled. "As if. More like a treat for

myself. Rob knows where I am. I'm not going to chase after him. But this teddy will bring me joy one way or another. I thought we said we wouldn't talk about Rob. Stop changing the subject from Ezra. Honestly, darling, you just need to get your confidence back. Alex is in the past. You know what you want now. You've had some detours, and you've learned the lessons. This relationship with Ezra doesn't have to be a huge, life-changing romance. You can just have some fun."

By now, I had an armful of underwear to try on too. "Changing room?"

I ignored the raucous group of girls, who were ogling our haul and giggling as if middle-aged women couldn't possibly want nice underwear.

Marina nodded. "Lead the way."

We made our way across the shop floor to the unstaffed changing rooms. I stepped over hangers strewn across the floor, ducked behind the curtain of an empty cubicle and stripped off, leaving my own underwear on. I sighed at the sight of myself in the mirror. My posture was good. I liked my curves and the thick waterfall of my dark, curly hair. But being here made me want to grab Marina and run screaming into the nearest cocktail bar. The claustrophobic space, enormous mirrors and harsh lighting of changing rooms didn't do anyone any favours. Unless you were Cindy Crawford.

I slid the first set of underwear off its hanger. A teal blue bra, with plenty of support and coverage, with a barely there thong I could have flossed my teeth with. It was a more adventurous choice than my usual fare, but sometimes a girl had to throw caution to the wind.

"How's it going?" called Marina from her cubicle opposite.

I grimaced as I fastened the back of the bra and shimmied into the thong over the top of my knickers. "Yeah, okay. You?"

"Not going to lie. I look like a sausage stuffed into a meringue."

I giggled, but my smile slid off my face as the curtain of my cubicle opened. I squealed like a pig. One hand flew up to cover my breasts, and the other flew to cover my nether region while my legs folded into a weird twist. "Oh, my god."

Marina's worried voice met my ears. "Alisha?"

The girls' eyes widened in glee as they gawped at me. Their translucent skin shimmered in the light.

"It's her. It's the granddaughter of Rajika Verma."

Fairies. A red blush of humiliation flooded my cheeks. "This changing room is being used. Bugger off."

One picked up her phone to snap a picture.

With a flick of my hand, I sent the gadget skidding across the floor. I would have given them an earful, but my arse was plain to see in the mirror reflection, and my exposed bikini line looked like an English sheepdog. So instead, I channelled my powers and sent the curtain shooting across the rail again, sending pretty underwear raining through the changing room like confetti.

"That's so cool," said an awestruck fairy.

Anger, red and hot, surged through me. "Get the hell out of here."

"You should chill out, or you'll lose your fans," said the fairy. "People are so uptight these days."

I poked my head around the curtain, quivering with rage. "I take it you're Wildwoods students? Rayna will hear about this."

They ran off laughing, having utterly humiliated me. Mission accomplished.

Marina tumbled into my cubicle, still buttoning up her jeans. "What was that all about?"

I tugged on my clothes with trembling hands. "Fairies, I think. They saw me starkers. I'm mortified. I blame Margola Silver. She's the one who's whipped up all this attention."

I looked at the state of myself in the mirror and almost cried. I had a right mind to ask Lavinia for a glamour until the interest had died down, but she'd probably land me with a turnip nose out of spite.

Marina laid a hand on my arm, and I felt immediately calmer, as if her very touch was medicine. "What knob heads. We should tell the security guards. Get them turfed out."

A rush of noise met my ears. A scuffling that I couldn't decode. "Do you hear that?"

I pulled Marina onto the shop floor, hoping the security guards had cottoned on and booted out the fairies. That would teach them.

A ginger-haired shop assistant froze in her act of restocking socks, mouth aghast. "Oh, my god."

I followed her gaze. Cameras filmed three well-heeled officials, but the officials had dropped any semblance of respectability or professionalism. As the cameras rolled, the trio had a very public spat. A stick-thin man with a mop of carefully combed hair shouted down at a petite woman, waving a phone in her face. To the glee of the cameraman, the woman snapped. She tugged the tall man's tie, hard. The third person bodily lifted her and dumped her in the homeware section like a discarded pillow.

I gawped. Marks and Spencer, the epitome of middle-class restraint, had turned into a hen house.

The shop assistant motioned to us from behind a display of tights. "They're Lambeth councillors on a filmed walk-about to boost the high street. All this argy-bargy. Aren't politicians supposed to be the grown-ups? We were all told to be on our best behaviour."

She gasped as the shorter man delivered a knockout punch to his colleague.

The cameraman looked thrilled to have footage that would inevitably be shown on prime-time television.

Marina nudged me. "Aren't you going to do something?"

I shook my head. "They're lawmakers. I'm not going to get involved. You could do that hand thing and calm them all down."

She shuddered. "No thanks. Maybe they'll feel better after they've worked out what's bothering them."

I kept one set of undies, tossed the rest and gave the shop assistant twenty quid before grabbing Marina's hand. "Come on. We're not hanging about here."

We strode through Marks and Spencer's with the attitude of two assassins walking through a hail of bullets.

6

The following afternoon, Echo, Marina and I scoffed down sushi in the staff room at Marina's veterinary surgery: avocado and cucumber rolls for vegetarian me and a mix of tuna and salmon rolls for Echo and Marina. She didn't usually open on the weekend, but ever since her patch-up job on Faeza, an influx of peculiar creatures had been turning up on Marina's doorstep.

"I always found English men and women a puzzle," said Echo. "Their emotions are laced up so tightly. In India, emotions are much closer to the surface. Indians say what they think. They wrap their unpalatable truths in charm and poetry. They don't hide them. But now, the people of this country are wearing their emotions on their sleeves. It makes me wonder..."

"If they are all on drugs?" Marina dipped a roll into soy sauce.

Echo gulped down a chunk of salmon. "Something has changed, has it not?"

Marina waved her chopsticks in the air. "Well, yes. I mean, the Prime Minister just reshuffled his cabinet. There was only a reshuffle last week. He's ousted some of his closest allies. There's definitely something funky in the air."

"It's the wind of change." Echo farted.

Marina didn't even blink. She carried on sucking out the shell of her edamame beans.

I gave a heavy sigh, accustomed by now to Echo's noxious gases and fluids. At least he didn't leave the toilet seat up.

"We've definitely had more clues recently about who would cannibalise their neighbours if society really were to break down." Marina waited, chopsticks poised in the air, while another flurry of sirens sped by. "So the pack didn't find any leads that could point to why wolves are turning up dead?"

"Afraid not. I suggested you could take a look at the body, but Gunnolf almost bit my head off."

"Wolves have a tight ranking. You probably overstepped the line," said Marina. "You need to tread more carefully if you're going to win Gunnolf's trust. Otherwise, it could make things hard for Ezra."

I grimaced. "I thought I was on my best behaviour. At least they're not blaming the dark elves this time. Ezra says Gunnolf will get to the bottom of it."

Marina raised an eyebrow. "That look on your face tells me you think otherwise."

I squeezed out some more wasabi from a sachet and popped in a mouthful of sushi. "My intuition tells me not to trust him. But Ezra trusts him completely. Gunnolf is not only his alpha. He's his uncle, his dead father's brother. Ezra is loyal to him. He doesn't want to see Gunnolf's faults, especially so soon after being disillusioned by Lavinia and her phoney war against the elves."

"If you're worried, you could pick up an object of Gunnolf's from the farmhouse. Something that's been close to his body, like a jumper or a watch. I can use it to get a reading about him." She used her powers generously in her veterinary surgery and out in the world without thought for the toll it took on her.

Echo gave a low growl. "The answer is quite simple, Alisha. If Gunnolf and Lavinia can't be trusted, you just have to open Ezra's eyes to it, or you risk being the one left out in the cold. Failing that, just say the word, and I will urinate all over that farmhouse. It will drive those territorial wolves crazy, and they won't be able to blame it on you."

I wrinkled my nose. "Please don't. Urination is not my choice of tactic."

Marina pulled her rainbow-coloured hair over one shoulder. "I think a much better approach would be not to jump the gun. Gunnolf is Ezra's uncle, after all. Give him the space to show you who he is without all the bluff and bluster that goes with being the alpha of a wolfpack. Just focus on Ezra. Forget about anything else."

"I would love to just focus on him. There's just a little performance of my animation powers in front of *the whole Wildwoods community* to get through first, thanks to you, Echo."

A string of tuna hung from Echo's teeth. "Stop exaggerating, druid. It doesn't become you. And don't blame me for your lack of libido."

I gave him a withering look.

"Don't look at me like that. There's a distinct lack of sex hormones emanating from your bedroom. And you're hardly going to do the dirty at a farmhouse full of wolves. Their hearing is as good as mine, and they would tease you far more."

I changed the subject with the subtlety of a ten-tonne truck. "Did I tell you? Dad seems to be doing better. I caught him in a Superman outfit painting a portrait of semi-nude Alma. My eyes were burning, I tell you."

Marina blinked. "He did *what*?"

Echo honked with laughter. "It is a long time since Joshi Verma has impressed me."

I grinned. "It's so good to see him painting again. Ravens are his new obsession."

Marina picked up her last roll with a deft pincer-like movement of her chopsticks. "Did you say ravens?"

I nodded. A familiar swirling started up in my belly. I pushed it down.

"That's funny," said Marina. "I saw on the news this morning that all six ravens, plus the spares, left the Tower of London."

"They're flying birds, aren't they? They must leave all the time," I said.

My best friend shook her head. "Sometimes they are dismissed for performing their duties poorly, but they can't leave of their own accord. Their flight feathers are clipped on one wing."

Echo swallowed down a chunk of salmon and tossed his head dramatically. "I would die if anyone took my freedom."

Marina's blue eyes grew troubled. "Legend says that if the ravens are lost or fly away, the Crown will fall and Britain with it."

My eyes watered as a dollop of wasabi hit my taste buds. "Oh, for crying out loud. I love you, but not even you can believe that nonsense, Marina. It's as bad as taking Fei Yen and Faeza's tarot reading and raven in the tea leaves seriously. Crystals, tarot and tea leaves are just a bit of fun. It's like horoscopes. They're comforting when they sound good, but when they sound bad, you just ignore them."

"You are foolish to doubt omens after all you have seen, Alisha," said Echo.

My stomach churned. I didn't believe in omens, but if I kept stumbling across the same image, did it mean the universe was trying to tell me something? Did true sight mean I had to listen to things I'd once ignored?

"We should be wary," said Marina. "In mythology, ravens are associated with Apollo, the god of prophecy and war. They symbolise death or bad luck."

Echo cleaned his paws with slow, deliberate licks of his enormous tongue. "The empath is right. Ravens are born of primordial darkness, and their jet black colour represents the night, the great void."

I shook my head. "Let's keep some perspective. Mythology is varied. I can point to as many myths that say ravens are a sign of good fortune. That they symbolise wisdom, longevity and healing powers. That they are symbols of metamorphosis, change and transformation."

Echo rolled over with the lethargy that came from a full belly. "All the more reason to tell the senate. There are those practised in divination amongst them. Let them discern the meaning of these omens."

"Can you imagine the raised eyebrows if I went to the senate with something as nebulous as this? They'd laugh me out of Wildwoods," I said. "Like you said, they have their prophets. Let them decipher their own omens."

Marina collected the rubbish from our takeout and swept it into the bin. "There's no time for a nap, Echo. We have an injured shifter to see at three-thirty p.m., and I'm nothing without the help of my consultant leopard."

Echo purred with pleasure. We'd learned that compliments, steak and salmon were key to keeping magical leopards happy. Well, that and the opportunity to maul prey.

I caught Marina's eye. "You are coming to the performance tonight?"

Marina looked at Echo. "We wouldn't miss it for the world."

I'D NOT SEEN Ezra since leaving the farmhouse. He and the pack had been preoccupied with wolf sleuthing, and Gunnolf demanded pack business come first. So we made a date to meet in Crystal Palace Park on the day of my performance.

I waited in a meadow of long grasses, knowing he'd find me. He told me once that as a boy, he'd been unpractised and had teleported into precarious situations, landing on people as if he'd fallen out of the sky. His father had schooled him then how to choose his locations more wisely. How to seek out quieter places to appear or to return to scents he recognised. To stay in the folds before emerging completely. Like a magician behind a curtain.

He said I smelt of wildflowers and cocoa, and I decided there and then to carry on using my Tom Ford perfume.

A whisper of noise, like the dissembling and reassembling of particles in the universe.

Ezra materialised next to me. He kissed me, his stubble grazing my cheek, and then he looped his arms around me, exerting gentle pressure until we stood chest to chest. His head dipped, eyes on my lips, and when he pulled away, I ached for him.

Grey eyes, flecked with copper, met mine. "I've missed this. I considered turning up unannounced at your flat last night to surprise you."

I gave him a shy smile. "Unannounced sounds just fine. I mean, so long as Echo doesn't mistake you for an intruder."

His hands rested on my waist. "So I don't need an invitation?"

I held his gaze for a moment. "I think we've passed that stage, don't you?"

"And I don't need to worry about what Margola Silver has been writing about you and Orpheus Might?"

I shook my head. "There's nothing there. He's just a weird old vampire."

Ezra murmured in my ear. "Good. One step closer to our happy ever after."

My heartbeat leapt, and I locked his words away to savour.

A young couple argued nearby. We grimaced and walked away to give them some space.

I entwined my fingers with his. "Everyone's a bit fractious at the moment. Have you noticed?"

The smile dropped from his chiselled face, highlighting the shadows there. "It's been pretty hellish running the investigation."

"Is the pack any closer to finding who killed the wolves?"

"Not really. We took a good look at the bodies. The wounds were jagged, not clean. That tells me they were killed by an animal. But then, vital organs were targeted. The neck, the heart, the eyes." He frowned. "So that points to a sentient creature. A peculiar, perhaps. A shifter. I was thinking of paying Robert a visit. The Shadow Squad might have some intel."

"He and Marina have drifted apart. He keeps ignoring her messages."

Ezra's brow furrowed. "I could have sworn he'd have bitten off his own hand to marry her." He paused. "Do you know what gets me? There was a rage in these killings. I could smell the lingering stench of fury still on the bodies. Like it was personal."

I shuddered. "That's awful. I bet Marina could get a sense of the emotional residue."

Ezra gave an exasperated sigh. "The alpha has spoken. Besides, there aren't any bodies to look at. We burned them on a pyre last night. Can't risk a humdrum uncovering a werewolf corpse. It raises too many questions."

Marina had counselled me to be supportive, but I couldn't help myself. "Isn't it a bit premature, cremating the bodies before the investigation has concluded?"

He stiffened. "We had to weigh the risks. But Gunnolf has it under control. He isn't the Justice Minister for nothing. He always finds the perpetrator."

I bit my lip. "If you say so. I mean, you do sound a bit like a propaganda bureau. Not even *CSI: Miami* has a one-hundred per cent success rate. And Horatio is good."

He folded his arms across his chest, and his biceps strained against his T-shirt. "Stop that."

I gave him my wide-eyed innocent look. "Stop what?"

A vein throbbed in his jaw. "You know exactly what. Gunnolf's not only my alpha—he's family. Promise me you'll try to be friends."

I sighed. "I'm sorry. I was just trying to help."

"I realised." He softened. "Shall we do what we came here for?"

Slipping into the rhythm of mentor and mentee came more naturally than creating a new musical score.

We flicked through Dad's catalogue of creatures, but I worried that expending my energy now would weaken me later, and I didn't want to be a laughingstock. I wanted to prove to all the naysayers that I could animate as easily as breathing when the truth was I'd only done it a few times.

"You're not a battery, Alisha. You don't need to worry about running out of energy," said Ezra. "Druids draw their energy from the Earth. And Earth's resources are infinite. I think it might be why Gaia has had a natural affinity with druids across the ages. Why she helped you. The trick is to relax and believe."

"You make it sound so easy. I can't see you going on stage and shifting in front of strangers to prove a point."

He laughed, and I enjoyed how his good humour rubbed off on me. He allowed me to blow off steam and didn't belittle how I felt but made me feel better just by being there.

"It won't be that bad. Come on, choose one of these and animate it. Just for me. To get your juices flowing. How about the beaver? Or the squirrel? Then you could let it go in the park."

How could I stay crotchety when a sexy werewolf-wizard was cajoling me into using my newfound magical powers? A million women would have bitten off my arm to exchange places with me.

I shook my head. "Just something small." I flicked to a page where Dad had painted butterflies in a myriad of styles and shades. My finger landed on a bronze-and-black one with elegant tiger markings. "I'll try with this one."

He nodded encouragingly.

I took a deep breath and closed my eyes. Motes of light played in the air, infiltrating the nebulous pink of my eyelids. I opened my eyes. The world slowed as I drowned out all the noise of passers-by lamenting the tech blackout, children playing frisbee and the chirping of crickets in long grasses. I focussed only on the tiger butterfly, blocking out even Ezra and the scent of cigarette roll-ups on his fingers and the taste of his tongue.

The threads of the universe loomed in my mind. I was no longer myself. I was a conduit. A harpist. A surgeon. A seamstress who crafted marvels worthy of royalty.

My fingers traced the painting, and the dimensions deepened into velvet softness and quivering fragility. An intake of breath, marvelling as I sensed rather than saw the veiny wings, antennae and fine legs of the butterfly, and the wings fluttered within the page, a secret only I knew. Instinct told me when to pull the threads, and the tiger butterfly emerged, small and perfectly formed. He came clean off the page and rested on my palm as if he were catching his breath.

And then he was gone, camouflaged amongst the flower borders at Crystal Palace Park.

I laughed because, as much as I sometimes feared and doubted myself, when my talents shone, it empowered me.

At that moment, I believed there had never been anyone like me.

Ezra's smile mirrored mine. "You're ready."

I reached for the catalogue of creatures and hooked my arm through his. We meandered towards Wildwoods, which beckoned to me like the sea calls to a mermaid.

7

———

The sphinxes stood vigil over Wildwoods in the summer sun. As we neared, I noted how their great, stone bodies shivered with intrigue. Only Mammatas brightened at our approach. His mood had improved considerably since a restoration funded by friends of the park.

"It is good you are here," he said. "Usually, the most exciting part of our day is when a child trips and swallows their teeth, but today we are witnesses to a true drama."

"It's the end of days," said Rhokon, the second sphinx, whose grumpiness stemmed from the fact that one of his legs was in a state of severe disrepair. "The ravens have fled the tower. Soon, the sun will fall out of the sky, and you will be turned to stone like us."

"Settle down, boys," said Ezra with a briskness that made me wonder if he'd ever been in the military. "Or you'll give yourself cracks."

I patted Rhokon soothingly and sensed the rumble of appreciation in his unyielding body. "I'm sure it's not as bad as that. Everything will be up and running soon enough. In the meantime, we can all enjoy some peace and quiet."

Rhokon's voice was as dry and gritty as sandpaper. "Have you looked at the sky this morning?"

I hadn't, actually. I'd had my head down on the bus and en route to the park. Once, I had relied on my wits, kickboxing skills and keys clutched in my hand to see me home safe at night. As a druid, I could stuff in my earphones with abandon, listen to podcasts or rock out to music, safe in the knowledge that I could triumph over most foes. And having headphones in meant I could pretend any peculiars stalking me didn't exist.

Rhokon sniffed. "Sorry to say, Mr Neuhoff, but werewolves always have their noses to the ground. But I thought better of you, granddaughter of Rajika Verma."

We looked up.

A message loomed against the sky, flamboyant and stark, carved into the vast blueness in a deep mauve ink.

RESCHEDULED OTEROR JIGOT TRANSPORT FEDORAN

My eyebrows disappeared into my hairline. I turned to the sphinxes. "Well, that's weird. Who's behind it?"

Ezra frowned. "Was that part of a Red Arrow display? Is it supposed to mean something?"

Mammatas's unblinking eyes regarded us. "The humdrums contemplate whether the fall anticipated by Nostradamus has finally arrived. The more obvious question is: when will we get our clear view back?"

"We are unsure where or when it originated," said Rhokon. "I can't tell you how hard it was for us to swivel our heads to take in the full effect. It was very frustrating not to be able to decipher it. It would have been much easier, of course, if they were hieroglyphics."

For two beings tasked with the job, the sphinxes had utterly failed at standing vigil.

Rhokon continued. "I know what you are thinking. Our

stone necks cope quite well with a 360-degree rotation, but angling our heads upwards risks cracks. We could discard these stone bodies, of course, but the humans have enough problems right now without a pair of sphinxes scaring the bejeezus out of them."

"So you see now, Ms Verma, why we've been feeling a frisson of excitement this morning," said Mammatas.

I cupped my hand over my eyes to squint at the message. Crosswords were my jam, but this was different. It could have been French or Latin or a made-up language. Maybe in all the chaos, someone really had stolen a Red Arrow plane and would spend the rest of their life regaling the geezers in the pub about the nutty message he had written in the sky over South London. But unlike the vapour in Red Arrow displays, this didn't dissipate.

I dropped to my knees in the grass and rummaged in my bag for a pen and a scrap of paper, then scrawled out the words.

"What are you doing?" said Ezra.

"Hang on a sec." I chewed the end of the pen, staring at the words, and then the old magic happened. The one that made me brilliant at crosswords, word searches and *Countdown*. The letters unscrambled, and I scribbled the options down, crossing out dead ends until I finally had the answer. I held the page aloft in jubilation. "I solved it."

Ezra grimaced. "I can't read that thing. Spell it out for me."

"It's an anagram." Excitement made the words spill into each other.

He nodded. "Okay. What does it say?"

Pinpricks of anxiety blurred my vision. "It says, 'Rejoice and prostrate. For the old gods return.'"

Ezra cursed. His grey eyes met mine. "Not again."

Mamatas turned his pharaoh head towards me like he'd

done dozens of times before. It still made me jump out of my skin. "Isn't she clever?"

Rhokon's deep voice rumbled through his body. "You should tell the senate."

I ignored them and focussed on Ezra. "I've probably got it wrong."

In fact, the sinking feeling in the pit of my stomach told me I was right. My teacher's brain was already breaking down the language. The words *rejoice* and *prostrate* were strangely biblical, and the *for the* construction was archaic. We were clearly dealing with a fruit loop.

And a god.

The swirling in the pit of my stomach grew stronger. *Rejoice and prostrate. For the old gods return.* But what did it mean?

I drew in a shaky breath. *It's not my problem.*

We'd tell the senate and then wash our hands of it.

In fact, if anyone suggested I get involved, I'd take a handful of crystals and shove them where the sun didn't shine. My priorities were clear. Survive the display of my magical prowess. Teach uneventful night classes. Enjoy long, lazy days in bed with Ezra. As wish lists went, it wasn't asking a lot.

I turned to the sphinxes. "The senate must be preoccupied with these developments. I'm sure a magical display is the last thing anyone needs."

Mammatas shifted on his platform with a grinding and shuddering I feared could be heard across the park. "To the contrary, I heard the Information Minister say that a bit of light entertainment is just what everyone needs."

I sighed. He made me sound like a kids' party entertainer. I leaned towards Rhokon. "You're my favourite."

His stone lips curved up in a smile. "Knock them dead, granddaughter of Rajika Verma. Blow them all away."

I gave him a jaunty salute. That was the intention. I would

dazzle Wildwoods with my skills and then take cover with my lover boy until the dust had settled.

AT THE GNARLED YEW TREE, Ezra stood back and waited as I pressed my palm to the rune. The cool bark reacted to my touch as the rune activated, recognising me and sending heat pulsing through my arm. Beneath us, the ground trembled, and the trees shifted. A blink and Wildwoods School of the Wondrous materialised, complete with its grand arena and myriad of cabins and rope bridges nestled amongst the trees.

Our hands entwined as we walked into the grounds. The circular motion of Ezra's thumb against the back of my hand sent a shiver up my spine. Our relationship was so fresh and new that this public declaration of togetherness felt big.

"You know, we could pay the detective a visit and find out what he knows about all this," said Ezra. "If a god is behind all this, we can't just sit on our hands."

I laughed. "You can't be serious. Weren't you the one that was a stickler for the Pragmatist's Law?"

We chanted together. "Never meddle in the affairs of the gods."

Ezra gave me a rueful smile. "Yeah, well. You're the one who taught me that rules are all well and good until they collide with reality. I think you'll find I've broken the rules a number of times for you."

"What happened to Ezra Neuhoff, Mr Black and White, he of the Justice Minister's wolf pack?"

The copper flecks in his eyes danced. "I met a wayward druid."

My heart expanded in my chest. A flash of colour caught my eye. "Will you look at that?"

The cabins at Wildwoods changed with the seasons and, on a whim, an evolving, blooming and shifting that took my breath away. Today, they had been painted with the bright stripes of beach huts and patchwork bunting fluttered in the wind, at odds with the sinister message in the sky.

It's not my problem. I said the words in my head like a mantra.

Margola Silver had outdone herself in organising the event. Together with Rayna, she had arranged for stalls in the arena for students who showcased their magic and learning. My heartbeat raced at the sight of a grand stage at one side, backed by the obelisk.

Ezra followed my gaze. "It'll be okay. You animated a dragon, Alisha. You can do this magic show."

I gulped. "I just can't wait until it's over, that's all."

A quick scan of the crowd told us that Dad, Echo and Marina had yet to arrive, so we set off to explore. I spotted alchemists brewing murky potions in tiny cauldrons and turning matter into tiny jewels. Vampires practised mind control on brave volunteers. Druids coaxed sunflowers and camellias to grow from seed to full bloom in seconds. Shifters —a bear and a bull—faced off against each other in a show of strength, speed and wits. Fairies instructed visitors to their stall on the wonders of a glowing, chattering caterpillar and an inky blue kingfisher with the power of invisibility.

How I wished at times to be invisible. How had I gone from a woman craving attention to an object of curiosity?

I sighed as whispers reached my ears.

"It's her. The druid."

"Rajika Verma's granddaughter. She's the main attraction today."

"Margola Silver splashed her all over the front page of *The Otherworld News*. Did you see?"

"You're quite the talk of the town. And you have Margola to thank for it." Disapproval coloured Ezra's voice. "She never was one to ask the stars of her stories if they want to be taken along for the ride. How about we head up to the library and find a quiet nook to catch our breath before your performance?"

I nodded, and he led the way to the cable cars. I loved him for not needing to spell out how uncomfortable the attention made me. There was a softness to Ezra that my ex had lacked. Losing his parents at such a young age had honed his intuition, allowing him to pick up on others feeling overwhelmed.

Ezra stole a kiss as we rode the cable car towards the heart of Wildwoods. When the doors opened, we stepped out onto a rope bridge, which swayed with our weight, and made for the library, tumbling through the cobalt blue arched door into the cherrywood interior with its endless rows of books. The boughs, vines and stone that entwined to form the skeleton for the room had sprouted foliage, and the carpet of desiccated autumn leaves had vanished. In its place was a floor of soft rose petals in peach and sunshine yellow.

He pulled me towards the travel section.

I trailed my fingers along the shelf, breathing in the heavenly scent of old books and flowers. "So, how do you decide which one to read?"

"I tend to choose the ones that are more damaged on the outside. A well-thumbed book means that what's inside is special."

God, he was sexy. I dropped my bag and melted into him amongst Lonely Planets, Rough Guides and Bill Brysons. When the door to the cabin opened, and voices came our way, it took us a second to come up for air. I giggled and put my finger to my lips. It was one thing coming in here to soothe my frazzled nerves but quite another to be discovered like horny teenagers creeping away for a bit of nookie when we were in our forties.

The voice that filled the library sent a frisson of fear up my spine, and I knew we'd made a terrible mistake.

8

I'd have recognised the Prime Sorcerer's voice anywhere. This wasn't the sort of conversation we should be a party to. Wildwoods safeguards meant Ezra couldn't teleport us out of there. We could have sauntered out of there clutching an armful of books as cover, but something about his tone rooted me to the spot. I clenched my butt cheeks together in fear.

"It is a shame so few of us are here for this discussion. The others are tending to pressing matters and will meet us in the arena," said Phinnaeous Shine. "We have full authority to proceed in this matter. You deciphered the code with typical speed, Orpheus."

"Indeed, Prime Sorcerer," said Orpheus. "Anagrams were a favourite pastime of mine back in the 1940s."

Phinnaeous harrumphed. "Well, thanks to you, we know the gods are stepping out of the shadows again."

I sucked in my breath and exchanged glances with Ezra. So it was true.

My first instinct was to call for Gaia, but I didn't always need to be in the cavalry. I repeated my mantra. *Stick to your goals. It's not your problem.*

"How easily the humdrums fall apart," said Phinnaeous.

"It was pathetic yesterday. I skin-walked into the Prime Minister's office yesterday pretending to be the Home Secretary. He was lamenting about the Queen's private secretary coming to fisticuffs with the head of the Royal Guard. The Prime Minister himself had only just dealt with conflict within his own cabinet and was spitting with rage about the conduct of the Environment Minister on WhatsApp."

Lavinia piped up. "Any trouble between the humdrums means peculiars are stronger in comparison. My rats tell me it seems centred around mobile phones, and even peculiars have seemed more ruffled than usual. I have advised our kind to refrain from using their mobile phones for important communication. I say we ride out the storm. It wouldn't be difficult to improve the magical post. My rats and Helio's birds could be trained to carry messages. We have a whole ecosystem that is not dependent on the human one."

Echo had told me about the cloud master and magical post. There was still so much I had to learn.

Orpheus sounded gruff. "We don't live apart from the humdrums. We live amongst them. Anything that troubles them is our problem too. Our oracle warns that Crown and country may fall. I say that if the message is true, if the gods are interfering in everyday lives, then we should take action. The Magical Constitution was written in a different time. The gods were stronger then. Now we stand a chance of winning if we stand united against them. What is power unless we use it well?"

Lavinia's laugh tinkled. "Underneath that fatigued, tragic exterior, you have a poet's heart, Orpheus. But you forget, there's an opportunity in every crisis. It would be advantageous to see how the situation plays out. Aren't you tired of living in the shadows? This could be our chance to swing the system our way. To come out on top."

"Hush, Lavinia," said the Prime Sorcerer. "Wasn't it you

who saved the humdrums along with the druid when the scientists were being targeted?"

My ears burned. I turned imploring eyes on Ezra. We should have left when we had the chance.

Lavinia's voice had the tartness of a lemon. She didn't like being challenged. "Indeed, Phinnaeous, but it wasn't a gesture of magnanimity. I weighed up what I would get out of it. And in this situation, the chaos suits us. Weakened humdrums mean that, in comparison, we are stronger."

The Prime Sorcerer struck out like a whip. "You have made many mistakes of late, witch. Without your cock-ups, we might have had a dragon. But as it happens, this time, I agree with you. Perhaps we should listen to what Margola has to say."

He must have been very secure in his ability to defend himself because Lavinia wasn't the type to let an insult slide off her back. She was made for revenge. I peeked through the bookcase. Margola's flame-coloured hair shone through green foliage.

"Of course, Phinnaeous, we would be in a different place right now if you had agreed to my proposal to launch a social media app, but the senate deemed it a low priority," said Margola archly.

My eye roll almost gave me a neck injury. Yeah, right. Or maybe it would just be another way for the senate to keep tabs on everyone.

"I thrive on discord. My readers love it. Conflict means friends turn on each other. They become loose-lipped about secrets they once would have died to protect." Margola's sultry voice belied her dark heart. "I care little for humdrums. It doesn't matter which god is behind this or how he is achieving this. I say let the world burn as long as peculiars survive."

Like I said, she was like Vladimir Putin in a Christina Hendricks body.

Anger coursed through my veins at her casual disregard for humdrums. I'd lived most of my life as a humdrum. I couldn't believe anyone could be so callous as not to lift a finger to help those more vulnerable. Wasn't she even curious as to what was going on? What kind of Information Minister was she anyway?

My rage propelled me into the open.

I gave Ezra an apologetic glance and slipped out of his reach, only to find myself pushed unceremoniously back onto his lap.

Orpheus stood glowering above me. "Just fetching a book, Prime Sorcerer." He hissed in my ear. "Your mind is as loud as a Mahler's Symphony no. 8. When *will* you learn to be quiet? If you know what's good for you, you'll stay here."

I clambered up and pushed past them both.

Their groans echoed in my ear, but sometimes you needed to stand up and be counted. Even if it meant you landed in hot water. And from the look on Lavinia's face, her cauldron was boiling. Her helmet of silver curls only just hid the steam coming out of her ears.

I didn't hold back. "You know the gods are up to no good, and you won't even investigate? Why would you hold all your power and not even try to help?"

Phinnaeous Shine's righteous anger was a sight to behold. "Of course, it would be you skulking in the shadows. How dare you eavesdrop on senate business?"

Ezra walked out from behind the shelving, his cheeks flushed. He avoided my gaze.

"What, Neuhoff, you too?" said Phinnaeous. "This is very unusual. It seems Gunnolf doesn't have his pack under control."

Ezra's head dipped. "My deepest apologies, Prime Sorcerer. It won't happen again. We were…reading when the senate contingent entered the library and were loathe to interrupt."

"Yes, well, Neuhoff. The druid has shown poor judgement, but I expected better of you."

I smarted. Was it just me, or had Phinnaeous Shine belittled the women in the room? Those succubi forced to be his house servants probably hated him. A question plagued me. "What would the Wildwoods community think if they knew you refused to help the humdrums we live side by side with?"

Phinnaeous Shine dusted off the shoulder of his robe like I was a mere gnat bothering him. "What makes you think Wildwoods is a democracy? The peculiars out there couldn't care less what happens to humdrums. They don't want us to waste time following a thread that could lead nowhere. So what if a god is up to mischief? We live a double life. It means if one combusts, we always have the other."

Orpheus stepped out. "Phinnaeous, you can't believe that."

"But I do, dear friend. We have survived all this time because we have chosen our battles carefully. But if the humans err, we could discard our double lives. Aren't you ever dissatisfied with only having a small part of the world? I agree with Lavinia. We do nothing."

"You are cowards." I turned to Margola. Her hourglass figure had been squeezed into a pencil skirt and silk blouse. "And you, Minister, have made my life hell by reporting on me. I mean, a small feature is one thing, but you have whipped up your readers with intrigue about my grandmother, my mother, the dragon, even my marriage and relationship."

Ezra shifted uncomfortably. Orpheus, at least, had the grace to look away. He couldn't have been happy that Margola had been gossiping about our supposed chemistry.

"Alisha, you are a funny old fish. Who told you news is fair? Or that it is about the truth? Of course, sometimes it educates. But it also titillates. It distracts. It muddies the waters. Depending on who it's in service to," said Margola. "And that's even more true of humdrums than of peculiars. A decade of immersion in the new technology has changed the way their minds and systems work. More fool them for growing used to the constant stream of communication and distraction. Whatever is going on with the mobile phones, let's take a step back and enjoy the show."

I flexed my hands. She was so smug and so utterly morally bankrupt that I itched to send her flying onto her arse. Just a little push. It wasn't like a selkie had powers that could retaliate. Not in this environment, anyway. But we weren't alone, and as much as I disliked her, Margola Silver had the power of the pen and microphone. She could shape opinions while filing her pretty nails. I couldn't declare all-out war.

I smiled. "Well, I can see I'm not going to convince you with rhetoric. So once I perform in front of the Wildwoods community tonight, I'm going to get to the bottom of this myself. It's not like I needed your help for Ra or Pan. And if you want to bring me up on charges for falling foul of the Pragmatist's Law again, I'll just tell the truth at trial—That you yourselves considered intervening in this matter. That you considered rewriting the law now that the gods are less powerful. And the reason you didn't was pure selfishness. And that little old truth tonic you knocked me out with, Lavinia, is used at trials, right? So you can't lie."

They looked at me in horror—all of them.

"Oh, shit," said Ezra.

Orpheus rolled his eyes. "Wow. Just wow."

Lavinia folded her arms. "I can't believe you gave her a medal of honour, Phinnaeous."

So much for my mantra.

ANY SECOND NOW, I'd step out onto the stage. The obelisk had been wrapped in fairy lights. There was a hush in the arena. The stalls had been cleared away, replaced by theatre-style seating. The semi-circles of green velvet chairs under the starry night and crescent moon took my breath away. My nerves, at least, had subsided. The run-in with the senate had been a good distraction, and now I couldn't wait to go out and show everyone what I was made of.

"I can't believe you did that," Ezra said. He usually couldn't keep his hands off me. Even with other people around, there'd be a frisson in the centimetres between us. A promise of what might happen if we were alone. But no. I had well and truly made his hackles rise.

Oops. "I didn't mean to put you in it. I mean, they would have discovered us eventually, right? Orpheus could read our minds."

"Correction. Orpheus could read your mind. I learned a long time ago to block out the voodoo powers of vampires." Ezra shook his head. "Orpheus is a lot of things, but he isn't a snitch. And for whatever reason, he seems to have a soft spot for you. I mean, didn't he use his faster-than-light speed to ask you to stay put? At risk to his own neck, I might add. His role as a history scholar means he is more aware than most about what disasters can befall the world when good men don't act."

I bit my lip. "You're right. He was the only one there who didn't sound like a psycho. I had to go with my gut, Ezra. We've seen it before. Bored gods are trouble. We can't just turn a blind eye."

"The investigation into the dead wolves is taking up all my time. I don't know if it's wise for you to get involved in this."

I perked up. "We could just give Robert a ring. Maybe have a word with Gaia. Ruffle a few feathers. Follow our noses."

"Stop. Just stop it. Put all that out of your head, go onto that stage and get through the next few minutes."

Goosebumps raced up my arms at the sight of the audience. "Can we talk about it later?"

He sighed. "Of course. Go thrill them."

I turned to the stage, where Wildwoods headmistress Rayna Willowsun, a silver plait trailing down her back, prepared to take the microphone. The audience twitched with anticipation: pupils and their parents, impassive senate members, lone wolves, raucous leprechauns, timid elves, sulking vampires and fairies whose wings glistened in the night. Margola's cameraman, the fallen angel from the medal ceremony, filmed the proceedings. Margola herself waited alongside him, twirling her microphone like a weapon.

Rayna stepped up to the microphone. "Ladies and gentlemen, welcome to the Wildwoods arena. First, an enormous thank you to Information Minister Margola Silver for arranging such an inspiring event for our pupils and their families. Now, without further ado, the woman you have all been waiting for. Put your hands together for the granddaughter of Rajika, fellow druid, animator, and winner of the Wildwoods Medal of Honour, Alisha Verma!"

I stumbled out under the bright lights in my slim black jeans and a button-up shirt, with the catalogue of creatures tucked under my arm. When I gave the crowd a wave, the applause ratcheted up a notch, and I wondered what magic prevented the late-night dog walkers in Crystal Palace Park from hearing us.

Marina and Dad gave me a thumbs-up. Echo quivered with excitement. He liked a display of pomp more than anyone, especially as he could bask in the glory of my achievements by virtue of being in my inner circle.

I shook Rayna's cold hand and stepped up to the microphone. A high-pitched squeal of feedback made me wince. I adopted a game show host persona to mask the sudden resurgence of my nerves. "Hellooooo, Wildwoods. For those who don't know me, I'm Alisha. I've only been a peculiar for a few months."

"Show off," shouted a stranger.

I braced myself and ploughed on. "I'm here to demonstrate what it means to be an animator. Like my grandmother before me, I am able to lift animals off the page and bring them to life. I have raised a dragon, a rooster and a butterfly."

"She's going downhill," said a voice from the back of the arena.

The audience tittered.

I located Orpheus in the audience. His granite face betrayed no emotion. "Orpheus Might told me once there haven't been many animators in history. They are scattered between continents and sometimes come only once in a generation. If they do not find an illustrator, an animator's powers lay dormant. Unused. There is no animator without an illustrator. We come in pairs. I just get to steal the limelight."

The crowd laughed. I didn't have them in the palm of my hands, but they were warming to me. The encouragement in Dad's eyes strengthened my resolve.

"Just as each illustrator has their own personal style and their own subject matter, each animator has different quirks. For example, my grandmother assigned her creatures a purpose as they were born. I am able to reassign a purpose after birth. Like those of you learning new skills, it has been a case of trial and error. Many errors." Teacher 101. Show that making mistakes is a path to learning.

I picked up the leather-bound catalogue of creatures, turned it outwards and flicked through some pages for the audience to see. There was a unicorn with a purple mane, a jellyfish with intricate veining and a stern eagle with ruffled feathers. "This catalogue of creatures was painted by my dad.

It was once my grandmother's, and now it's mine. There is one cardinal rule of animating. We may not bring to life a creature unless it can be useful, happy or free." A bead of sweat rolled down the side of my face under the hot lights. I gave a shaky smile. "So now it's over to you, Wildwoods. I will now animate a creature from the catalogue for you. One creature only. Chosen by you, as agreed by my very naughty magical leopard, Echo."

Echo gave a roar of approval.

Another titter of appreciation.

I held a hand up. "Just remember the cardinal rule. I ask you, Wildwoods, would it be wise for me to animate a jellyfish here?"

"No," came the united response from the arena.

"That's right. Because we are not close to the ocean." I was enjoying myself now. I was a teacher, after all. I just had to remember how to handle the performance like a lesson. "How about a giraffe?"

Mirabel's voice met my ears. "A giraffe is not native to this country. Unless you wanted to gift it to London Zoo."

I nodded. "Excellent analysis, Mirabel. You're getting the picture. Now, over to you, Wildwoods. I'll flick through the catalogue so you can see your options."

Lavinia stood up and raised her umbrella, which I knew now to be her broomstick, her wand and her weapon. "And I will project the choices into the sky."

I nodded my thanks, but the smile didn't reach my eyes.

Neither did hers.

I flicked through the options as the catalogue of creatures became a projection in the night sky, sitting amongst the constellations. "How about a snail?"

The arena groaned. "No."

"Too boring," said a voice.

I held up a page full of insects. "Or a beetle."

"Too small."

On and on the list went as if it were a cinema reel or a gallery of Dad's works, the exhibition he craved. The crowd booed or applauded based on their preferences: a bear, an owl, a kraken, a vulture, an otter, a fox, a nightingale, a zebra, a phoenix, a hippo, a pegasus, a bee, a monkey. Judging by the peaks and troughs of the applause, the owl seemed a favourite. Dad had painted one that filled the page, its feathers an inky blue, with large amber eyes set in a flat, grey face and a small, sharp, orange beak. Who didn't like owls and their night-time calls, reputation for wisdom and entanglement with tales of old? It was the perfect choice for pupil demonstration.

I could sense the threads of the owl, its talons and its tufty plumes, leaping under the pads of my fingers. I took a deep breath. "An owl. I will animate an owl."

Suddenly phones started pinging all over the audience. Little rectangles of light appeared in the arena as they checked their messages.

Margola, too, checked her phone, then abruptly turned to address the audience, her sultry voice drifted over the audience. She lifted her phone into the air like a call to arms. "A fox. It has to be a fox."

"Fox. Fox. Fox." The chanting started slowly but quickly gathered pace, like the demented crowd at a gladiator fight.

If I could animate a dragon, why should I be afraid of a fox? It was much better than being asked to animate a pegasus or a phoenix because what the hell would I do with those even if I managed it? Surrender them to the Bestiary Master for captivity? Foxes—not my *hu hsien* fox friends Fei Yen and Faeza, of course—were ordinary. I could manage that. A fox could be freed after the performance and would blend in. The London streets were full of them.

I ignored the churning nerves in my belly. "Agreed."

A small smile toyed at the corner of Margola's painted lips.

Lavinia sat down, her job done, with a quizzical look at Margola and me.

My heart hammered in my throat as I returned to the page featuring a skulk of foxes. Dad had drawn four variations. A rusty vixen with a snowy white tip to her tail. A few cubs with slanted eyes and too-big ears. In the centre of the page, a rangy male with a bristly unkempt coat and whiskers was ready to leap off the page. I chose him, knowing my animation powers did not allow me to assign sex. The fox's sex would be the luck of the draw, just like in nature.

I sat cross-legged on the stage, with the catalogue in my lap, and blocked out all those present until they were in my peripheral vision but blurred out. No longer important. I heard the sway of the trees in the wind and sensed the presence of the stars above. My breath became one with nature, with the heartbeat of the Earth. Only then did I allow my fingers to drift over the page, to call the fox forth, to imagine who he was and who he could be. Like a mother envisaging her child.

But the pull and tug of the threads were strangely absent.

I doubled down, determined, trusting that my skill would not let me down. My fingers searched the page. Where were his blood and veins, his wily, resourceful nature, teeth like tiny knives, and eyes that knew all the secrets of the universe?

I grew desperate. I couldn't fail. I had talked myself up. Hell, Margola had talked me up.

My fox would appear like magic any second.

The audience leaned forward, eager to see the marvel. Believing and not believing.

But my fingers couldn't coax the fox into being.

Orpheus's voice filled my head. *Focus, druid.*

My eyes flashed to him. *Get out of my head.*

He came at me again. *The stakes are too high for you to fail now.*

I chewed the inside of my cheek, willing my fingers to do

their thing. To be the harpist. The midwife. The giver of life. The page remained dimensionless, however much I sought its depth.

Closing the catalogue, I looked up, tears blurring my vision.

The audience gawped at me.

My toes curled. I tried to brazen it out and stop the flush creeping up my neck.

One unkindness could make the difference between holding your head high and being crushed.

"She's bottled it," called a gleeful voice.

I died inside.

I let the whispers wash over me as I stumbled to my feet.

Orpheus rose from his seat and bellowed at the audience. "I think that's quite enough for one evening. The children should be in bed."

I caught Margola's smile of triumph as I fled the stage into the shadows.

9

———————

The audience dispersed at Orpheus's command. My ears burned as fragments of whispers floated my way. Pupils and their families, some enjoying the schadenfreude, many angry I hadn't delivered as promised, and others crowing they'd known I was a fraud. It didn't seem fair to have been put on a pedestal only for it to come crashing down so publicly. I hadn't asked for the extra attention. I was only trying to live my life.

It needled the part of me that still doubted myself. Were my wins down to luck or talent?

Ezra put his arms around me. "This will pass. It'll be okay."

"Will it?" I wished he could whisk me out of there, away from prying eyes—the sort of eyes that ghoulishly turned to look at car crashes as they pass—but the defences of the yew tree blocked teleporting. "Can we get out of here?"

He nodded. Heat spread through me as he threaded his fingers through mine, and the meaty part of his palm pressed against mine. We waded our way out of Wildwoods, my thoughts like treacle.

But my humiliation wasn't yet over.

A senate contingent floated towards us as if a rogue god hadn't written a message in the sky. As if they didn't have a care in the world except for me and my misdemeanours.

Ezra murmured into my ear. "Let them say their worst. I believe in you." He put a protective arm around me as they closed in. "Ministers, whatever needs to be said doesn't have to be tonight."

Cillian O'Meara, Minister for Finance, patted me awkwardly on my arm. He was a short, stocky sort, with a peach fuzz of beard growing in scraps across his face. "Your charge could have done with the luck of the leprechauns tonight, Neuhoff."

Phinnaeous Shine's lips twisted in the moonlight. "All those threats she made have come to nothing. How can she expect to challenge a god if she can't even perform a few tricks to dazzle Wildwoods pupils?"

Rayna put a hand on the Prime Sorcerer's arm. "Leave her be, Phinnaeous. At her age, our mouths also ran away with us. That must have been a hard lesson out there, Alisha. I was sorry to witness it. Take heart; you are still learning."

I gulped. "I appreciate that, Minister."

"Now, if you'll excuse us, we have business to attend to." Rayna ushered the Prime Sorcerer and Finance Minister towards the cable cars.

That left Gunnolf and Lavinia.

Oh, goodie, my favourites.

Plus Orpheus, whose brooding eyes searched mine.

I shuddered, wondering if he viewed me as prey after my humiliation.

He pushed his voice into my head. *You've always been prey to me, druid. I just choose not to take advantage of you.*

I balled my fists. *Seriously? You're sticking the boot in too?*

Orpheus gave a sardonic smile.

Ezra looked between the two of us, instinctively sensing that he was missing something. A tiny part of me enjoyed his hackles rising when Orpheus showed an interest in me.

Lavinia distracted Ezra by throwing her arms around him, sending a cloud of berry-scented hairspray over us. "You should be more careful where you stick your tent pole, Ezra. Even I thought the druid was something. But she is nothing."

A growl. "You are wrong, auntie."

"Take this as motherly advice, given my dear sister is no longer with us. Who you spend your time with has a direct impact on who you become. So be careful where you lay your head to rest each night." She stood between Orpheus and Gunnolf, a pint-sized pocket rocket in pink between two dark, brooding men. She twirled her umbrella and gave Gunnolf a dazzling smile. "You have told Ezra the news, haven't you? You'll be very excited to hear this too, Orpheus, given your oversight of genealogy for the senate."

Gunnolf searched Ezra's face. "This is best discussed back at the farmhouse, Lavinia."

My toes curled. I could sense this display was for my benefit. I guess she still blamed me for Elvira's death. Or simply thought I wasn't good enough for her nephew. Lavinia might look pretty in pink, but she was as much a strutting cock as the rest of them.

"Spit it out, auntie. You obviously have something on your mind." A growl laced Ezra's words. His thumb drew comforting circles on the inside of my hand as though he was trying to tell me to hold on just a little longer.

"Very well, if you insist. Your aunt Isadora has been doing some work. You know what a talented matchmaker she is. She's practically the godmother of a dozen peculiar children. And it so happens that the sexy red wolf Rashida you once dated has been meeting with Isadora. Their bloodline work has shown that the two of you are wonderfully compatible.

Not only that, but Rashida is fertile. Almost unheard of for a female werewolf. Isadora's dark arts show your children would survive the birthing process." She gave me a triumphant glance. "The first wolf born—not made—in a generation in this city. It's quite magnificent."

My humiliation was complete. My posture slumped, and my vision blurred. I didn't often dwell on not being able to have children. My life was full, after all. But to be completely cast aside while Lavinia discussed Ezra's ex-girlfriend's fertility was too much to bear.

"This is ludicrous." Ezra looked from Lavinia to Gunnolf and back again. His grip tightened on my hand, but all I could think of was how he'd choose Rashida over me.

Gunnolf addressed Ezra as if I didn't exist. As though this conversation had nothing to do with me at all and I was simply an object to be discarded. "It pains me to break it to you this way, Ezra, but the witch is right. Have your fun if you must, but in the end, you must choose duty to the pack. You loved Rashida once. It is obvious to all that your mate bond is strong. You will love her again. And we will have pups running around the woods once more."

The black night seemed even blacker to me now. Ezra and the red wolf already had chemistry, or they would never have been together in the first place. She could give him children. I couldn't. His alpha wanted them to be together. The senate was excited about the union. I didn't stand a chance. It was case closed.

Breathe, druid. Orpheus sighed. "This is welcome news, Lavinia, but quite odd for you to share it this way and not in a formal meeting."

I waited, stunned into silence, hoping Ezra would come through for me.

Lavinia pouted. "Always such a killjoy, Orpheus. You should be pleased. You know as well as I do that the senate might turn a blind eye to rumbles between the sheets but magical unions are only blessed between peculiars of the same sort. It's too much of a risk to bring a mixed-race mewling into the world when they might have uncontrollable or demonic powers."

Was I just a rumble between the sheets? What I wouldn't have given for the chance to have a mixed-race mewling with someone I loved. My emotions stretched taut, almost at breaking point.

Ezra bristled. "Sometimes it works out just fine. Or are you wishing me away too, auntie, as well as Alisha?"

"Why so prickly, nephew? Of course, I'm not wishing you away. You're all that's left of my sister," said Lavinia. "I'm only trying to help. I truly want you to succeed."

"I'm not sure you could have handled this any worse." The vampire's look would have made a lesser women wither.

Ezra ignored him. "When have you ever helped me, auntie, without wanting something in return? Your love, too, Gunnolf, has never been without conditions. So can you speak to me of love?"

The alpha released a growl of warning. "This is not a discussion. You will do your duty."

Ezra's posture changed. His grip on my hand loosened, and grey eyes no longer challenged. The alpha had spoken, after all. His biology compelled him to be obedient.

I couldn't stand it anymore. Something in me broke.

I wrenched my hand from Ezra's, and it slid away like butter, no friction, no attempt to hold me back.

I ran, tears trickling down my face. I pounded through the empty woods and past the yew tree, past the sphinxes whose stone heads didn't bother to turn my way, through the park and towards the double-decker buses hurtling down the main road. I wanted to be in my flat, with Marina's arms around me. I wanted to nuzzle against Echo and pretend he was still just my Bengal cat—just my friend. I wanted to leave all the magic behind me. All the pressure to succeed and battle, the relentless quest to improve.

Wasn't that what I wanted?

No children. No magic. No lover.

My fight drained out of me like water down a plughole.

When I heard footsteps behind me, my heart ricocheted inside its cage.

My fragility scared me. I didn't want to be found. I didn't want to be strong.

A hand caught mine, and I jerked to a stop, a cry on my lips as I spun against a man's chest, and his arms closed around me.

Ezra's heart raced against mine. "Why did you run?"

I looked up at him. The wind rustled his brown hair, and the shadows played in the crevices of his face. We could have been something. I knew it in the deepest parts of me. I'd known it from when we'd first saved Melissa. I wanted so much for him to be mine. For him to stand at my side and look at me like I was his world. To protect me.

Not that red-haired hussy.

I drew in a shaky breath. "You have to choose her. It's the only thing that makes sense."

"It doesn't make sense to me."

"Don't you ever think about children, Ezra?" A deep, shuddering breath. "I can't have them."

His eyes on mine. "I haven't thought about children. But I do think about you. All the time."

A catch in my voice. "I don't want my heart to break. I won't recover again."

Serious grey eyes compelled me to believe him. "Your heart is safe with me."

"Prove it." I knew how strong the alpha bond was. I didn't want to be hurt again.

He inched forward, less man than wolf, his eyes full of raw intent, until there was no one else, no noise in the world except his breath and mine. He kissed me, teasingly at first, not giving me enough, until I wrapped my arms around his head and pulled him closer, deeper. My salty tears ran into his mouth.

Then he pulled away. "I know you're scared, but I need you to know I'm more my father's son than my uncle's nephew. Your heart is as important to me as my own. I would disobey pack law and the Magical Constitution to put you first. Does that make me weak?"

I searched his eyes for the truth. My heart fluttered. I knew I'd pushed him, but he'd not pushed me away. Not yet.

The copper flecks danced in his grey eyes. "It's not up to Gunnolf and Lavinia to decide who I love. It makes me proud to follow my heart, just like my parents did. Their love burned so brightly that it was worth the fallout. I would take risk after risk for you, Alisha, because I love you. I love your passion, your belief, and your sense of humanity. I love your stubbornness and the way you shoot off your mouth." He swept back the tangled mess of my hair and pressed a kiss to my forehead. "It makes you real. I feel more alive than I've felt in a decade, and it's all down to you."

My heart expanded in my chest until I thought it would explode. How long had it been since a romantic partner had told me they loved me without prompting? I trusted that he meant every little syllable. I wrapped my arms around his neck and jumped up, entwining my legs around his waist. My joy bubbled.

I took his face in my hands, raining featherlight kisses over his stubbly cheeks. "You love me."

His hands splayed across my bum, holding me in position. He nodded solemnly. "I do."

I looked at him from under my eyelashes. "Can you take me to bed now?"

His eyes darkened. "Soon, hellfire. If that's our first lover's quarrel, I want to settle it properly. You wanted proof of my intentions, didn't you? Well, I have just the thing in mind. And aren't you going to tell me you love me back?"

I gave him a teasing look. "Soon, Ezra. Soon."

10

Marina and Echo waited at the flat for us. We piled into the living room, undone by the events of the night. I put on the kettle as we picked over the bones of what had transpired: the message from the god in the sky over Wildwoods, eavesdropping on the senate, my grand-scale humiliation and finally, Gunnolf and Lavinia's declaration that Rashida was the one for Ezra.

Not even a never-ending cup of tea, a foot massage from Ezra, or a tin of shortbread could lighten my mood. Okay, I lied. The foot rub was pretty amazing. I had to stop myself from moaning in pleasure. There was a promise in how Ezra's hands kneaded the arch of my foot and in the light in his eyes.

I hugged the three little words he had uttered close to me.

Marina wasn't fooled. She grinned as she soaked up the chemistry between the two of us. "The senators were out of line, of course, but it doesn't seem to have pierced your little love bubble."

Echo pored over a copy of *The Otherworld News* fresh off the press that had magically appeared in my living room. As if out of spite. The front page featured a picture of me on my knees at the moment my skills had failed me, and the headline sent colour rushing to my face.

Washout at Wildwoods. Can This Really Be Rajika Verma's Granddaughter?

"I just want to crawl into a hole and never come out." I chomped on another biscuit. "You know those dreams people have about being naked on stage? Well, it was worse than that. Do you know what really gets me? Dad was just getting back on his feet. He was happy and excited, and now I've crushed him."

Marina reached over to squeeze my hand, and calm washed over me. She didn't even need to focus anymore to do her empath thing. It came so naturally to her. "You're not responsible for Joshi's feelings. He'd be the last one to want you to pressure yourself that way. So what if you messed up? Nothing worthwhile comes without a struggle."

"Look on the bright side. It should put an end to all the fans." Echo began whistling. "Do you know the Monty Python tune? Whistle with me. It will cheer you up. Or we could go and hunt poodles."

Marina sighed. "Not the time, Echo."

He looked up hopefully. "Is it time for steak?"

I shook my head. "Not yet. I can say one thing for sure. All that self-confidence I had about taking on the god has drained out quicker than air leaves a balloon. I thought I was Wonder Woman there for a moment, but the universe taught me a lesson."

Ezra tugged my feet in reproach. "I'm not having you doubting yourself. It was a blip, that's all." He pushed my feet off his lap and motioned to the three of us. "Come on, Alisha's not going to sit around here feeling sorry for herself. I made her a promise. I'm due at the farmhouse at dawn, but there are still a few hours until then."

I exhaled in a huff of air. "To do what?"

He held out a hand. "To visit your most brilliant creation."

I met his eyes as my black feelings dispersed, letting in a little light.

Marina grinned. "Atta wolf boy. Can we swing by the surgery first to pick up some roadkill and my gear?"

Ezra nodded. "Your wish is my command, Ambrose."

EZRA'S olive skin was pale and clammy when we emerged on the green bank of a river in Bulgaria. He'd confided in me how teleporting was easy enough for him if he was alone or going short distances. Teleporting groups of people, however, took a toll on his body. Teleporting three people, plus a leopard, across Europe was a mean feat.

But my heart sang with joy. We were here to visit the dragon in his safe haven. It was exactly what I needed to buoy me after the evening's disaster. It had been weeks since Gaia had brought Tielbu here for safekeeping. The senate still hadn't forgiven me for not turning Tielbu over to them, and I didn't put it past them to attempt to capture him themselves. Secrecy was of paramount importance. It was risky coming here. I could tell Ezra knew it, too, by the set of his jaw.

He was taking the risk for me.

Though a blanket of night masked much of the view of the village, I spotted chalets, quaint hotels and a church with a bell tower in the shadows. The evening was warm and made lovelier by snow-capped mountains in the distance and the sound of the gushing water.

Echo's jaw dripped with drool as he surveyed the landscape with the demeanour of a creature about to evacuate its stomach contents. Luckily, we hadn't fed him the steak. "What fresh hell is this?"

"It's beautiful," I said. "No wonder your parents holidayed here, Ezra."

Ezra's grey eyes grew melancholy. "They loved the summer trekking and hot springs here as much as the winter skiing with its crystal white ski trails lined with trees."

Bulgaria was a special place. It had both mountains and plains. It had the Black Sea coastline and the Danube and was a melting pot of diversity, with Greek, Slavic, Ottoman and Persian influences. Bansko was the perfect hiding place for a peculiar community.

"Come on," said Ezra. "We have a dragon to find."

"Tielbu's going to love the roadkill I've stashed away in this cool bag for him," said Marina.

"It'll mean we are off the menu, at least." The sheen had returned to Echo's lustrous coat. He bounded ahead through a lane of pine trees. "Follow me. I have caught the dragon's scent."

We trudged through an eerie forest, not a soul in sight, with glee in our hearts and pine needles crunching underfoot. At the mouth of a cave, Echo unleashed a roar and forged ahead into the even deeper darkness within.

"These mountainous regions with their plentiful forests and water supplies are renowned brown bear habitats." Ezra raised a wry eyebrow. "Let's hope it's the dragon and not a bear that the leopard is tracking."

I scanned our environment, alert to every footfall. "Now you tell us."

Her expression grim, Marina zipped open her vet bag and loaded a tranquilliser gun. "We have plenty of weapon options between us, what with wolf man, leopard teeth, dragon-fire and whirlwinds. But it makes me feel better to have this in my hand. Just as a last resort."

"Let me carry this." Ezra picked up the cool bag of roadkill. "Stay behind me, ladies."

I lassoed him to me with a draught of wind. "Forget that. You stay behind me."

I didn't wait for an answer. My dragon and leopard needed me.

The temperature cooled as we entered the cave. We stepped over stalagmites emerging from the floor. Icicle-like stalactites grew from the cave ceiling, too, although some of the rock formations had crumbled onto the cave floor as if something large and clumsy had come this way. A layer of smoke lingered at our feet.

Tielbu. I ran through one cave hall into another, deeper and deeper, my heartbeat pounding in my ears. I blinked as my eyes struggled to adjust to the change in light. Goosebumps ran up my bare arms when I spied three bodies around a small fire.

A smiling old woman.

A snorting dragon.

A purring leopard.

"Hold on!" called Ezra.

Deep-set amber eyes glowed in the darkness. The dragon lifted his head in recognition and snorted rings of smoke towards me in greeting. "I have missed you, druid."

I laughed and ran towards Tielbu to press my cheek against the iridescent turquoise scales of his cold reptilian skin, drinking in the scent of smoke and meat.

Not so long ago, he had been mere lines and paint on paper. I might have failed at animating the fox, but I couldn't be a complete failure. I had managed this. His bulky frame told me that he had been well nourished. His teeth and horns had retained their menace, and his wings hadn't withered away.

I drew away from him. "Are you well?"

"I am," the dragon said.

A bubble of tension I hadn't known I was holding evaporated.

I turned to Gaia and bowed my head, joined by Ezra and Marina as they caught up behind me. "Goddess. I am glad to see you. I thought of you just today."

She smelt of hair oil and curry spices. Her plump midriff spilt out of her sari blouse, and shadows cast by the fire swept across her lined face. "The universe told me you were on your way, and I thought it would be a nice evening for a reunion. I visit the dragon often for a cup of chai. He is accomplished at reheating a lukewarm brew that would otherwise be ruined."

Echo had rolled over at her feet like the hussy he was.

"Yes, Chanakya, I have missed you too." The goddess tickled his exposed belly, and he unleashed a purr of ecstasy.

The cave was alive with warmth and friendship, although I had been shivering only a few minutes before. We gathered around the fire in the cave that Tielbu had made his own. Marina checked him over with her stethoscope and various gauges, cooing all the while. When she had decided all was well, she tore open the bag of roadkill and encouraged the dragon to eat to his heart's content. The dragon used teeth and talons to devour the deer carcass, leaving scraps for Echo.

"Are you happy here?" I asked the dragon.

Tielbu lifted his rounded skull. His table manners left a lot to be desired. Lumps of flesh landed in the hissing fire and inches from the goddess's luscious peach-coloured sari.

Gaia didn't flinch as if she was accustomed to the grime of living.

"I am." The dragon's voice was an ancient rumble in my ears, like the moving of mountains.

"And have you found your purpose?" I didn't mean the question to sound weighted, but as soon as the words spilt out of his mouth, I knew I was talking about me as much as him.

Tielbu snorted twin rings of smoke. "The goddess tells me that sometimes it takes a lifetime to find one's purpose. A dragon can live for centuries. I have food, freedom and friends. The Bulgarian witches here have conjured a glamour for me. I am told humdrums see me as a black vulture. I am judicious about how often I prune the herds in neighbouring villages, and I have found a way to be useful in heating the hot springs for the tourists to enjoy. I have only one worry."

I frowned. "What is that?"

"That I will be too far away to protect you when you need me." He bent his head to his meal. The bone-crunching sent shivers up my spine. So did his use of the word *when*, as if he knew with certainty that my peace wouldn't last.

Echo licked the blood off his jaw with relish. "There is no need for you to worry, dragon. Alisha has many allies. I have been at her side since the very beginning."

"The leopard is right," said Ezra. "It is far more important that you stay here, out of the clutches of the senate. There is little you can do from a continent away, but rest assured that I can be at her side in a flash."

I glanced at Marina and rolled my eyes. What was it about the protective urge of the men around me? I appreciated their care, but it was like they had completely forgotten that, even before I had magical talents, I had been slinging right hooks and putting my shoe in sorry behinds. Hell, the first time I had met Ezra, I'd flipped him on his back. "It's okay. I'm not planning on getting embroiled in any more Otherworld fights."

Gaia's dark eyes hid the secrets to endless worlds. "And what, pray tell, makes you think you have a choice?"

My voice was small and hollow. "There's always a choice. My run of luck is over. I completely failed in front of the Wildwoods community tonight."

The goddess's eyes gleamed. "That's what you're worried about? Progress is never a straight line. It comes in fits and starts. That's the way the world has always been. It's the way it has been programmed since the dawn of time."

"Be that as it may, I almost went into warrior mode again,

but my failure reminded me to focus on my personal needs. The world doesn't need me to save it. There are plenty more qualified people." I shrugged. "I thought growing older would make life simpler, but somehow I've ended up in a soup of competing needs. I have an ageing dad to care for, a wayward brother, a classroom of students and a hot boyfriend." I smiled shyly at Ezra. "Tonight sealed it. I'm going to put a huge sign in my lady garden to tell everyone to go and knock at someone else's door. I prefer a quiet life."

Gaia's eyes twinkled. "Good luck with that."

Tielbu snorted. Not a snort of disdain or mirth, more like an anxiety hiccup. "When we journeyed to Bulgaria together, you told me who the druid is. She should know the truth."

Marina looked at the goddess in alarm. "If there is something we should know, a heads-up would be brilliant. As the empath in the group, I end up a little exposed. Like a snail without a shell. There have been bad omens in the tea leaves, and I saw on the news the ravens have left the Tower of London."

Gaia's back had been curved as a question mark, but she suddenly sat as straight as an arrow. In her eyes was a warrior of the ages, all trace of the cherubic old woman gone. "No need to plead with me. Is it not obvious to you all by now? If the ravens have fled the tower, then that thieving old bastard Hermes is up to his old tricks."

My brow furrowed. Hermes. The messenger god?

Marina clapped, pleased to have her superstitions confirmed, even though I had pooh-poohed them. "I told you the ravens leaving the Tower of London was bad news."

"That's who wrote the message in the sky tonight?" I asked.

"That old codger. He always did like grand gestures. Less than a day old, and he stole Apollo's herds then turned a witness to stone." Gaia fixed me with a stare. "Whatever shapes you twist yourself into, Alisha, whatever doubts plague you or humiliations you suffer, you must know by now that you are the eternal girl. You may resist your calling, but you cannot escape it."

Ezra cursed under his breath.

Echo shivered with pleasure. He would have given the spots on his golden coat for this to be true, particularly if the goddess had taken an interest in the proceedings.

Marina looked from me to Gaia, a stupefied expression on her face. "Err…what on earth is the eternal girl?"

I grimaced. "A saviour fable that has the senate dumping little girls into a tank with an octopus."

I knew it to be bollocks. How could I be the eternal girl? I was hardly fresh as a daisy. My arse ached if I sat on the floor, my eyesight had deteriorated something rotten, and my skin was starting to head south. Anger coursed through my veins like molten lava. "That's the most ridiculous thing I have ever heard. There's not even a cat's chance in hell I'm the eternal girl. I'd know if I was. I'm in control of my own fate. You're not going to make me a central character in some fairy tale handed down through the ages."

"*What?*" Marina pinched her arm hard and twisted. "Just checking I'm actually awake."

Gaia ignored her, adjusted her sari and wrapped the train around her waist. Evidently, even a goddess could have dirt under her fingernails. "Some things are written and always have been. You are an accomplished woman, Alisha, but even you cannot withstand a current that has been churning for centuries. You must understand two things."

The fire no longer warmed me. A coldness seeped into my very bones. "And what are they?"

"You're only as powerful as the weakest link in your circle. And that weak link is a pigeon."

I frowned. I still hadn't sent Sahil that text. "A werepigeon?"

Gaia blew out a huff of breath in exasperation. "Am I

speaking Aramaic again? There is only so much I can tell you, druid, or the Fates will scold me for intervening."

I chewed my lip. All this intrigue was enough to make me want to head out on an expedition to the artic where no one could find me. Possibly with my wolf in tow. And I was a beach lover. "And the second thing?"

"We are all cogs in a grand scheme, and only one path is blessed. You see, human lives aren't just reliant on talent, sheer willpower or choices. More often than not, it is a thought, a prayer, an alignment of the stars or the sneeze of a god that means the difference between jubilation or devastation." Gaia's brown eyes blazed. "Your ego, your exhaustion and your preferences have nothing to do with it."

My chest tightened. "You don't believe in choice?"

The goddess gave a sad smile. "To the contrary. But choices are only available within the parameters we set ourselves. And you're a heroine, are you not?"

I resented her for asking me to give more of myself than I was willing to. "I'm just a middle-aged woman."

Gaia's voice reverberated around the cave as her body faded into nothingness. "And the possibilities are endless."

11

———————

The air in the cave suffocated me. The thought of being tied to an inescapable fate made me shrivel with terror. I was finally the mistress of my own life, and I didn't want anyone else, not even a goddess, manipulating me. Had I made the choice to involve myself in this Hermes business, or was I only walking a path that had been marked out for me? If I didn't have agency, what was the point of anything at all? I laid my head against Tielbu's dry turquoise scales.

"Fly with me," I whispered against his sternum.

"You are upset, druid," said Tielbu. "We will fly."

Ezra stood, his forehead creased with worry lines. "I'm coming with you."

I nodded. We had a mutual love of heights. Usually, a werewolf would have preferred being grounded, but Ezra's ability to teleport had changed his nature. We followed the dragon out through the cave chambers, over the smoke-filled floors, past the stalagmites and stalactites out into the clear air that tingled on my skin, a far cry from the smog of London.

Hermes is up to his old tricks.

You must know by now that you are the eternal girl.

She is nothing.

A sharp intake of breath. It wasn't my problem.

Tielbu waited in the clearing outside the cave, and when we reached him, he bowed and flattened himself to the ground so we could clamber onto the space between his fragile wings. My wind powers gave me the ability to propel myself up and lower myself down, but it was safer to climb. I had to focus to keep my trajectory clean and not end up on the floor like a pancake. Besides, I savoured the feel of Tielbu's skin against my palms. The scent of musty dragon smoke mingled with Ezra's cigarette roll-ups as I nestled against him. No sooner had I steadied myself than Tielbu made a running leap, launching into the air.

I lurched. Ezra's arms clamped around my waist. A lifeline.

You must know by now that you are the eternal girl went through in my head like a merry-go-round.

We soared above a rippling lake and circled the snow-capped mountains. The cave in which Marina and Echo waited was a distant speck. Tielbu dipped and curved through the starry sky. The wind rushed in our faces. He swooped, his wings beating to the time of my heart, and before I knew it, my anxiety fell away and bubbled out of me like a fountain.

After the first rush of energy, the dragon snorted and stilled, catching the slightest current of air, like a paper plane floating on a breeze under the watchful eye of the moon.

I turned to Ezra. "I don't believe it, do you?"

He gave me a grim look. "I should have known that whenever the goddess appears, there is more trouble coming our way. She speaks in riddles and then disappears. I know from experience that when a god speaks, the rest of us just fall into line. We keep this under wrap for now. No need to rock any more boats than necessary."

We glided through the sky, and when the cave came into sight, Tielbu angled his wings and dove towards the earth.

Ezra clutched me tight. "It doesn't matter what I believe. Whatever my reservations, if you need me, Alisha, I'll be there."

Midnight neared as we returned to my living room, grimy from our journey into the Bulgarian cave. I longed for a scalding shower to cleanse my body and mind. I sighed at seeing Echo's discarded copy of *The Otherworld News.*

Ezra's deep voice was a growl. "So we're agreed? Not a word of the eternal girl to anyone. Alisha doesn't need any more heat from the senate or the Otherworld press."

It made sense to keep quiet. "There's no way she's right. We're all taking an oath of silence here and now. I mean it. Promise me."

Ezra had reacted with incredulity to Gaia's revelation, just as I had, but Marina and Echo seemed to be having a whale of a time imagining the what-ifs.

Marina blinked in awe. "How awesome would it be if the Chameleon Tale was real? An eternal girl who blends in even though her talents are brighter than the sun. Who, once she has a disintegrating tome in her possession, can stop the coming dusk when Death opens the door. You'd be part of a myth, Alisha."

Echo fizzed with glee. "I have long mourned my choice to follow Rajika Verma across the globe merely to pretend to be a cat. This revelation would validate my life's path. I wouldn't have merely been a babysitter to snotty Verma children. I would have had the eternal girl as my charge. Somebody put on the Supremes so we can celebrate."

My nerves were frazzled. "I'm so tempted to stuff a sock in your mouth. Not a word to anyone. I mean it, you two. Promise me."

Empath and leopard both gave a solemn nod.

"Thank you for taking me to see our friend tonight. I hope the dawn meeting at the farmhouse is fruitful." I pressed a kiss to Ezra's lips and Marina's cheek. "Now, scoot. This tired body is crying out for sleep. And stay off mobile phones. We can't trust that our messages are private or free from tampering."

When Ezra had melted into the hidden realms, I escorted Marina to her van and waited until she drove off before returning to the flat. I showered, slipped into a nightie and went into the hallway to check my answerphone machine. There were a handful of messages from Dad.

Echo padded past. "I thought you were tired. Do you need a lullaby? I can offer you 'Moon River' or perhaps 'Somewhere Over the Rainbow.'"

I scratched his ear. "Go to sleep, Echo. I'm just checking the answerphone."

He sighed. "Humans and their gadgets. If it's not mobile phones, it's blenders or vibrators. I despair."

"Actually, would you mind taking a letter to the postbox? I should stick to old-school means. I thought I'd drop Sahil a note. You heard what the goddess said tonight. It made me worry again why he's gone off the radar. Mum would expect me to check up on him."

"You and he are not so dissimilar. The werepigeon is just spreading his wings, that's all." Echo's lips pulled back into a gurn, his version of a grin. With his crooked teeth, he didn't exactly have an American smile, but at least his gums were pink.

"Maybe you're right. Can you do me a favour?" I pulled out a postcard, my address book and a stamp from the sideboard and scrawled a few lines. I blew on the ink and set it down. "The postman comes at six a.m., I think. Can you send it off by then?"

He snorted. "This task is beneath me, but I will do it for you."

I kissed his head. "Scrubbing your urine off the wall is beneath me, but I do it for you."

"Goodnight, Alisha."

"Goodnight, Echo."

He wandered down the corridor and, within seconds, snored on the sofa, grunting like an orc worthy of Tolkien.

I listened to my answerphone messages from Dad. He had always preferred calling my landline. I suspected it harked back to wanting to check I was home and safe and not boozing in some bar.

10:05 p.m. "Alisha, this is your dad. Call me when you get this."

10:38 p.m. "Wake up. Are you asleep already?" A pause. "Is the werewolf with you? Make sure you use protection."

11:42 p.m. "Darling, call me whatever time you receive this. It's your dad, by the way."

My hands turned clammy as I dialled. Maybe something had happened. Maybe he'd needed me. The dialling tone went on for an age, and just as I was about to give up, Alma answered the phone. Had she stayed over? Alma, hanging about my dad like his wife hadn't just died. I wanted him to be happy, but slower steps would have been nice.

She sounded sleepy. I pictured her picking up the telephone in the bedroom. "Hi, Alisha. I hope you're eating your greens."

I did a poor job of masking my grouchiness. "Can I speak to Dad?"

"Of course. I'll fetch him. He's been in a tizzy in his studio all evening." Rustling and heavy breathing came down the line as she made her way to the studio. "Here you go, love. It's Alisha on the phone."

Dad grappled with the line. "Alisha. Finally. Wait a second." The line grew muffled as he spoke to Alma. "You go on baking your pie, Alma. I'll be right in there to taste it." He came back on the line. "Alma's been working very hard making apple pie for the neighbour's party. She's very good at bringing people together."

I sent a silent apology to Alma for jumping to conclusions. "I got your answerphone messages, Dad. Did you need me?"

The sound of a door closing came down the line. He dropped his voice. "Yes, love. It came to me in a flash after the performance. Once I'd had my dinner. It really was awful to see you so upset on the stage. You know how I think better on a full stomach."

"Dad, what came to you in a flash?"

"Darling, what if the reason you failed to animate was because you can only animate winged creatures?"

My heart pounded as a moment of silence stretched between us.

His worried voice came down the line. "You're not offended, are you? I should have thought of it straight away. It makes sense, doesn't it? You said it yourself. Not every animator is the same. Just because your grandmother could animate all creatures doesn't mean you can."

I thought back. I'd managed a dragon, a rooster and a butterfly. I had failed at a fox, but before that too, when Dad had attempted to teach me to animate. There'd be a frog in his attic I'd not managed either.

"Wait a second. I have to try something." I ran to my bedroom for the catalogue. I'd hidden it in my knicker drawer alongside Death's sword, the choker necklace Mum had left me and my Wildwoods medal. I really did have to find a better hiding space for them.

I bounded back to the hallway and opened the catalogue, Echo's snores filling my ears. I searched for the unicorn, my pulse a hummingbird in my throat. There it was, in all its purple-maned glory. It would be very, very reckless to try to animate a unicorn in my bedroom, but what girl wouldn't love to see a unicorn? And after the day I'd had, the universe couldn't hold it against me if I threw caution to the wind.

I breathed deeply, shut my eyes and pictured the unicorn in my mind's eye. Then I focussed on the page, stroking my fingers across the unicorn's rump, its elegant back, and the horn that protruded from its forehead.

Nothing. Nada.

No ripple in the page. No warmth of a beast's skin. No neighing that precluded a mystical creature coming to life.

More fool me.

"Alisha, are you still there?"

"Just one more minute, Dad."

I turned a few more pages until I came to a swarm of bees. I'd always been afraid of that end scene in *My Girl*. But bees were inherently good. They were central to our ecosystem. Without pollination, wildflowers and food sources decreased. Not to mention honey production. And I liked honey in my tea. The universe would thank me for animating a bee.

I picked a little fellow and focussed on his mustard yellow-and-black-striped jacket, his antennae and tiny legs. He flew off the page before I could blink. I attempted it again and again until the bees buzzed around the hallway, and Echo stirred. The bees flew out to the open living room window in formation. I picked up the handset, full of wonder.

"You're right, Dad. You're right. I just animated a family of bees. I don't know how, but you did it."

He whooped like a man decades younger. "It's entirely logical that you should only be able to animate winged creatures, now I think about it. Life and colour always found you. Before the witch bound your powers, you went through a spell of winged creatures following you. Ladybirds, crickets, house flies, you name it. In the end, your mother took you to the doctor like you had a common cold. She was always looking for a scientific reason for anything." He giggled. "Anyway, the doctor thought your mother was barking mad. He was quite perplexed. He'd never seen anything like it. At first, he put you on a regime of daily baths, like uncleanliness might be the reason insects were following you."

"Charming."

"Eventually, he suggested you wear insect spray year-round. In the end, we just used mosquito nets to keep them out of the house at least." He gave a contented sigh. "It's funny how comforting those memories of your mother are now. Sahil was different, of course. He hated flying creatures with a passion, even as a boy. His fear made him wheeze. When he was really scared, he'd pinch his eyes shut and hold his breath until someone tapped him on the back, and he popped like a cork. It must be so hard for him to accept his werepigeon nature now."

I sighed. "Yes, poor Sahil."

Dad's smile came through his voice down the line. "Anyway, darling, it's simple, really. You are a mix of your mother and me. The vampire told you your mother's line traces back to virgin priestesses in Brittany, the Gallizenae. They could calm the winds, predict the future and take the form of different animals. Your mother didn't know this, of course. That culture had been lost long before she was born, but it remained in her blood. You have your wind powers through her. And your animator powers come from my mother."

My head spun. I had thought it was my fault for failing to pull off the performance, but it hadn't been in my capabilities all along. The knowledge empowered me. It gave me a starting place. Maybe my powers would grow to match my grandmother's. Maybe they wouldn't. But somewhere in my cells, I had something from my grandmother and my mother, and that made me more powerful, not less.

"Dad, I don't know how to thank you," I said.

"You don't have to thank me, love. That's what fathers are for. A little bit of support, a little bit of elbow grease and belief in your brilliance. I knew that you had been short-changed at Wildwoods tonight, and I wasn't going to let it stand."

"I love you, Dad. Listen, I need you to avoid mobile phones for now. Can you do that?"

"I love you too, Alisha. And you know I rarely touch my mobile phone. Frustrating thing."

"Do you think you can paint some of your ravens into my catalogue of creatures?"

"Of course. Now I must go and eat some pie. Otherwise, Alma will never let me go to bed." He paused. "And Alisha?"

"Yes, Dad?"

"Beware of Margola Silver. I think she's sabotaging you on purpose."

12

———

I rolled out of bed at the crack of dawn before my alarm sounded. A few minutes later, I had thrown on a hoodie and trainers and headed out to the high street in my PJs. With any luck, my misfire at Wildwoods meant that my fickle fans had found another target. The last thing I needed was to be caught in public without a bra on. I was pretty certain Mum tutted down at me from the heavens for my impropriety.

I eased into a red telephone box and fed it some change. It paid to be cautious. The god wouldn't control me. I dialled the detective's landline number. His role in the Shadow Squad meant he worked ungodly hours. My words flew out, garbled and anxious. "Robert. I know you and Marina have fizzled out, but I hoped you wouldn't mind me ringing."

"Alisha? You don't usually call me on this line. Slow down, will you?"

I sighed. "Did I disturb you?"

He sounded exasperated. "If you're asking me if you pulled me out of bed, then no. I've not had a wink of sleep. I've been working on a case. Now, what was this you said about Marina? Are you saying she dumped me? That cuts deep. We're not teenagers. She could have told me herself."

I frowned. "That's funny. She said you'd ignored her messages, that she was the dumpee, not the dumped."

"What nonsense. The thought of that woman has been getting me through the day. It's only been just over a week since we saw each other. I've been trying to chisel out time to go and steal a kiss." He paused. "Although what you said chimes with what we're uncovering in the course of the investigation. There's been a severe unravelling of trust in this country in the past few days. And I think normal people like us are just as impacted as those in the upper classes."

"What's good for the goose is good for the gander."

"Huh? Anyway, the Prime Minister is on his third reshuffle in as many days. The Lords were uncharacteristically venomous during a debate in the Upper House yesterday. And a fight broke out between the Royals in their private box at Ascot. Camilla lunged for Charles, but Princess Anne caught the brunt of it and gave as good as she got. There were hats flying everywhere. You wouldn't believe how many everyday people are in lock-ups at the moment. Local police stations are packed to the brim. The courts can't process cases quickly enough. At first, the Health Minister wondered if it was perhaps an airborne virus that triggered hostility. It wasn't farfetched. There's a lot of chaos in the natural world. But then, the message in the sky appeared, and my eyes opened."

"Oh, so you're good at anagrams too?"

He grunted. "So you deciphered it?"

"Well, yeah. On the hoof. With a scrap of paper and two scary sphinxes and a werewolf-wizard eyeballing me," I said breezily.

"Fair play to you," said Robert. "I might have got there sooner if we weren't so short-staffed. Once it was clear gods were involved, it was a case of tracing which one. I had a hunch, but I couldn't interrogate the Prime Minister and his cabinet. Or the Lords or the Royals. There's strict etiquette to these things. The higher up they are, the more difficult it is to question them. Plus, there's the issue of the veil. The hidden world must stay hidden. It was only when I picked out some low-level delinquents out of lock-up that I realised mobile phones, specifically messaging apps, were at the root of all the disharmony. Distorted messages, fabricated ones, and messages that fell into a black hole. And then it all came to me. It's related to tech."

I butted in. "It's Hermes. The trickster god. The messenger god."

There was a moment of disbelief. "Dammit, Alisha, will you just once—*just once*—not steal my thunder? I was just about to tell you that. I should bloody well recruit you to the Shadow Squad. At least then you'd be on the inside of the tent pissing out."

I grinned. The situation was serious, but I could still take a moment to revel in being right. "That's what I was ringing to tell you. Gaia confirmed it last night, but the truth is there have been signs everywhere. I just hadn't put the puzzle together. However, we shouldn't say his name. Gaia told me once that the gods have an inkling when we name them."

"I should have realised when the ravens left the Tower of London. He's the Ravenmaster there. All those birds have buggered off because he's busy causing chaos, and they won't listen to anyone else." A slow exhale of breath. "I wonder if the goddess could be convinced to be a source. So you're calling to offer your help, Alisha? Because we sure as hell need it. There are very few people at Number 10, the PM included, who are in the know. He's very worried that any number of countries—China, Russia, Saudi Arabia—will be champing at the bit to destabilise this country, and Hermes has given them the perfect opportunity."

"You've been in this game longer than me. You must have a plan, Robert."

"Very clever of you to use a landline, by the way. I'll

suggest that at once. We can't just confiscate mobile phones or shut down apps. I raised it with the PM, of course, but the general public won't stand for it. For now, I'm going to treat the symptoms. Arrange for mediators and therapists to calm matters down. I was hoping Marina could help with her empath talents. Maybe Fei Yen and Faeza can concoct some tea from Shanghai Moon for me. But cauterising the wound has to be down to you. I'll do what I can to help, but I don't have your skills. And this is a powerful enemy. We need you in this, or we don't stand a chance."

I sighed. "Has the Prime Minister been to Phinnaeous?"

The detective groaned. "Why would he, after what happened with the earthquakes palaver? Phinnaeous Shine didn't exactly cover himself in glory when he pretended the elves were behind the tremors. That relationship isn't getting back on track any time soon."

"Probably for the best. The senate are well and truly up their own arses."

Robert blew out his breath. "Fighting a tech war isn't like arm-to-arm combat. If all enemies could be dispatched with a Walther PPK and silencer—"

"—or Death's sword." I'd been practising with Ezra and was keen to use it.

"Then the world wouldn't be as dangerous. But tech is an invisible enemy. We are fighting in the dark, and the enemy is in each citizen's hands. From ten-year-olds to pensioners."

"I didn't think the Queen would have a mobile. I pictured her as a landline-only type of gal."

Robert gave a sardonic chuckle. "Her handbag holds a handkerchief, a pistol, a powder puff and a mobile phone. Word is, shortly after Tony Blair won the 1997 general election, he convinced the Queen to get a Nokia 6110. Soon afterwards, palace officials started complaining about how much time she spent in the loo. They almost called the royal physician, but it turned out she was addicted to playing Snake."

"Better than shooting grouse, I guess."

"Whichever way we play it, Alisha, this is going to be a tough ride. I don't see how we're going to come out on top."

What was that saying? The only thing necessary for the triumph of evil was for good men—or women—to do nothing. It didn't matter if I was being manipulated or pulled along by fate. It would be wrong to sit this one out when I knew I had the power to help.

"That's easy, Robert. I'm going to visit Hermes." I sounded braver than I felt, but it was clear we didn't have any other options. What kind of woman was I if I sat pretty while my country suffered?

Robert hesitated. "Marina will hate me for sending you into danger." A rustling of pages came down the line as if the detective had opened a file. "Our intel tells us he's still living at the tower. His previous professions were calligrapher, forger, head honcho at Royal Mail and Senior Manager of the Nokia text message team. He's not to be trifled with. He's clever, resourceful, and gifted in translation and interpretation, trading and thievery. Some say he escorts the souls of the deceased to the afterlife. Roads and boundaries are his bread and butter. Perhaps that's why he excelled at Royal Mail. His winged cap and boots give him flight, and his staff has the power to make people fall asleep or wake."

I gritted my teeth. "Sounds delightful."

Robert paused. "Alisha? Over the centuries, he's been known as a god of the winds, but I don't believe he has power over them."

I sighed. "That's something, at least."

"I hate to do this to you. But it's for Crown and country, you know?"

I ignored the knots in the pit of my belly. "Well, you know

me. I like a challenge. I just need you to do one thing for me in exchange."

A note of determination. "Name it."

"Go and see Marina, will you?"

13

With its moats, two concentric walls and protection towers, the Tower of London remained the most heavily fortified place in the city. It had a formidable reputation. Henry VIII had sent two wives and dissenting clergymen to be imprisoned and executed there. I had visited as a tourist to see the crown jewels and armour displays, view the poppy installation and ice skate in its moat under twinkling Christmas lights.

Once, I would have worried about what to wear to face a god. I knew now that all we had been told about respect and rituals should be labelled myth and dogma. Some of these gods were as flawed as the rest of us. It didn't matter that I hadn't washed my feet or prepared an offering. It didn't matter that I wasn't wearing virgin white or flowers in my hair.

All that mattered were my intentions and those of the gods.

As a precaution, we arrived under the moonlight when Ezra would be his strongest. I carried my catalogue of creatures in a satchel and wore my baldric and sword on my back. Echo had been tempted to wear the armour Rajika had commissioned for him, but we didn't want to give the impression of war, not when the Ravenmaster might be amenable to peace. I hadn't even told the goddess we were coming here. It was a scoping mission only.

We gathered by the Starbucks across from the Tower of London. That hadn't been there in the thirteenth century.

Like me, Ezra had dressed all in black. His chin-length hair, usually loose, had been tied in a man-bun. He obviously meant business. "I can't believe you talked me into this."

"You're coming because you know me well enough to know I'd go through with it without you."

Ezra grimaced. "If you're getting into trouble anyway, I'm going to be there to protect you. Think of it as penance for setting you up to fail at the performance. I should have realised your animation powers might differ from your grandmother's."

"How could you have known? I don't blame you."

A vein throbbed in his neck as if his perceived failure pained him, but he tried to lighten the mood. "We get in. We find the Ravenmaster and figure out if he's a friendly. We fix this, if only because I can't take another one of the PM's reshuffles. I'd rather Mr Bean ran the country than him at the moment. In fact, I might go and find Rowan Atkinson after this."

"If we get out alive, young wolf." Echo's emerald eyes scanned the coffee shop as if Hermes might be picking up a latte.

I bit my lip. "At least the ravens should be gone. They have some of the biggest bird brains in the animal kingdom. If that wasn't scary enough, even the English language calls them a murder of crows or unkindness of ravens."

Ezra raised an eyebrow. "I'm pretty sure they brought it on themselves by eating the flesh of the dead. It probably began with them feasting on human flesh after bloody executions in the tower."

"All carnivores eat the flesh of the dead. In their eagerness for carrion, the ravens have no airs and graces about it. They are simply opportunistic survivors. It's quite commendable, really."

A coffee-slurping customer emerged from the shop and did a double-take at my sword and the cat.

"We're off to a fancy dress party. The cat wanted to come," I said.

"Looks like you're in for a wild night. Have fun, lass," said the man.

I waited for him to disappear around the corner and gave a grim smile. "Come on. Let's get this over with."

The keys to the Tower of London were kept on an enormous iron ring, guarded by Beefeaters in their dark blue-and-red tunics, topped by a round-brimmed hat. Once inside, the building was a maze with endless stairwells and arrow-slit windows. But with Ezra at our side, we didn't have to worry about walls, security or even floor plans. As a creature of the night, Ezra knew the scent of ravens, which was our key to entry and placement. The ravens may have fled the tower, but their night enclosures remained in situ, together with their fallen midnight feathers. Ezra only needed to orient himself to their stench, and with a sense of smell a hundred times greater than a human nose, this would be a home run. He could smell prey over a mile away.

We teleported and materialised within the inner walls. The room was vast and dull, with the night enclosures taking centre stage. Travel-sick Echo heaved onto the stone floor, leaving his dinner spattered there. Meanwhile, Ezra checked the room. His body moved differently in here, alert to potential threats, and revealed his predator nature, however gentle he was with me.

Ezra's tense whisper reached me. "Not a raven in sight."

"Then that feast is mine." Echo devoured some chick and quail carcasses with a side of bird biscuits soaked in blood.

I shuddered at the sound of odd knocks and bangs that grew ever closer. The Ravenmaster came for us. I could feel it in my bones. "Quiet, Echo. We're not here for a luncheon. It's spooky enough in here without you chomping on those bones."

A knock sounded inches away.

A chill ran up my spine.

We spun, standing back to back to cover all angles of the room: the wolf, the leopard and I. The knocking echoed in my brain. I focussed on keeping my breath calm. I wanted to exude power, not fear.

There had been no reasoning with Ra, but Pan had been different. I hoped Hermes, too, would be open to conversation. Our plan was to establish a rapport and trick him into revealing his motive and end game. Everyone wanted someone to listen to them. It had been one of my most important life lessons.

The Ravenmaster walked straight through the door, like a ghostly apparition, and then hardened in form. A round-brimmed hat perched on a head of strawberry blond curls and a clean-shaven face. His blue eyes had the brilliance of glaciers.

I almost wet myself.

"Why the surprise? Boundaries are no barrier to me." His voice was throaty and thick, like he'd spent an eternity walking through the halls of the tower. The shadows deconstructed and remoulded themselves around him. "Did you not come here, to my home, with the intent to see me?"

I trembled. "We did, Ravenmaster."

The Ravenmaster stepped closer. He wore the distinctive Yeoman Warder's Tudor-style tunic in dark blue with scarlet trim. A scarlet crown and the Queen's initials EIIR embellished the chest area, and a belt accentuated his slim build and broad shoulders. In his manicured hands he held a short staff entwined with two snakes and topped by a pair of ornate wings. Knock, knock went his staff on the stone floor.

He towered over me. "Why did you break into my home, druid?"

Echo and Ezra bristled next to me, but we had a plan: keep the peace and make him talk.

I held my ground, although there was a hair's breadth between us, and I could see tiny golden wings fluttering from his hat and boots. My heartbeat drummed in my ears. My mum had taught me to be polite. "We wondered if you could tell us what happened to the ravens."

"Pah," said the Ravenmaster. "The ravens. I have lived through centuries, known countless kings and queens and the All-Father himself, yet all anyone wants to know about is the ravens. How I tire of this world."

"You don't seem to like ravens very much," said Ezra.

"So you might surmise, wolf. I feed those creatures, tend to them when they are poorly and counsel them when stressed. I bury their bodies in our raven cemetery and utter a prayer. Ungrateful swine. Did you know how mischievous those creatures are? Raven George was dismissed for eating television aerials, and Raven Grog was last seen at an East End pub called the Rose and Punchbowl. He had a penchant for a pint of Fosters."

I frowned. "Are you saying that your ravens went for a drink?"

His eyes flashed. "Of course not. Ravens can't just disappear. I clipped their secondary flight feathers myself to limit flight. They're only capable of short flights. It's not like they can go for a jaunt across the countryside. Pesky little creatures."

"Ungrateful too," Echo purred. "Having snacked on some of their food, I feel you treated them very well."

The Ravenmaster glowered. "Mice, rats, quail, even an egg a week and they still act like strutting deviants. I didn't serve twenty-two years in the military and achieve an exemplary record for those fools to make it look like I can't do my job. Last week, Raven Merlin attacked Yeoman Warden Harold's lip just for looking at him the wrong way. I had to pull him off and hope Harold would still have some lip left."

Echo growled. "The ravens do seem like scoundrels of the lowest order. At least in this job, you get to eat beef every day."

The Ravenmaster gave a heavy sigh. "Leopard, the origin of the Beefeater nickname does indeed stem from beef-eating. The king wanted to ensure the Yeoman Wardens were a muscular type. But sadly, nowadays, with veganism running rampant through the palace officials, we now only eat it twice a week."

I'd been hyper-alert since he'd entered the room, but I started to relax. Whatever was going on, the Ravenmaster seemed like a grumpy old man. "You still haven't told us what happened to the ravens."

Blue eyes narrowed at my tone. "I broke their necks."

I sucked in my breath. Maybe this god was a killer, after all.

"Or maybe I didn't." He smiled, and his large, pearlescent teeth glimmered in the moonlight. "All that matters is that, with their absence, I gave fair warning of the coming calamities, just like I did during my years of service on the battlefield. It would be ungentlemanly to attack Crown and country without warning."

"And the message in the sky?" I said.

"Just a little fun. I invented the alphabet, after all. I knew it would tickle your fancy. You are a linguist, after all, as am I.

You, too, have an affinity with the winds. In another universe, we could have been friends. It was I who escorted your mother's soul to the afterlife."

A knife twisted in my gut. I found no depth in the Ravenmaster's glacier eyes. The longer we spent in his company, the less I trusted him. "You're lying."

He leaned so close I could smell the sweat from his pores. "Not this time."

Echo snarled in warning, but the Ravenmaster didn't flinch.

Ezra reached for my hand as the air left my lungs.

His bulky form, clad in navy and red, added to the oppressiveness of the raven's quarters. "It was she who told me what your weak point is."

The wound in me, caused by Mum's death, stung. "I don't believe you."

He shrugged. "Suit yourself."

Stick to the mission. Don't get distracted, I told myself. "Why have you been disrupting our communication?"

His blue eyes were overly bright. "Because I am a nostalgic old man who misses the old ways."

"You make it sound like you're harmless, but you're not, are you? You gave Pandora the gift of curiosity, which is why she unleashed the sorrows into the world...greed, envy, hate, pain, disease, hunger, poverty, war."

He was peeved. "When will humans understand that it was a jar, not a box? It wasn't all bad. Pandora unleashed hope into the world after all." The shadows shifted, and I wondered whether his role as an escort of dead souls made shadows dance around him as fire danced around wood. "It is true—I'm not harmless. All gods have the power for creation and destruction in them. For millennia, we have been lambs, but I am enjoying this new era. It alleviates the boredom."

"Boredom?" said Ezra. "Boredom is your reason for wreaking havoc on a country you have served?"

"There speaks a wolf who understands duty. But do you understand desire? Let me spell it out for you. There was a time when I would carry letters sealed by Zeus himself. What a golden age it was. I was revered and trusted with great tasks. I knew things that no one did." The Ravenmaster sighed. "Once, humans communicated over distances by smoke signals or drumbeats. I trained whole flocks of birds to carry messages. Then came telegraphs and fax machines. How I hated their sound. The headaches they gave me. But they were still slow and ponderous. So I adapted. Telephones rendered me somewhat obsolete, but I am an inventor. I appreciate progress, within reason. I championed postmen. I was the Head of Royal Mail. But then came the internet." His thick voice brimmed with disgust. "Does anyone ever thank me for paving the way? Men have forgotten what they owe the gods." He shook his head. "All these messaging apps. Hundreds of millions of messages sent globally per minute. Meaningless messages. Memes. Emojis. Gifs. I took a job at Nokia, but the other companies accelerated past us. I couldn't keep up. I want to go back to the old ways. How better to do that than to destroy trust in the new technology?" He glanced at the night enclosures and jerked his staff into the air.

I instinctively recoiled, my hands aloft, ready to go on the offensive.

He widened his posture and raised his staff again. "Now get into the cages."

A vice tightened around my chest. "Excuse me?"

The Ravenmaster smoothed out his tunic. "Did you think I'd tell you all that and let you walk away? I've very much enjoyed getting to know you, druid, but your time is up. Meeting the enemy is key to understanding them, and I understand now why you defeated Ra and Pan. You might be a woman, but you have gumption. This is my chance to prove

I am stronger than those who have rolled over before me. I will not underestimate you." His voice hardened, and he waved his staff. "Now get in the cages. A little nap until this is all over. I promise you'll be safe."

Echo growled and whipped around. Captivity was a death knell for him. "We cannot trust this god's promises. He has as much integrity as the raven faeces lining the cages."

The Ravenmaster struck a fist against his heart cavity. "It wounds me to hear you say that, leopard. I promise I will provide you with all the chick and quail meat you desire. Your safety is guaranteed. Once you are in there, no one can tamper with you. No mortal nor immortal will find you unless they have this key." He showed us a large key on an iron ring. "No soul can escape. These enchanted enclosures are one of my cleverest inventions."

Ezra gripped my hand tighter. His other hand flew to his charm necklace. He was ready.

"There's no way we're going to sleep in this creepy little haunted tower." I raised my hands. We hadn't come for war. It didn't mean we were going to leave peaceably, but I didn't want to make the first move.

The Ravenmaster nodded. "I respect those who choose death over captivity."

A trickle of wee definitely escaped me. This god was a heathen.

His thick voiced boomed, and I crumbled inside. "I will not kill you here. There has been enough blood shed in this palace through the centuries. The old laws state that to skin a visitor to one's home is the foulest sin. So I will give you a chance." His sensual lips parted, and his words were a whisper. "Run, little mortals, run!"

I blasted the god with wind, hoping to force *him* into the cage.

His tunic fluttered, but he held his ground easily.

"Run." This time his voice was a foghorn.

Ezra's hand became a vice around my wrist. Echo leapt against his chest, and we fell, fell between the seams of the world, out of the tower, that dark place of blood and torture, bright jewels and black feathers. The breath left my body as we tumbled through the mists and the stones, and I didn't know if the grasping hands were Ezra's or mine or the Ravenmaster's.

We emerged by the coffee shop, spluttering and sprawling on the floor, with Ezra's chest slashed red by Echo's leap.

I looked at him aghast and pulled off my scarf so I could wrap his torso.

He winced. "There's no time. I'll live. My thistle charm will heal me."

Echo swayed with motion sickness. "I am sorry, wolf."

And then the Ravenmaster was there, in his Beefeater tunic and hat, his face contorted with malice. He lunged for us, and we scattered under flickering lamplight in the now deserted courtyard.

I gasped, unleashing a whirlwind that tore branches off nearby trees. "We have to split up. It's the only way."

The god kept coming, murder written on his face.

"Don't go home, Alisha." Ezra had already torn off his clothes, a grim look in his grey eyes. A sad smile. He looked up at the moon, and already his body contorted, hair sprouting and bones cracking as he took on his wolf form.

My heart twisted. He could have teleported somewhere safe. To the Parisian café we had dined at or the top of the Eiffel Tower. The Ravenmaster had flight, but he couldn't have followed him there so quickly. Except he was protecting me. As I watched, my brave, silver-copper wolf launched himself at the Ravenmaster with a growl that shook me to my core.

I pushed Echo's rump in the opposite direction. "You heard what he said. Go. We're safer if his attention is divided."

Echo bounded off, gathering speed. I winced as the sounds of the fight behind me grew more intense.

A tearing of flesh. Could a god bleed?

Intent laced through every sinew of Ezra's silver-and-copper wolf. He sprang at the Ravenmaster, knocking off his hat. Then he rounded back, attempting to disarm the god of his staff. When that failed, the wolf twisted, clamping his jaw on the Ravenmaster's forearm, where the birds had found a home over the years.

The god struggled to control the beast, frustration chiselled into his features. He might have lost his wide-brimmed hat, but the wings on his boots gave him an edge. He was spritely for an ageing god—and cunning. The Beefeater's uniform hung in shreds, but its wearer remained determined. He shook off the beast time and again as a bullfighter taunts a bull.

The god raised his staff.

Claws and teeth and the wolf's eyes implored me to make use of his sacrifice, and then he went limp.

Grief wailed inside me as I ran, the image of Ezra's limp body in my mind. I wanted to turn back, but I pressed on, my mind whirling. The catalogue of creatures bumping against my thigh as I ran was useless in the heat of battle. I needed calm to animate. Doing it while running was next to impossible. My wind powers had little effect. I pulled my sword. I could run with my sword and poke the Ravenmaster in the eye before he waved his staff.

I didn't stop to look behind me.

The shadows twisted. My heartbeat thundered like hooves.

I ran through cobbled alleys and past closed pubs until my chest heaved, and I didn't know where I was. I was a forty-year-old woman whose legs were already jelly from my sprint. My eyes blurred with tears as I tripped over a homeless woman. I didn't apologise but raced on, my lungs burning.

I'd been stupid to attempt this. I'd been stupid to put my friends in danger. I couldn't do this without them.

Just when my legs were about to give out, a hand reached for me in the darkness.

I unleashed a blood-curdling scream.

14

———

The hand, consisting of four knobbly grey fingers, pulled me onto a ledge in the darkness.

I cried out as a triangular head with large, milky eyes loomed into focus.

"Flinar!" I threw my arms around him, forgetting for an instant our precarious position in the black hole he'd created.

The elf smiled with delight. "I like helping my druid friend. The elves remember what you did for us when we were blamed for the tremors. Thanks to you and the wolf, we have a community now. I was drinking mead when one told me you were running through the streets like a madwoman." He hiccupped.

I put the sword back in my baldric and peered at him in the darkness, my pulse still heightened. "Are you drunk, Flinar?"

He hiccupped again. "Just a little. The elven community is a very merry sort, especially now we have you as a friend. We feel understood." He leaned his wispy head against my shoulder. "I feel loved."

I clutched his tiny muscular body. "A god was chasing me, Flinar."

Flinar's sail-like ears, situated high up on his skull, twitched. "Many elves, including me, have had run-ins with Hermes. It started when he was at Royal Mail. He hated mischievous elves who spun road signs or created dead ends and lost pathways with their black hole magic. He takes roads and boundaries very seriously. He never gave us credit for how we clean the streets of cigarette butts, splatters of pigeon poo and gloopy chewing gum."

I shook my head. "I can't get my head around the fact they've been walking amongst us for so long."

His ashen face creased into a smile. "We all have, Alisha. You just weren't alive to it before."

My chest remained tight with fear. "Can the Ravenmaster find us here?"

"I was a naughty elf. I created a black hole for him too." A throaty chuckle bubbled out of him. "It was deeper than this with no ledge, so he must have fallen like a stone in a well unless his boots and hat stayed on. My magic can't hold him for long, though. I think he's escaped already. We can stay here for as long as you like, but we would get hungry." He patted the ledge from which our feet dangled. "And uncomfortable."

I stood up on the ledge, a sense of urgency in every fibre of my body. "I have to get back to Ezra. I have to help him."

Flinar's milky eyes widened. "The wolf is in trouble?"

"I think so. He shifted to fight the Ravenmaster. He was bleeding. He went limp."

His nostrils flared, and he set back his knobbly shoulders. His knickerbockers had been updated. He wore leggings with his tunic instead. "I will take you to him. Where did you leave him, Alisha?"

"The Starbucks. Outside the Starbucks by the Tower of London."

His four fingers wove through mine.

We vanished, and a popping sound filled my ears as we emerged on the forecourt where Ezra had bled.

Flinar's eyes swept the area, his billowing ears alert to every sound. "No wolf. And no blood. Are you sure it was here?"

Sorrow and panic swept through me. My eyes blurred with tears. "He must be here. Or in the Tower. Maybe the Ravenmaster took him back there."

He reached for my hand. "Or maybe he went home. You need to tell the alpha."

ECHO HAD BEEN TOLD NOT to go home. I needed to make sure he was okay. I had a hunch that he'd head for Marina's surgery. It was nearing the dead of the night, but we found a phone box and telephoned Marina anyway. It wouldn't have been the first time. Flinar pointed out which women were his friends from the postcards from sex-workers in the telephone booth while we waited for Marina to pick up.

"What do you mean Ezra has disappeared?" Worry clouded her usually sunny voice. "Yes, yes, Echo's here. He disrupted my reunion with Robert. I'd only just slipped into that lacy teddy. Thanks for egging him on, by the way. What a swine the Ravenmaster is. What can we do to help?"

"Stay put for now. Don't let Echo out. I'm not sure it's safe. I'm heading to the farmhouse to tell Gunnolf what's happened. Maybe Ezra's there."

A rush of words. "You're going to walk into a den of wolves without Ezra at your side? No way, José. Over my dead body. I'm calling Orpheus at his club to give you some backup."

I grimaced. "Why would you do that? I don't need Orpheus to daddy me."

"Talk sense, Alisha. Orpheus is one of your few allies in

the senate. He cares about you. You don't need to be an empath to feel that. And he has real clout. You need him in your corner when you face the alpha."

I swept back the escaped tendrils of my hair with a shaky hand. "Okay, okay. You win."

"Head to his club. I'll ring ahead and let him know you're coming. And Alisha?" Her voice came down the line, a caress that made me long for a hug. She gave the best hugs. "Echo said Ezra might need stitching up. I'm only a phone call away."

I hung up. "Flinar, will you take me to Orpheus Might's gentleman's club in Charing Cross, please?"

He reached out his hands. "It would be my honour."

We appeared with a pop in front of Orpheus's three-storey Georgian building.

Flinar bowed. "I wish you luck, Alisha. I must leave you here. The senate are no friends to elves."

I crouched down to his height. "I understand."

The elf pursed his lips. "It might be nothing, but tonight, as the elves indulged in mead and merriment, a redhead arrived to speak to one of them. I heard snatched conversation. I think she means you harm."

"The wolf, Rashida, perhaps? She's in love with Ezra," I said. Ezra wouldn't tolerate open warfare, but I wouldn't put it past Rashida to be underhanded. "Pale skin, big brown eyes, flame-red hair."

He nodded. "That's her. I'll find out what I can. Be careful."

"Thank you, Flinar. You saved me tonight."

"As you have saved me many times before." He hiccupped, stepped into a slice of night and was gone.

I dusted off my trousers and scanned the house. A single candle burned on an upper floor, visible through the netted multi-pane windows. The last time I'd been here, I'd had my friends in tow, and now they were scattered god-knew-where across the city. I recalled the business card Orpheus had once given me and rapped on the door seven times in quick succession.

Silence reigned, and I raised my fist to knock again when the door opened with a click.

Orpheus opened the door with a tumbler of whiskey in his hand. He wore a slick tuxedo. His bowtie lay undone around his nape, and his unbuttoned collar revealed the pale skin beneath. "What brings you to my door at this hour, druid? I was relaxing with Charlotte Brontë's *Jane Eyre* after hosting a rather fractious casino night here. Of course, I first read it almost two centuries ago. On my copy, the author is known as Currer Bell."

"Didn't Marina call ahead?"

"The landline rang, but the lackey who answers it was already in his coffin."

"Sorry, do you mind?" I took the whiskey from his hand and downed it in one fell swoop, wincing as I handed the empty glass back to him.

"Whatever is the matter, Alisha? It can't be that witch Lavinia's meddling." His brow furrowed as he read my thoughts.

I allowed him to delve into the horrors of my night without a word of censure. If I asked him to come with me. I owed him that much, at least.

Orpheus swore under his breath. "Wait here. I'll get my keys."

He was gone and back in a flash and pulled the door closed behind him before ushering me into a panther-like vehicle at the kerb.

I wasn't good at cars. After all, I didn't even own one. It was only when I climbed into the swanky, dark leather interior and peered at the badge on the steering wheel that I realised it was a Lotus.

Orpheus threw me a glance. "Extravagant, I know, but I only own the one. I like my cars to go as fast as me."

He reached across to fasten my seatbelt, and I caught the scent of his dark chocolate-and-sweet cherry beard oil from his goatee.

Goosebumps raced up my arms. Ezra smelled of mountain air and cigarette roll-ups. Or maybe he didn't anymore. Maybe he was just ashes scattered in a raven cemetery by now. I shuddered.

Orpheus turned on the engine and put his foot on the accelerator. "The wolf knows how to take care of himself. You did the right thing coming to me. The motorway will be clear. We'll be at the farmhouse in no time." He threw me a sideways glance. "Lavinia went out of her way to hurt you at Wildwoods. I don't agree with the purity decrees regarding mating, even if genealogy is my responsibility. Diversity in nature is of great merit. And I understand carnal desires more than most men."

I gulped. It probably wasn't my best idea to be locked alone in a car with a vamp at night.

He sighed. "I learned long ago to control my desires, druid."

We sped down city roads until we reached the motorway. The Lotus purred like a cat, lulling me into a daze, with my thoughts fracturing into tiny horrors of what could be.

Orpheus's piano-player hands rested lightly on the steering wheel, although the speed gauge showed we were well over the speed limit. His profile, with his Roman nose, stern lips and longish black hair, fell alternately into shadow and amber light. "I want to chastise you, Alisha, but you're more courageous than those with thrice your power. This city has been my home for centuries. How can I admonish you for standing against those who wish to harm it?" He sighed. "It pained me to see you fail at the Wildwoods performance."

"It doesn't matter. It pushed me to realise I can only

animate winged creatures. That's why I failed, Orpheus. An owl would have worked, but a fox…a fox set me up to fail."

His heavy brows pulled together. "Margola's manoeuvring forced your hand. It is not like her to be so obsessed with undermining someone. She usually has a better relationship with the truth. Senate members are too advanced for me to read their thoughts. Perhaps there is female jealousy at play."

I laughed. "She has no reason to be jealous of me."

He shrugged. "When does jealousy ever need a reason? Isn't it more about the jealous person's insecurities than it is about the recipient of the ire? Although, Margola is well within her rights, of course, to suggest you are terrible at being told what to do. I will try to smooth things over with Gunnolf, but I need you to follow my lead. Can you do that?"

I nodded. I couldn't get the image of Ezra's limp body out of my mind.

"I need you to say it, Alisha."

"I can do that. Thank you, Orpheus."

Orpheus grunted. "We only tell the alpha as much as he needs to know. If you need to pass something by me, you do it telepathically. I can read your thoughts and push my own thoughts into your head. Do it casually. It's a trick the alpha dislikes. It reminds him of how basic his own talents are."

He turned onto a slip road, manoeuvred a roundabout, past a set of traffic lights, and soon we pummelled down a dirt track towards some woods. A few minutes more and the pack farmhouse appeared.

Orpheus parked the Lotus next to a pick-up truck and let the engine idle for a moment longer as if collecting his thoughts. Then we climbed out. As the car doors thumped shut, the wolves howled in response.

The sound made me tremble.

"Here. The night is chill." Orpheus draped his jacket around my shoulders.

We trudged across the lawn where I'd been only days before when Ezra introduced me to the pack. The sprawling, white farmhouse lay ahead, bordered by the orange dahlias, and already, wolves waited on the dilapidated deck. Gunnolf stood in the centre, dressed in head-to-toe denim. On his left, Dominic, the huge, tawny wolf, bristled. On his right stood Rashida's beautiful red wolf and Maximillian's silver-white wolf, their eyes never leaving our faces.

"We could smell you a mile away." Gunnolf turned his nose up at us. "You know I don't like unannounced visits, Orpheus."

Orpheus raised an eyebrow. "Who does?"

"I could have made an exception for a game of cards, but you brought the druid." His lip curled at Orpheus's attire. "A little overdressed for a trek in the woods, aren't you? And you dare to bring a sword to my house, druid?"

Deirdra, in human form, waved from the kitchen window.

I didn't dare wave back.

"There is no time for our usual games, Gunnolf," said the vampire. "Is Mr Neuhoff here?"

The red wolf showed her teeth and emitted a low growl.

Gunnolf frowned. "I am not my nephew's keeper, as you well know. He is less obedient than the other wolves."

I clenched my fists. Anxiety made half-moon imprints of my nails in the soft flesh of my palm. "So he isn't here?"

The alpha's gravelly voice pulsed with irritation. "No, druid. My nephew is not here."

I cried out in anguish. The Ravenmaster had taken Ezra—perhaps worse—and without his teleporting skills, there was no way to return to the tower. To check if he was okay. In my hurry to solve this crisis, I had assumed my lucky innings against Ra and Pan meant I would always succeed.

And now Ezra had paid the price for my hubris.

Next to me, Orpheus stiffened. *If you want to save your boyfriend, stop drowning in pity. We have no choice but to tell him.*

And by that, I mean me because the alpha's disdain for you is obvious.

I flinched. *You really need to work on your sensitive side.*

Orpheus stepped forward. "We should go inside."

Gunnolf's hackles rose. "Just spit it out, old man."

"As you wish. Mr Neuhoff was on an unsanctioned mission tonight with Ms Verma here. They got into trouble and scattered. The Ravenmaster captured the wolf."

A growl ripped from Rashida's red wolf. She lunged forward, flying through the air.

Gunnolf sprang forward off the deck, plucked her mid-leap and held her to the ground. His hand lingered on her panting body, both a scold and a caress.

She whimpered and quietened.

He straightened up, his dark eyes brimming with hatred. He pointed a finger at my chest. "You convinced my nephew to go after a god? We told him you were bad news. We told him to walk away. Are the two of you incapable of listening? We should cast you out." He swung around to Orpheus. "She is consumed by her desires and has no thought for duty. I stood against her at her trial vote, did I not? And yet the fools amongst us decided to give her a cloak of respectability. Well, look where it has led us."

The timbre of Orpheus's voice was a sharp prick of warning. He flicked Gunnolf's finger away from my chest. "Careful who you call a fool, alpha."

Their eyes met, and neither backed down.

Gunnolf glowered. "There will be consequences for this lack of discipline. First, I will need to interview the druid to find out what she knows. You may leave, Orpheus."

"On the contrary," said Orpheus. "The druid need not stay. I have read her thoughts and can tell you what has occurred."

"I will not let the druid leave unless she makes an oath on her father's life not to go after Ezra."

I won't abandon him, I thought.

Then you will never leave here. And what good will that do your wolf? Orpheus nodded at Gunnolf without a step change. He'd been practising this trick for centuries. "You mean to find the wolf?"

The alpha's lips twisted. "How do you expect us to track a teleporting werewolf? It is suicide challenging a god. How are we supposed to get inside the tower undetected without my nephew's skills? It's not like the wolves can storm it. No, Orpheus. We won't seek Ezra." He cast me a glance. "As much as I love my nephew, he made his own bed. I will not sacrifice the pack in a hunt we are sure to lose."

He would leave his own nephew to rot, I thought.

Don't do anything stupid. Orpheus inclined his head. "Then I am sorry, Gunnolf. Your nephew is a good man."

"My nephew should have known better who to trust. Like his father before him, he let his desire for a woman stand in the way of his duty."

Orpheus searched the alpha's face for a fraction longer than comfortable. "I heard about the murder investigation. You are no closer to finding the culprit."

Gunnolf gave a bitter laugh. "You are right. I have my own troubles here, but even with a closed case, my answer would have been the same."

One thought rolled through my head. *What an arsehole. He's known Ezra all his life.*

A nerve twitched in Orpheus's neck. *The alpha is merely putting his own skin above his nephew's.*

I tried hard to swallow my emotions, but they broke the dam of my control. It didn't matter that the alpha and the god scared me or that I ignored Orpheus's counsel.

Druid, don't—

I squared my shoulders to hide my fear. "I won't leave Ezra's survival to fate, even if you are willing to."

Orpheus dropped all undercover communication and

spun towards me. "Don't be ridiculous, druid." *I can't help you now.*

Gunnolf's eyes lit up with unconcealed malice. "Then welcome to your new home, Alisha Verma. I hope you don't live to regret your decision."

15

Gunnolf flung me into Ezra's room. "You'll be staying here. I've confiscated your sword until this is all over. You can keep your little book of creatures. Fat lot of good it does you. We'll make sure you're fed and watered. I promised Orpheus I wouldn't harm you, but if you try any funny business, I won't be responsible for what follows. Rashida is on first watch outside your door, and she doesn't need an excuse to rip your throat out."

I ached for Ezra.

Would I even know if he had died?

I sorely regretted not keeping my mouth shut. I could have grabbed a cat nap in Orpheus's Lotus on the way back to London and gone after Ezra without Gunnolf being any wiser. I had to find out what happened to him and make the Ravenmaster pay. "How can a Justice Minister think it's okay to lock away a person without due process? What kind of archaic system is this?"

Gunnolf smirked. "I can do whatever I want, Alisha. Who's going to stop me?"

He strode out of the room, giving me a glimpse of Rashida still in wolf form.

The door clicked shut, and a key turned in the lock.

This wasn't how I had imagined alone time in Ezra's room. I'd only been here once before on my whistle-stop tour, but this time, I surveyed my surroundings properly. It was a spacious room, furnished simply, the stripped floorboards topped with a threadbare rug. A king-sized bed with charcoal bedding took centre stage. A small chest of drawers had been placed on one side of the bed, a lamp and framed picture of Ezra's parents balanced on top. There was a slim wardrobe, a sink, and a cracked mirror in the corner. The window had been left open just a sliver—the whole house reeked of damp wolf—but I had no hope of escape with the pack lurking on the decking below. Not when there were so many of them. Not when I was alone and didn't trust my own powers.

I sighed and dumped my satchel on the bed before pulling out my mobile phone to check my battery life. Thirty-eight per cent. Enough to get me through the night. Then I'd be well and truly cut off from help. Orpheus was long gone. He'd been pissy about me ignoring his instructions and roared off into the night in his Lotus like a bat out of hell. My instinct was to ping a text to Marina, but I held back. The Ravenmaster could alter the intent of my message, block its sending or track me here, where I was a sitting duck. Even a phone call would be risky. Not to mention that Rashida's wolf hearing meant nothing would be secret.

Ezra's limp wolf body flooded back into my mind.

A sense of urgency came over me. I had to get out of there.

I could try to blast myself out of the room, like a twisted Dorothy from Oz creating the tornado that ripped through Kansas. But I was pretty sure Ezra loved this place. Targeting my wind powers could work against the pack if they were one-on-one, but they worked as a team, and I was all alone.

I screwed up my face, trying to ignore the *rat-tat-tat* of my heart, willing me to be quicker, cleverer, and braver so I could save Ezra. I could feel the silent tug of my connection to

Tielbu, but his journey here could last through the night and every second counted. It stung my pride that the wolves hadn't even bothered to confiscate my catalogue of creatures in case I tried to animate a giant getaway goose or something. However, when I opened up the catalogue to instil life into a winged creature, my fingers couldn't find the dimensions I needed, and I felt like a screw-up all over again.

But when I barely had time to go to the loo in peace, how on earth was I supposed to find time to train?

Love had been a good emotion to ground me when I tried to animate, but how could I feel love when separated from and fearful for my loved ones?

No, my escape would have to be more humdrum.

I sped around the room, checking for anything that might give me an advantage. In Ezra's chest drawers, I found rolls of boxer shorts, like he was some sort of Marie Kondo folding genius. I uncovered a plentiful supply of grey socks, a man-bag of toiletries, a packet of flavoured condoms that made me blush and a stash of Stephen King books at the bottom of his wardrobe.

Nothing to help me escape. No knives, no whips, no handcuffs. Nada. What was that man thinking?

A cooing at the window caught my ears. I swivelled and noticed a set of enormous teeth and fiery eyes. The creature squeezed in through the open window and perched on a small chest of drawers beside the bed, its pink claws scratching the surface. It looked rabid, with unkempt feathers, a muscly chest and an orange beak that barely contained its huge gnashers. Then it transformed before my eyes, stretching upwards and outwards, his beak, teeth and feathers morphing into his human self in a mind-boggling feat I would rather not have seen.

I sprang forward just in time to prevent a framed picture of Ezra's parents from clattering to the floor. "Sahil."

My brother cupped his hand over his bits and darted

across the floorboards to grab a pair of jeans from Ezra's closet. "Hello, sis. I don't suppose the werewolf would mind me borrowing these? A little birdie told me you needed my help."

I averted my eyes. "Orpheus?"

Sahil pulled on Ezra's trousers. "The vampire? Of course not. Marina called me."

"I'm surprised you answered. I wrote you a postcard this week. You used to love them when we were kids. I figured you'd respond to that."

He shrugged. We had the same mouth and slim nose, but his eyes were more almond than round. "It's probably buried under a pile of junk mail at the penthouse." He might not have been my favourite person, but it was a relief to see his face. "So they put you in Ezra's room, eh?"

"I think they want me to drown in guilt. Trapped in a nest of vipers, and I only have myself to blame. Keep your voice down. I don't suppose you're here to break me out."

Sahil dropped his voice to a whisper. "I'm afraid I'm not the Tarzan type. I can't carry a fully grown woman on my werepigeon back, either. I'm here to make up for abandoning you during our Wildwoods trial. I did feel a bit of guilt about that, you know."

I hugged him. "I should have been there for you more after Mum died. I've been distracted. You know I love you, though?"

He regarded me quietly for a moment, and then his face broke into a smile. "It's not easy when your little sister suddenly becomes a star in a world neither of you knew existed."

I grimaced. "I think you'll find my star is falling fast."

"My powers are developing too, you know," he said. "We seem to be a family of secrets and surprises."

"I saw. So you're a shapeshifter with shield skills. That's pretty damn cool. How did you get them anyway? They don't seem…you know…in line with the family genetics." Even Ezra, with his experience of mentoring initiates, and Orpheus, with his knowledge of genealogy, had been surprised at the unnatural medley of skills Sahil possessed. I had my suspicions Lavinia was the one who had supercharged Sahil's powers. It was the only thing that made sense.

He grinned. "If you must know, I had a little nudge in the right direction after the dinner at Baba Yaga's. The night you animated the dragon. Funny, isn't it? How we were pimping our powers at the same time."

Fingers of apprehension crawled over my skin. I knew we shouldn't have left him alone at Lavinia's, but if he were here to help, I wouldn't be a sourpuss.

"Listen, when Marina told me your predicament, I had an idea. I'm going sneak into the Tower of London and check whether Ezra is there."

A chink of hope opened up in me. "You'd do that for me?"

"It'll be a cinch. I can go wherever I want to these days. I don't need tickets or invitations for anything. You just need to tell me how you hid from the Ravenmaster. In case he comes for me too."

"Flinar the elf helped me."

Sahil nodded slowly. "Of course he did. Black hole magic?"

"Yes. He trapped the Ravenmaster and created an alternate pocket for me."

"Right, I'll be off then and will report back."

I gripped his arm. "Just be careful, will you? I can't lose anyone else. And I *really* want to fill you in on Dad's shenanigans with Alma."

He dropped his trousers.

"Jesus, Sahil. Keep it clean, will you?"

"Sorry, sis. Shifters get used to the nudity pretty quickly. We don't have much choice."

Even as he spoke, his voice transformed from intelligible

and manly to a pigeon coo. He sprouted feathers in his nether regions first, his nose flattened, and his mouth became a beak.

Then pop. He was the size of a Wellington boot.

We were, without a doubt, the weirdest family ever.

He looped around the room to show off and then soared out of the window. I watched his progression over the sleeping wolves and into the woods, feeling both proud and envious. He'd just disappeared from sight when my phone buzzed in my pocket.

"Alisha?" came Marina's voice through the line. "Orpheus told me you're a fool who asked to be imprisoned."

"You shouldn't be calling me on this."

"What choice did I have?" she said.

I cupped my hand over my mouth. "They've got me holed up in Ezra's room."

"Listen, I made a mistake. I was worried about you. I called Sahil and told him what happened, but I shouldn't have, Alisha. I really shouldn't have. I sensed something down the line—a blackness. Don't trust him. And don't tell him anything."

Oh, shit. I listened, my ears burning.

She hurtled on. "Echo's out trying to get Ezra's scent, so we'll get to the bottom of this. You hear me?"

"Yeah, I hear you." I cast my mind back through my conversation with Sahil. What had I told him? Had I willed him to be on my side when he really wasn't?

"I'm going to hang up now. Just stay safe. Tell me you're safe."

"I'm safe." I'd mentioned Flinar, but his black hole magic had grown stronger and he knew this city better than anyone. He could look after himself.

"Stay that way." Marina ended the call.

I had to get our lives back on track. I couldn't sit around waiting to be rescued. What was I missing? I had to be cleverer than I had been with Pan, and my allies were scattered everywhere. I had no idea anymore who was foe and who was friend.

The Ravenmaster's whole reason for messing with humdrum lives—and ours—was because he felt out of control in this new world. He'd been at Nokia, but that meant the world was progressing too fast for even him to keep up. Which meant his skillset fell short. It suddenly seemed so obvious. To intercept messages in a city the size of London, he needed expert help. But who could be helping him?

The seeds of a plan took root in my mind.

If my brother was playing both sides, I needed to find another way to help Ezra as well as flush out our enemies. As far as I could tell, there were three of us who loved Ezra and would move mountains to help him.

A few hours later, when the moon revealed the wolves asleep on the decking and the house was quiet, I slung my satchel on, splashed water on my face at the sink to chase away my drowsiness and knocked on the bedroom door.

Rashida's sleepy voice filtered through the hard wood. "I have my orders. I'm not opening up, druid."

"Do you always obey orders when the life of someone you love is at stake?"

A pause, and then the lock clicked open.

I stood back just before Rashida shoved the door open.

She stood barefoot, in light joggers and a T-shirt, her red hair cascading across her shoulders. Her lips formed a snarl. "I should tear you apart for what you've done to him."

I nodded. I'd feel the same way. Ezra had followed me into battle. We'd been unprepared. I wouldn't make that mistake again. "How about we work together to save him instead?"

Her brown eyes narrowed. "Why should I trust you?"

"We both love him, don't we? And as far as I can see, Gunnolf is doing zilch to rescue him."

"Gunnolf hasn't been himself recently. He's under a lot of

pressure." She hesitated. "But that doesn't mean we leave Ezra in the lurch. Pack is family. All right, druid. Let's hear your plan."

"You have a better relationship with Lavinia. I'd like you to ask her rats to report on Ezra's whereabouts. Or she can get one of the witches to scry for him. We need to know where he is and if he's moving."

Rashida nodded. "Say I agree. What next?"

It was true. In a way, we were on the same team, but that hadn't been the main reason for me to reach out to her.

She'd unlocked the door just as I wanted her to.

I channelled calm and stepped back slowly towards the window. The wolves were still sound asleep on the deck. Rashida was on the rug, just where I needed her. My hands tingled as I raised them. Before Rashida could react, a gust of wind knocked her off her feet, and another one rolled her into the rug, wrapping her tight, with her hands pinned against her sides. Not so much sexy lady as sausage lady.

Her muffled cry followed me out of the room. I locked it behind me, pocketing the key. Even in her human form, Rashida would be a formidable adversary. I didn't know how long it would take her to unravel herself or rouse the sleeping wolves, but she wasn't getting out of that room until someone helped her.

My heart hammered out of my chest. I crept down the stairwell, cringing with every creak lest I rouse the pack. My back lay flat against the wall as I rounded corners, and I chose the back door to give the sleeping wolves a wide berth. A triple padlocked door caught my attention in the downstairs hallway, given the wolves were so lax with security, but I didn't have time to linger. I swept my sword out of an umbrella stand and swiped the pick-up keys from a hook on the wall by the back door.

Easing the door open a fraction, I slipped through it and fixed my eyes on the pick-up in the distance. When I reached the lawn, I ran like the devil was after me, hoping the long grass would muffle my footsteps. The pick-up was parked at the top of the estate, not more than a few minutes away at a run.

I had to make it.

I thought I was going to until a crash sounded behind me. I risked a glance and almost collapsed there and then.

Rashida had jumped through Ezra's window in wolf form. Clean through it, as if her anger at me had made her invincible. There was resolve in her eyes and every leap. She howled as she ran, stirring the other wolves to action.

I was an English teacher, not a bloody warrior. Fear made my knees wobble. My satchel bounced against my thigh, and the sword in its baldric poked my back. I desperately began pressing the automatic door button for the pick-up, hoping I had the right one. Hoping I'd make it to the car and remember which peddle was the accelerator and which was the brake. Hoping the damn wolf wasn't going to bite my arse off.

Up clicked the locks.

Copper eyes in the woods beyond caught my attention, but there was no time to think.

I dove for the door, my feet sliding in the dirt, and wrenched the handle. The door flew open, but just behind me, something in the air changed. I turned, my sense of dread surging.

The red wolf launched herself at me, teeth bared, drool frothing at her mouth.

I lifted my hand, instinctively sending her spiralling into the dirt with a furious wind.

The red wolf bounced off the earth, her bloodlust for me driving her on, the other wolves almost at the pick-up.

I had no choice. I drew my sword, just as Ezra had trained me to do. In the heat of the moment, it felt heavier than ever before. I swung it clumsily as the red wolf charged at me, slicing her front leg.

She howled in pain as she collapsed in a heap on the cold earth under the starry sky.

I tossed the sword into the open pick-up, clambered into the driving seat and stuffed the key into the ignition.

Let there be fuel. My fingers fumbled to find the headlights. I released the handbrake and slammed my foot on the accelerator, pulling away in a whir of wheels as a tawny wolf leapt for the back of the pick-up.

He missed, landing in the dirt next to Rashida.

I sped towards the motorway, jerking and cursing as I got to grips with the truck.

The wolves didn't let up, muscles pounding, gaze fixed on their prize: Gunnolf's big black wolf, Maximillian's tawny one and Ruud, the small grey wolf with the white muzzle. Each of them wanted a piece of me. I ran a red light ahead of a roundabout and prayed the road would be clear. It would have been insane to stop with those beasts in my rear-view mirror. Ezra's wolf had the capacity for gentleness, but I couldn't be sure with these ones. The pick-up swerved as I tried to maintain my speed on the roundabout, and the wolves parted ways to corner me, ruining borders in their wake.

Gunnolf leapt at the side of the truck and clung on, hitting the window with his muzzle, his wolf eyes red in the darkness.

I couldn't have him hanging on like a leech until London. The car swerved as I used one hand to manually roll down the window a third of the way.

The black wolf lunged for me. There was no mercy in his eyes.

Power pulsed through my palm as I sent a tornado to take him to the ground. Just like I'd wanted to do ever since he told me to clean the pack kitchen. His body turned through the air like a ping pong ball, and I returned my focus to the road, pressing hard on the gas, a scream building in my throat. Only when I reached the motorway did Maximillian and Ruud lose ground, slipping away amongst the grasping trees that lined the road.

Exhausted from the impact of the adrenalin, I kept one hand on the steering wheel while I called Sahil for an update on Ezra. It went straight to answerphone, and I had the sinking feeling again that Marina was right.

And Gaia.

And Orpheus.

Hadn't they all told me my brother couldn't be trusted?

Had I been wrong to pooh-pooh all the warnings about him? The cogs of my brain blipped, and not even Smooth Radio could settle my fraught nerves.

Think, Alisha. What are your priorities?

Ezra. Hermes. Sahil.

The empty expanse of the motorway, in noir colours and lighting, acted as a balm for my soul. I reached London as dawn broke over the city, my sword—sticky with Rashida's blood—on the passenger seat.

16

———————

My foggy, sleep-deprived brain fought to stay awake as I wound through the streets of Balham towards my flat. I'd been surprised on my drive through the city to discover how many more homeless people lined the streets, as if overnight. Where once there had been the odd person in a doorway with a sleeping bag and collection bucket, now there were tenfold more. The same was true of every town I drove through. Sad, cold, lonely faces poked out of charity shop doorways, railway bridges and bus stops. Had I become so used to being whisked between destinations in Ezra's arms that I'd not noticed the change in the city?

At a red light, a bus driver peered into the car and baulked at the bloody sword lying on the passenger seat. I gave him a wave—hoping that nonchalance would stop him from reporting me to the police—and pushed the sword onto the floor, letting him pull ahead of me as the lights turned green.

A surge of light filled the cab, and I shut my eyes for a moment against the bright dawn. I opened them and jumped out of my skin.

"Sorry it took me so long to get here." Gaia plugged her seatbelt in, despite her immortality. "I was slightly irked that you went to the undead for help. I did hear your prayer while you were being chased into the pick-up truck, but I decided you could handle it alone. I find succeeding during the heat of battle does marvellous things for one's confidence and aptitude. I didn't want to take that learning opportunity away from you. And I hadn't finished my cup of chai. It is such a shame to let that beautifully stewed concoction with all its spices go to waste. I would never have forgiven myself."

I stared at her. "I could have died."

Her cherubic face broke into a knowing smile. "Oh, I doubt it. They might have given you a spanking, but they wouldn't have stooped much lower than that. You're not any old peculiar, after all. You're the granddaughter of Rajika Verma."

"I have to say my grandmother's legacy is more of a burden than a gift."

"But you have so much in common. She, too, fought injustice. Isn't it terrible how many more homeless people have appeared on the streets from London to Leeds, Bath to Belfast, Southampton to Swansea?" Gaia shook her fist. "I have a right mind to cut Hermes apart and bury the pieces of him in pits so far apart that it takes him millennia to reform. But that would blacken my own heart, which I fight so hard to keep clean."

"Why has there been a surge in homeless people? I don't understand it."

"People nowadays never talk to each other. Even in tea shops, where you are supposed to sit face-to-face. All they want to do is stare at their devices. To interact electronically. With strangers. With their mothers, even. I've never seen human nature change. Humans need touch. Now they get most of their touch from screens and tablets. Can only blame themselves, really. Little addicts. Don't they know that a hug is much more satisfying than a game of Candy Crush? Add Hermes to the mix, and of course, these people are on the streets. A few crude texts exchanged for real messages, and he's engendered a family fallout. Or an irate, trigger-happy boss. It's not like warring people pick the phone up to each other anymore. They block away. Wipe the offending person clean out of their life. Et voilà. Relationships fractured overnight."

"The Ravenmaster's doing all of this?"

"Well, of course, he is, child. He's a devious god, after all. Did you expect him to be sitting around twiddling his thumbs, waiting for you to get around to standing up to him?"

I gawped at her. I'd been expecting a shoulder to cry on, and here she was, just prodding me onto a quest that surely should have been hers. The cheek of it.

Gaia rearranged her sandalled feet in the footwell to avoid the blood-stained sword. "I see you've not yet unlocked the full potential of Transcender, but you will. It is forged by a god after all and blessed by another."

I indicated left to turn into my street and swallowed my frustration. I'd seen some of Gaia's faces—the mother, the crone, the warrior—and I knew how quickly she could swing between her personalities. I decided to ask nicely for her support. "Are you here to offer your help? I'm in quite a quandary. Ezra is missing. Hermes is after me. My brother might be a wanker."

Gaia tutted. There was something about her matter-of-fact persona that brought me comfort, even on a night like this. "Language, Alisha. A talented linguist like you should be able to come up with other ways to express yourself."

"Yes, but swearing is good for stress release. And I like the way it emphasises a point."

The goddess nodded. "In all my years, I have only sworn once when Death refused to change the burning pyres of hell into a more environmentally friendly option. It really was very stubborn of her."

Despite my sluggish brain, I logged away the information that Death was female.

Gaia continued. "I did tell you to beware of the pigeon. A trifling but vexatious little creature. But no, druid, I'm just here as a cheerleader. A little bit of motherly support. You're the eternal girl. This is all playing out exactly as I hoped it would. Although I have one piece of advice: don't believe anything Hermes told you unless you see it with your own eyes."

"I think he killed the ravens." A painful lump in my throat. I couldn't let myself imagine it. "Does that mean he'll kill Ezra too?"

"Pah," said Gaia. "That god is a gifted liar. He loves those birds. He loved that job."

I sighed. "Who knows what he's done with them. Or if Crown and country will fall without them."

"I see the superstitious empath is rubbing off on you, druid. It's like seed dispersal in nature. Ideas spread based on who we spend our time with. They catch on like wildfire. Just remember, stories are not all as true as the Bible or Torah or Qur'an. But you must stop the miscommunication, Alisha. Without reliable communication, whole empires can crumble. I have seen it time and again through the ages. I have seen how one cross word tears apart a family. How misreported facts turn communities against one another. How even a king can be manipulated by a carefully planted lie in his mind. He who controls communication controls the world."

A shudder ran through me as I pulled up to the kerb outside the flat. A light shone from inside. I knew my friends awaited me there. "Goddess, I need to know what drives him."

"To Hermes, this is just a game. Do you think he cares for mortals? We all miss the heavens, but some of us learned to care for life. Not Hermes. Mortals are just pawn pieces to him.

He is a master of chaos. He won't kill unless he has to. If he has taken the wolf, it is merely to distract you. He saw how easily you dealt with Ra and Pan. His ego drives him to be the one to beat you, and he will want to see your pain and humiliation."

"And the ravens?"

"They are a symbol, that's all. But they are important to him." Her eyes darkened, and she looked down at her fingers, still caked with mud. "If they were dead, he'd have buried them in the raven cemetery, but they are not there."

I gawped at her, imagining her in her sari, knee-deep in bones and feathers and soil-slick with gore.

She frowned. "Don't gawp at me, druid. I've been seeding a meadow of sunflowers. I'm not a grave robber. The soil spoke to me. I am the Earth goddess, after all."

"Of course, goddess." I turned off the ignition.

"Do you know what I find, druid? Often, with mysteries, if you pull one string, the whole ball unravels." She unplugged her seatbelt. "Now, aren't you going to help me out?"

I clambered out of the pick-up, opened the door for her and held out my hand. Her outward appearance gave the impression she was in her seventies after all.

She leaned heavily on my hand as she climbed out and smiled at the tweeting of the early morning birds. The winds quieted at her smile as if to allow her to hear the chorus of the birds better. Gaia stepped onto the pavement, rearranged the folds of her sari and stretched her back.

I reached into the footwell for Transcender, and when I turned, she was gone. There wasn't any point looking for her. The goddess only appeared when she willed it. I sent her silent thanks and staggered up the path to my building, dragging myself through the hallway towards my flat.

Marina, Robert and Echo rushed at me as I tumbled through the door. I sank onto the chair in my hallway as my legs turned to jelly. I didn't have to be strong with my friends here to hold me up.

Marina's hug squeezed the air out of my lungs. "We've been keeping vigil all night. I thought the worry would kill me."

Echo licked me, his dry tongue seeking out any bare skin he could find. My arms, my ankles, my neck. Less ferocious leopard than pussy cat right now. "Let us never split up again, Alisha. In the heat of battle, it was my duty to obey your command, but I have lost a decade of life not knowing how you were faring and not being there to help."

"You look like you've been in the wars," said Robert.

"Yeah, well, we're here to take care of her now." Marina took off my satchel and shoes. Then she unpeeled my fingers from the hilt of Transcender, her mouth a grim line at the sight of the blood, and left the sword in the bathtub.

My whole body trembled.

"Make her a hot cup of tea with lots of sugar," said Marina to Robert. She led me into my en suite bathroom, helped me undress, and then pushed me under the hot jets of the shower while she and Echo paced my bedroom.

I scrubbed myself until my skin was red and sore, gave my hair a cursory wash and grabbed a towel before my legs gave out. In the bedroom, I slipped on knickers and a sports bra over my damp skin with some help from Marina. The clock on my bedside table said it was nearly six a.m. "I have to fill you in."

She bundled me into my bathrobe, fussing to make sure I was wrapped up warm. "We know everything. *The Otherworld News* arrived an hour ago." Marina popped her head out of the bedroom door. "That tea ready, Rob? Bring the newspaper, will you?"

I sank down on the bed. "Already? She keeps making every situation worse."

Echo padded over to sit by me and nuzzled against me.

"Deliberately, I fear. My gut tells me she is mixed up in this. Although, my gut is not very reliable when it is empty."

"You know that old saying? I'm not sure if it stems from Socrates or Buddism, the Bhagavad Gita or whether it's just perennial wisdom—before you speak, consider: is it true, is it kind, is it necessary?" Marina sighed. "Well, I'm pretty sure, for someone whose words are currency, Margola Silver has never considered those questions in her life."

Robert came in with the steaming cup of tea and pressed it into my hands. He chucked a newspaper onto my bed.

The hot, sweet tea soothed my aching body as I read the headline.

Trouble at Dawn: Druid Heir Deals Deathly Blow to Wolf Lovers

I sighed. Hadn't Flinar said a redhead had it in for me? I'd assumed he meant Isadora, who'd meddled with matchmaking Ezra. But could he have meant Margola? "Is it too much to ask her to get my version of events? And how did she get that hideous picture?"

She'd chosen one of me running through the woods after Gunnolf and Lavinia's revelation of who Ezra's mate should be. Had she been eavesdropping?

Echo nodded. "You are quite right, Alisha. That is not your best look. Pity it's gone out to the whole of the UK like that. Less Donna Summer's 'Hot Stuff' than Celine Dion's 'All by Myself.'"

I grimaced while skimming the paper. "No need to hammer it home, Echo. Well, she got the basic facts right. I did abandon Ezra, steal the pick-up and wound Rashida. Looks like she's going to be all right, though."

I wasn't sure how I felt about that.

Echo inclined his head. "Wolves heal quickly, even those who aren't in possession of a healing charm like Ezra."

I flicked through the rest of the newspaper. The inside pages devoted coverage to seven girls who would be facing the Kraglek trial at Wildwoods after the summer holidays. The back page summarised the peculiar sports fixtures, and tucked into a small space next to a crossword was the briefest mention of the communications fall out impacting the humdrum world.

Robert shook his head. "We're coming up to eight cabinet reshuffles, the PM's been caught with his trousers round his ankles after he texted his wife, not his mistress, and there's been a tenfold increase in the number of houses going on the market and petitions for divorce submitted. With the number of petty arguments, I'm worried the birth rate will be impacted. And we can't even tell the population there is a god behind all this, or they'd either label the PM insane or go insane themselves." He reached for Marina's hand. "Marina's been helping out with her empath skills, of course—without her, I'm pretty certain the PM would have thrown in the towel and called a general election by now—but he's exhausted, and we can't afford an election right now. It takes months for a new PM to recover from the shock of hearing about the Otherworld."

Marina's wan face softened into a smile. "I am tired, but you introducing me to all these powerful people is quite an aphrodisiac, darling."

The detective flushed. "Oh, stop it."

She kissed his cheek. "No, you stop it."

"Urgh," said Echo. "Both of you, stop it."

I took a slurp of my tea, my insides warmed by more than the hot brew. Marina glowed at being reunited with the detective, and her happiness meant the world to me. I made myself concentrate on the matter at hand. "When I was trapped at the farmhouse, I was trying to work out who could be helping the Ravenmaster. We know that he's not tech-savvy. At least, not tech-savvy enough to disrupt modern comms all by himself." I hesitated, gathering my thoughts. "What if Margola Silver has taken this dislike to me because she is the Ravenmaster's secret helper? We know how adept she is with tech. We know she operates in the shadows just like him. And we know she has thrown curveball after curveball at me."

The detective nodded slowly. "It makes sense that Margola's knee-deep in this. We used to take a spin class together at Baba Yaga's, and she always struck me as a neutral force. Neither benign nor evil. Just someone who could be manipulated either way. Her coming after you is out of character unless it serves some unknown purpose."

Echo growled. "Then you need to isolate the selkie and speak to her when she is vulnerable, Alisha. And I know just the place to do it. A selkie needs access to the water, and it so happens that I know, from my hunting of the deer at Richmond, where Margola Silver lives. She has a place there that backs out onto the river, and she swims there each morning."

I screwed up the newspaper and arced it into the bin with a display of wind precision that surprised even me.

"I am coming with you," said Echo. "I will not take no for an answer."

"Then the answer is yes." I buried my head in his neck, but even as I did, my head whirred like a computer running different programmes. I remembered Durga, the multi-armed Hindu goddess that Dad had once read me stories about. This must have been what it felt like to be a mother: the competing priorities and the striving to do my best by everyone. "But first, we must move the wolves' pick-up truck. It's a dead giveaway out there. And I must call Lavinia to find out if she has been able to track Ezra. She does have a landline, doesn't she?"

17

———————

Richmond, which sat on the south bank of the Thames, was one of the most affluent boroughs in London, with breath-taking open spaces, a royal palace, riverside views, boating, bridle and cycling paths, independent shops and a weekly farmer's market.

Of course, Margola lived there. She was hardly the sort to be slumming it in the poorer parts of London, with her push-up bra and perfectly coiffed hair. I bet her handbag drawer was full of Louis Vuitton, and I'd definitely seen her carrying a Hermes Birkin, which now seemed like an indisputable link between the two.

I would have liked to have napped at home, as Marina had implored me to do. There was a reason sleep deprivation was delineated as a torture method in international law. But it was only a matter of time before Gunnolf's wrath caught up with me, so I had to make every minute count.

We rode up the tube escalator with Echo in his cat carrier.

"So the witch sent her rats into the tower?" His miaows attracted the stares of a cleaner. "They must have been in good company there."

I kept my voice low and melodic as if I was comforting my

stressed Bengal. "She said countless rats had searched for his whereabouts, and not one had made it out alive. The witches' scrying yielded no results either. Maybe the tower has its own magical defences. Or maybe Ezra is…"

Echo growled. "Don't think like that. The wolf might not have a cat's nine lives, but he is an impressive warrior, with wit as well as great natural strengths and the charms given to him by his aunts. We must hope he has survived. As for the Defence Minister, at least she tried. It's more than we can say for his uncle."

"Lavinia said Rashida called her, you know. Even after I sliced her leg. She called the witches before she'd even been patched up. She loves him too. I was right about that."

"I can hear your doubt, Alisha. You love him, but you don't believe yet you are worthy of him."

"Well, I put him in danger, didn't I?"

Echo pawed at the zipper of the cat carrier. "No. He put himself in danger for you. There's a difference. Now, will you please let me out of this wretched thing?"

I unzipped him as we exited the station.

He sprang out and stretched luxuriously like we had all the time in the world.

"Come on," I said. "We have to get going. You know, cat prams are now all the rage in the USA. I could get you one if you like."

Echo's lip curled in disgust. "Why not get me a bonnet and a dummy too? Need I remind you that I come from a regal family? A pram. A pram! What has my life become?"

"I was only asking, Echo." I rested a soothing hand on his head. "Tell me what you know about the apartment."

He tossed his head, a little touchy still, but rumbled on. "It's in an Edwardian mansion block on the banks of the river. Four bedrooms, fireplaces in every room, beautiful stained-glass windows in the entrance hallway, ceilings not out of place in a maharaja's palace, hardwood flooring, three floors including the basement and gated parking to boot."

I stared at him. "How do you know so much about it?"

Emerald eyes glinted. "She leaves the sash window in the kitchen open a fair bit, and sometimes I come by after hunting deer in Richmond Park for a nap in her back bedroom when my belly is full. She doesn't use it for anything other than airing the laundry. Since I served your grandmother, it's been part of my job to keep an eye on senate members. The Otherworld is a cutthroat place. Every piece of information might contribute to our survival."

My voice was a high-pitched squeak. "When were you going to tell me that? And how many other senate members do you snoop on?"

"The leprechaun. He has no sense of smell, so I can rub myself all over his bedding, and he is none the wiser. The druid headmistress. Her abode is as fragrant as they come, and I like how she is not materialistic. Most people are hoarders, but somehow, she has retained an admirable simplicity. Oh, and the fallen angel. He's a slob. He stays up all night playing video games and is addicted to wasabi crisps. It's harder to spy on the ones who live in a community, like the witches, wolves and vampires. I have a healthy fear of the Bestiary Master. He's wily and has too many tricks up his sleeve to be easily fooled. Phinnaeous Shine's house is in Marylebone but teeming with succubi, and Calypso resides in the Celestial Library with better security than Alcatraz."

I whistled in awe. "We really need to talk more."

"I dislike verbal incontinence, Alisha, but if you book a karaoke booth and marinate a steak to Michelin standard for me when this is all over, I may well be convinced to prise open my clam heart and share some secrets."

I shook his paw. "Deal."

"We're almost there," said Echo. "For a dwelling in the heart of London, Margola's flat has ample privacy. She swims most days just after the sun has come up to avoid detection. Although the local papers have a running joke about local loonies reporting seal sightings."

"She turns into a seal?"

Echo sighed with the heavy burden of someone explaining a matter which should be common knowledge. "You grew up on these isles, didn't you? A selkie always longs for the sea. Though she may choose to live in her human form, the sea calls to her. Usually, selkies can only remain in their human bodies when the conditions of the tides are correct, but she is more gifted than most." Echo's teeth clamped around the edge of my T-shirt and pulled me behind a bush. "There she is."

The Thames, a quiet river that was neither deep nor wide, glistened under a sky peppered with candy floss clouds. A few canal boats bobbed on the water. Margola Silver stood at the edge of the river in a silk kimono with her back towards us. She had twisted her flame-coloured hair into a topknot. She let the kimono fall from her shoulders, revealing her alabaster skin. Then she stepped into the water without a scrap of clothing on, shoulders back, pointy breasts leading the way, without any shame for her state of undress or any hurry. She didn't flinch at the cold and soon was submerged, swimming in a dolphin stroke.

"That's funny," said Echo. "Why isn't she in her seal form?"

I frowned. I had always found Margola's confidence off-putting. It bordered on arrogance, with no chink of vulnerability in her personality. But when she came up for air, her puffy eyes, drooping shoulders and empty stare were a far cry from the armour she presented to the world. I thought I hated her for highlighting my mistakes and weaknesses in her newspaper for all to see, but seeing her mask slip made me wonder what I had missed.

Echo's whiskers drooped. "I rather fancy a swim in the river."

"Maybe later." I hid the cat carrier behind the bush.

We edged towards Margola's apartment, taking care not to be discovered.

Echo nudged me towards an open sash window. "She swims for twenty-five minutes on average, so we have twenty minutes tops to find any clues."

I pushed it down and hoisted myself up on the ledge and into a kitchen of sleek grey lines, hanging pendant lights over an island and copper accessories. I moved aside a lonely cactus from the windowsill as Echo squeezed himself through the opening. The most recent edition of *The Otherworld News*, with my face plastered on it, lay abandoned on the worktop next to a lukewarm cup of coffee.

He landed on the marble floor and extended his claws to scratch a kitchen cabinet. "I have the *Mission Impossible* theme tune in my head. Do you?"

I swatted him. "Focus. No marking. We leave everything as we found it."

"Spoilsport." No sooner had he retracted his claws than his ears twitched. He leaned his head against the floor, his rear end still pointing in the air. "Do you hear that? From the basement."

I shook my head and held my fingers to my lips. Echo's hearing was remarkable, but he wasn't the only creature in the Otherworld to possess acute hearing. We crept through the house towards the basement stairs at the other end of the corridor.

The rooms were sterile. There were no pictures of family or friends, no vases filled with flowers, and the only artwork was of the sea, slashes of blue and black on mammoth canvases. A meagre bookshelf in the dining room had been filled with back copies of magazines—such as *Private Eye, The*

Spectator and *National Geographic*—and current editions of newspapers. But no fiction.

As beautiful as the bones of the apartment were, the overwhelming impression was of lovelessness.

I didn't know what I expected to find here. It wasn't like Hermes would be lounging in Margola's roll-top bath with a single malt by his side or that I could somehow disrupt her next edition from here. Gaia had told me to pull a string, and the whole ball would unravel. And so I was here on a wing, a prayer and pure instinct.

Echo searched the bedrooms while I sank onto my knees to leaf through past editions of *The Otherworld News*. Margola's coverage seemed to have only recently taken an overtly gossipy and vitriolic turn. Her coverage of the tremors, too, had been even-handed.

So what had caused the change?

I looked at my watch. Eight minutes before we had to scarper. The furtiveness of our act wasn't good for my heart rate. I wasn't even good at sneaking snacks into the cinema.

Echo urged me towards the basement, his wet nose in the small of my back. We crept down the stairs, side by side. I'd always hated basements. They brought back suppressed memories of horror films I should never have watched as a child. A tapping reached my ears the nearer we got to the door at the bottom.

Echo's nose twitched, and his tail swished, making my own anxiety peak.

Six minutes before Margola returned.

A concert of sounds reached me as we grew closer. The tapping noise. A humming of machines. A cooing. I crouched at the door and leaned my ear against it. My mouth grew dry.

Echo hissed. "We have to go. She'll skin us alive if she discovers us here."

I shook my head. We were so close. A small square window provided a view into the dimly lit basement. There was no time to dilly-dally. I had to peek inside the room if we wanted answers, even if we risked discovery.

I inched upwards on the right side of the window. Echo stood on his hind legs to view the left side.

My eyes widened.

The basement ran the length of the apartment. Computers and servers lined endless rows of tables. Cables ran like snakes from computer to server, server to computer. In front of each computer, basking in the glow of the screen, sat an elf, grey fingers flying over the keyboard.

The elves didn't talk to one another. Their pallor was dull, and their eyes glazed over with focus. Their screens showed familiar typography and branding colours. On the back wall, seven ravens perched in seven cramped cages, doors ajar, their beady eyes watching the progression of the elf workforce.

I scanned the elves for Flinar, but he wouldn't be caught doing something like this.

I dropped down to the floor. "Holy cow."

Echo followed suit, growling. "Not cows. Dark elves."

"The Ravenmaster has employed them as bots. That's how he is disrupting communication."

"The birds live." Echo grinned. "Who would have thought it? They are not victims of a massacre. They are cunning, bloodthirsty taskmasters, much like the Ravenmaster himself."

"We need to get in there, destroy those servers and free the elves."

The three-inch scar from the corner of Echo's eye reminded me of how ferocious he was in battle. "You—or those feathery balls of murder—will be the death of us. But I will follow a Verma where she leads."

I turned the door handle. To my surprise, it wasn't locked.

Then why hadn't the elves already escaped? It wasn't like Margola had guards upstairs.

The elves looked up, ghostly grey faces zapped of energy by the screens. God knew how many hours they had been sitting there. The poor things looked dazed.

The ravens did not look dazed. They looked and sounded furious, judging by the cacophony coming from their midnight bodies.

I raised my hands, and a gust of wind surged from them, slamming shut six cages just in time but missing the last one.

Echo roared as he leapt against the last cage, slamming an emerging bird back into its enclosure and nudging the door shut, but not before he received a gory peck on the nose that made him howl.

"Are you okay?" I asked.

"No thanks to you," he said.

I crouched down next to an elf. The screens flashed with branding from different social media sites and telephone companies. There was code and text and icons that didn't match the elvish faces. But with the ravens taken care of, why were the elves still staring at the screens, still typing away?

"Pull out the server cables," I said to Echo.

He leapt over to the humming machines, tearing out cables with his teeth.

I prayed he wouldn't be electrocuted but didn't utter it to completion.

The elves—there must have been twenty of them—emerged from their trance, fury written into their usually benign faces.

"What are you doing?" the one nearest me asked.

I didn't expect a thank you, but this was a little odd. "Rescuing you."

The ravens' clamour continued.

Echo's tail swished as he reached my side. His emerald eyes caught mine. "I think we may have misjudged this."

I frowned. "No kidding."

Shit, they were doing that winding thing Flinar did when

he produced a black hole. What happened when they did it together?

"Oh no," said Echo. "Where is the wolf when you need him? Run!"

We scampered down the corridor and knocked over the cactus in our hurry to escape through the kitchen window. I shoved Echo's rump onto the driveway and used my wind powers to vault over the ledge myself.

"What are we running from anyway?" I bent over, panting, my hands on my knees.

He hissed at an eerie sound like the stars had been sucked out of the universe. "That."

I turned around. The ledge I had just jumped from no longer existed. Neither did the three floors of Margola's flat. They had clean been sucked away. "What the hell?"

"Now do you realise why elves give many peculiars of other races the heebie-jeebies?" said Echo.

I gawped. "I mean, how cool would it be if they could suck the world's litter into a black hole and then just inferno it?" I hiccupped, still struggling to calm my breathing. "Did we actually beat the Ravenmaster at his own game? You did quite a number on the cables, *and* there's no internet in a black hole. Even if they pop up again, they are screwed. Pretty weird, though, that they didn't thank us for the rescue. It's almost like they wanted to be there. I'm feeling kind of shitty that we pretty much destroyed Margola's home."

Echo spat out the plastic coating of some cabling. "I know you're excited, but you should probably stop talking."

I frowned. "Why?"

A scream of rage pierced my eardrum. The selkie had returned.

Fear snaked up my spine. I was in for it now.

Echo bounded away and then launched himself into the river with the gusto of a toddler at a waterpark. So much for backup.

"What on earth has happened to my apartment?" Margola tied her damp kimono, her voice a screech. Brown eyes flashed with horror. "This is *your* fault, druid. What were you thinking coming here? Where is my home?" She balled up her fists like she was going to explode.

I hadn't seen a selkie fight, but seals could be vicious. I'd seen a brutal battle on a nature documentary once. I winced and put up my hands in defence. "About that. The elves in your basement went nuclear."

A look of doubt darted across her face. She frothed with rage. "They wouldn't. They *couldn't*. This is you. You're a tsunami of trouble." She grabbed my shoulders and shook me. "Wait until Phinnaeous and Gunnolf hear of this. The whole Otherworld will give you a whipping by the time I've finished with you."

I accepted her mauling for a moment. I had been partially responsible for her home disappearing, after all. Then I looped two currents of wind around her wrists and pinned them to her side. "I expect your apartment will pop back eventually. I have it on good authority that the elves never stay in their black holes for long. There's no food or water in there, and they're not cannibals. At least, I don't think so. I mean, they did have ravens with them. And ravens are opportunistic survivors, I'm told, so that doesn't bode well for the elves…" I took a deep breath to stop my rambling.

Margola stared at the remnants of her home, words failing her. Not only that, a shadow of guilt crept across her face.

I leapt on it. What was she wrapped up in? "Minister, why were you harbouring a room full of elf bots? Are you working with the Ravenmaster?"

She baulked. "You don't know what you are talking about."

I sighed. "I saw the evidence with my own eyes. I saw the ravens. Sooner or later, your home will return like a pop-up shop, complete with its basement of evidence. You might as well own up to it. You know as well as I do that getting ahead of the news is your best bet right now."

She shuddered. "The Ravenmaster and I have always had a natural affinity. We both deal in information. His rumours have powered my news. He is a maverick, a lover of language and an inventor with a flair for the dramatic. If someone like that asks me for a favour, I'm not going to say no. All I had to do was provide him with my unused basement." She hardened. "Not that you deserve an explanation. Why are you here, druid? I can't decide if you are foolish or brave."

Behind her, Echo frolicked in the waves.

I pursed my lips. "I came to find out what you were hiding and why you've spent the past few weeks destroying my privacy. I guess I know the answer to one of those questions."

Her brown eyes narrowed. "I'm just doing my job."

"No. It's more than that. It's personal. I've seen your work. You're not a common hack; just writing for paymasters.

"We do what we have to do to survive." Her voice cut through the morning quiet, defiant. "Isn't that why you stabbed the wolf last night? Unless you enjoyed it." She turned to track the whereabouts of the leopard in the water, and a fleeting expression of melancholy slipped across her face.

My thoughts whirled. She had emerged from the river in her human form. "You're trying to rile me. Why would a selkie who longs for the water swim in her human form?"

Margola's eyes grew dull. "Leave it alone, druid. You'll only make matters worse. You know nothing of my culture, my way of life. You know nothing about the call of the sea, the compulsion that haunts me every second of the day or what it costs me to stay in my human skin."

I didn't expect the swell of sympathy that washed over me. "Tell me what I am missing."

"Why? You and I are nothing alike. How many men have stolen your skin to make you do their bidding?"

"Who would do that to you?"

"Selkie folk have always suffered. I am no different. My skin has been taken by sailors, by men who profess to love me, and by my own child to stop me from returning to the sea. It is always men. Always men seeking control. Humdrum, peculiar, it doesn't matter. They are all the same. This time, too, you know nothing about what levers are being pulled behind the curtain."

"I am sorry you lost your home. How are you going to explain this away to the humdrums in this community?"

"I'm a newsmaker, aren't I? I suppose I'll have to say it's a gas explosion. The truth is, there is only one of my possessions that is worth saving, and it wasn't in my house."

I sucked in my breath as the penny dropped.

That was why she hadn't transformed into a seal in the water. That was why her behaviour had changed. "Who stole your skin, Minister?"

The particles shifted behind me, a moving of molecules to make space for something else.

Goosebumps ran up my bare arms as I recognised the sensation. The scent of the wilds came with him, but I didn't dare turn around just in case disappointment crushed me. I thought I'd never hear his voice again.

"It was Gunnolf, wasn't it, Minister?" said Ezra. "He stole your seal skin, and that isn't even the worst of it. And when we steal it back for you, you're going to tell us everything."

18

I held it together until Margola left our sightline, picking over the foundations of her lost home. Then euphoria crashed over me like a wave, and I threw my arms around Ezra.

I kissed him. "You."

His smile chased away the darkness in me. He wore the same dark clothes from the night we sneaked into the Tower of London. His T-shirt was ripped. My fingers pushed it aside. Underneath, his torso had healed, leaving no scars.

Echo raced from the river. The wet leopard launched into the air and knocked Ezra onto his arse amongst a smattering of daisies, then proceeded to nuzzle him in rapture. "We feared you were dead, dog. I am sorry for maiming you. I see you have healed."

"I'm okay, Echo." Ezra pushed him off, his grey eyes focussed on me. "I need to speak to Alisha, though."

His tone made me wary. "Where've you been? I thought the Ravenmaster had captured you. The worry almost killed me. I went to see Gunnolf and even called Lavinia."

"I know, hellfire." He reached out to me. "I'll tell you, but you have to promise to stay calm."

I nodded but kept my distance.

"It goes back to the investigation with the dead wolves. It's when you said that we shouldn't have burned the bodies that it clicked. The reason we couldn't sniff out a perpetrator for the murders. The reason Gunnolf didn't want Marina involved. The way how from the very beginning, he's been all talk and no action to get to the bottom of it. I mean, the Gunnolf I know is *all* action and no talk, and that's a change in behaviour, right? But any time I wanted to speak to other packs about which wolves were missing, to put names to those bodies, he shut me down."

I frowned. "But what has this got to do with the Ravenmaster? With him capturing you?"

He sighed. "Nothing and everything."

"Spit it out, dog," growled Echo.

He bowed his head as if he was ashamed. "The Ravenmaster didn't capture me. I just needed everyone to think he did. Even you."

I saw red. The wanker. Endless hours of guilt and fear that he'd met a sorry end, that I'd never hear his voice again or experience the exquisite pleasure of disappearing into the folds of the universe with just his arms to hold me. He'd been just fine and dandy all along and not even bothered to let me know. I flew at him like a banshee, raised my fists and pummelled him, not caring if I hurt him, wanting to hurt him like he'd hurt me.

"You show him, Alisha. The wolf is an imbecile. I always suspected it," said Echo.

When my energy was spent, he caught my wrists and placed a kiss on each palm. "Don't be angry."

I pulled back to search his face, panting hard. "Why, Ezra?"

He chewed his lip. "Because I knew you'd go to *him* for help, and he would read your mind, and that would give you the alibi to keep you safe while I solved the case."

I frowned. "Orpheus? You knew Orpheus would read my mind?"

Ezra nodded. "You can't deny that he is your closest Wildwoods ally after me."

I swallowed hard. "There's nothing between us."

"Can't you see? It's not about what you feel for him. It's about what he feels for you. I knew he would protect you when I couldn't and that he is powerful enough to make a stand against Gunnolf and vouch for you. It bought me time to investigate the murders without Gunnolf breathing down my neck."

I clenched my fists. "You didn't have to go through this ruse. We could have found a way to figure it out together."

He shook his head. "No, Alisha, you have your path, and I have mine. The alpha was *my* problem to fix." He softened and reached out for me. "But even then, you threw in a curveball when you refused to give up on me. You distracted Gunnolf with your tenacity just when I needed him to be distracted. Almost as if we were working in tandem without even realising it."

I had a lightbulb moment. "That was you in the woods? I felt watched just as I made it to the pick-up."

"I heard the call of the pack. I had to make sure you were okay."

Echo inclined his head. "I spoke in haste. It was a good plan."

Relief that Ezra was safe vied with bitter disappointment for his choices. He could have involved me. We could have found a way to figure out what was going on together. His instinct to protect me had belittled my power. Even Orpheus hadn't tried to be my saviour when I had decided to shoot myself in the foot.

"Was it worth lying to me?" My voice was the cut of a cold knife on warm flesh. "Did you have to put me through an emotional wringer to achieve your goals?"

Ezra scraped a hand through his hair. "That's not fair, Alisha."

"It is fair, wolf. Her pain was clear for all to see," said Echo. "However, let it be said, I am not a monogamous creature. In fact, my happiest coupling was with three sisters. But despite his machinations, the wolf has eyes only for you, Alisha, and you would be foolish to let this relationship swirl down the toilet pan like human faeces."

"I solved the case. But if this is the end of us, then no, it wasn't worth it," said Ezra.

My heart did a black flip in spite of myself, but he wouldn't win me over so easily, even if I were a gooey puddle. "And what did you find out?"

His expression tightened, and his words slowed as if it pained him to say them. "That Gunnolf is the murderer. Those poor wolves wanted to join our pack, but Gunnolf was worried he wouldn't be able to control the... His strength isn't what it was. He was worried he wouldn't survive an alpha challenge, so he killed them. They didn't even see it coming."

Echo growled. "If what you say it true, this will have wide-ranging consequences, dog. An indiscriminate murderer cannot be allowed to remain on the senate. We must do everything in our power to bring him down. But it will be difficult. It is Gunnolf, after all, who presides over justice in our world."

A vein pulsed in Ezra's neck. "A beta wolf can call the Court of the Wolves. I need the backing of the Prime Sorcerer, but I think I have enough evidence for him to be tried." He hesitated. "And that's not all. Gunnolf was always possessive of me. He fought tooth and nail to make sure I grew up with the pack and dissuaded me from claiming my witch heritage. He hated the closeness between Alisha and me. He's right. I have grown more distant from the pack."

"At this precise moment, you would be wise to focus solely on Alisha rather than your family sagas."

"That's just it. Tell me, leopard, what is the Jailor's Law?"

Echo lifted his magnificent head and recited with ease. "It is forbidden to interfere with the compos mentis of another peculiar."

A vein throbbed in Ezra's jaw. "And what would happen to a peculiar if you took away the very thing that makes them magical?"

I frowned. "You have no evidence that Gunnolf has taken Margola's skin."

"Did you not see the look of fear on Margola's face when I suggested it?" Ezra implored me to believe him. "Gunnolf made no pretence of the fact he didn't want us to date. He sees you as a threat. He voted against you at your magical trial. When all else failed, he and Lavinia used fertility as a wedge between us. Just before Margola egged you on to attempt to animate a fox at the Wildwoods trial, she and Gunnolf exchanged glances. I think Gunnolf stole Margola's skin so she'd agree to discredit you."

My heart raced as I recalled the padlocked room in the pack farmhouse.

Echo hissed. "That is unconscionable. I would die if I were stuck as a Bengal cat forever."

A small, sad smile on Ezra's lips. "So you see, I might have lied to you, but I did it for us."

I wanted so much to believe him. He was so focused on the pack that he'd lost sight of anything beyond the end of his own nose. "Echo and I found out today that Margola is hiding something in her basement."

"Unfortunately, we don't know precisely what. But whatever was in there hummed and throbbed."

I grimaced. "For all we know, it could be a room full of sex toys à la Christian Grey. But she's in there now. We'll have to find out another day."

"Just tell me what you need from me." Ezra's face tightened with resolve. "But I need to face Gunnolf first."

I let out my breath in a whoosh. "Then I'm coming with you. I know where the selkie skin is."

<hr>

WE MUST HAVE BEEN stupid to go back to the pack farmhouse. As if we were invincible. As if we didn't bleed. As if our enemies couldn't wound us. Yet, standing beside Ezra, I didn't think anyone could. We were so powerful together. If we couldn't fight, then we could flee. He could teleport us anywhere in the world, couldn't he?

But he'd tangled me up in his ploy to get the bottom of the wolf murders, and I didn't know if I could accept it. It was a bitter pill to swallow. I'd wanted Ezra to choose love over everything. Even though his eyes—and his mouth—told me he loved me, I couldn't help but think he had put his duty to the pack above me. That his love and desire for me had come a distant second to his responsibilities to his wolf family and that I could never compete.

We walked across the lawn to the farmhouse. Ezra's broken window had been boarded over. This time the border of orange dahlias didn't seem romantic, despite the noon sun that lent warmth to the building. The flowers turned and twisted like they had agency of their own accord. Like they could leap from the earth, as treacherous as the wolves inside. I held Ezra's hand, but our fingers hung limp. They didn't mesh together. Distance had set between us, even though we walked side by side.

My voice quaked. "I stole the pick-up and wounded Rashida."

A vein throbbed in his neck. "I know. The pick-up was a pile of junk, and Rashida will heal. You did what you had to."

I stopped to dig in my pockets. "The pick-up keys. And your room key."

He accepted the car key but handed me back the rusty old silver key to his bedroom door. "Keep it."

I gulped and slipped it back into his pocket. How could his timing be so off? "Ezra, why did you and Rashida break up?"

A weighted sigh. "She didn't trust me. I couldn't breathe in that relationship with her."

My brain told me to back off. My heart wanted me to dig deeper. "How long were you together?"

I could cope with two or three years. It took that long sometimes to work out if something was worth fighting for. Hell, it had taken me twice as long as that to work up the courage to leave Alex.

"Six years."

Oh shit. They were serious then. I shrank into silence.

Mere yards from the farmhouse, his hand tightened around mine. "You've got to stop this. Gunnolf will take advantage of any split between us."

I bit my cheek as the pack came pelting out in their human forms: Gunnolf at the apex, with the two strongest males, Dominic and Maximillian, in formation behind him, and finally, mousy Deirdra, her boyfriend Ruud and a wan Rashida. Not even Deirdra raised a smile for Ezra.

Gunnolf spoke first, glowering with anger. "The prodigal son returns."

Ezra nodded but kept his distance, every nerve in his body alert and ready to defend us if he needed to. He didn't give Rashida a sideways glance. Yes, he was focussed on Gunnolf, but his heart was with me.

Gunnolf sneered. "That slut turned you against me, just like I knew she would."

That was a bit rich, given Ezra and I hadn't even gone the whole way.

Ezra didn't flinch. "You drove a wedge between us yourself. I wanted us to stay family."

The alpha let out a mirthless laugh. "I wanted you alive. I've known you since you were a babe in arms, nephew. I raised you as my own, but there you stand, not rushing to me. Returning with the druid, as if to rub salt in our wounds. Do you know what she did?"

"I know what you did." Ezra's voice was a statement of fact, not recrimination, and all the stronger for it.

Maximillian frowned, suddenly unsure. "What's he talking about?"

"Tell them." Ezra stared at the alpha and didn't back down. "Or I will."

Suddenly I realised what this encounter would do to their relationship. How there would never be a going back, however it played out. How Ezra wasn't acting like the beta of the pack anymore. He'd made the decision to be something more.

I fancied the pants off him, but lust had to wait. Obviously.

"He's out of his mind," said Gunnolf. "The Ravenmaster has broken him."

Ezra shook his head. "I found the traps you set. It took me a pretty minute to work out it was you, but once I had, the evidence was hard to ignore. Even if you had rushed into burning the bodies. You taught us those skills yourself. Your knots. Your ambush places. Your prints in the mud. We couldn't smell the perpetrator because we were looking for an outsider. It was you all along."

The deck creaked as the pack backed slowly away from Gunnolf. They, too, could sense the tide turning.

"You're not going to listen to him, are you? It's ludicrous. Why would I kill my own kind? I taught you how to be wolves. I protected you. And now you believe this halfling?"

Sadness tinged Ruud's quiet voice. "He's not a halfling. He's our family. And we can smell the fear on you."

Rashida looked from Ezra to Gunnolf. "Ezra is many things, but he is not a liar."

A roar ripped from Gunnolf's throat. "You turn my own family against me? You ungrateful swine."

"I have to fight him," Ezra murmured to me. The pack will wait to see who is crowned alpha. Get the selkie skin."

A primal scream built in me as Gunnolf leapt from the decking and transformed into his black wolf.

Ezra's clothes ripped, and his bones cracked as he, too, transformed into his wolf. His grey eyes met mine as they changed shape, and then he turned to meet his match.

I backed away, shuddering to see how the black wolf was bulkier and aimed to maim or kill, whereas the copper-grey one was loathed to strike a deathly blow. They circled each other and flew through the air in a tangle of limbs and teeth and claws.

Grunts and growls filled the air. A battle of rage, resolve and skill.

It was impossible to tell from the horrified expressions of the pack who they wanted to succeed.

I prayed to Gaia that Ezra would come out on top.

Bodies slammed against each other as I ran around the back to the door I knew was open and the padlocked one I'd have to break into. The selkie skin had to be behind that door. Why else would it be padlocked? There was no time to look for bolt-cutters, and I had the strength of a gnat. The monkey bars at school had been my nemesis.

But Gaia had taught me that I didn't always have to win with brute strength.

I had another idea. My hands quivered as I took the catalogue of creatures from my satchel and chose a pair of woodpeckers on the central spread. I closed my eyes to ground myself, pushing away the images I knew played out on the lawn.

Dad's painting on the page fluttered in my mind's eye, telling me I was ready. I waved my hands over the page. The threads waited for me there and leapt into my fingers as if they longed to be made real. To be born into this world of pain and power. I sensed the chisel-like beaks, the tiny bodies, the tail feathers and their tongues. Two palm-sized woodpeckers with black-and-white markings—one with a crimson head—came to life beneath my fingers. A sense of elation came over me. I whispered their purpose to them and pulled them out of the page.

They greeted me with a churring sound and then flew to the padlocked door in a fierce beating of their wings. The woodpeckers worked in tandem, laser-focussed, drilling with their beaks in a semi-circle each. I stashed away the catalogue of creatures in my satchel as they toiled. My anxiety rose with every second. How long until the drumming sound of the beaks against the wood roused the pack's suspicion? How long before I would be discovered red-handed and alone while Ezra fought for his life?

The woodpeckers had no thought except to break through the door. The tempo of their drilling reached a crescendo as they neared the finish line, and the circle they had excavated, complete with the three padlocks, fell to the floor with a thud.

"Thank you." I held out my hand, and they flew to me, tiny feet on my palm, purring with pride next to one another. I took them to the back door, released them to the woods, and then returned to my task.

I pushed the door open and stepped over the obsolete padlocks.

The scent in the room made my stomach turn. It stank of old boots or something worse, and there were no windows to let in fresh air. The room itself was no bigger than a box room in an old Victorian house. Shelves lined the walls, stacked with dusty accountancy notebooks—squared paper filled with sums and household calculations. I frowned. There were much better apps for that sort of thing nowadays. A humming came from the far end of the room. An industrial-type freezer had been squeezed into the space at the end, the sort of one that was more horizontal than vertical.

Dread stirred in the pit of my stomach.

I made a beeline for it and reached out to hoist up the lid when a voice behind me gave me pause.

"Haven't you done enough?"

I swivelled to find Deirdra there.

At least it wasn't Rashida. I wasn't sure how I would have managed that rabid redhead in such a small space. I'd already pissed her off enough without burying her in accountancy notebooks. Death by maths wasn't a way anyone wanted to go.

I raised my hands in surrender. I could talk Deirdra around. She'd been the friendliest pack member right from the get-go. She hadn't been wary of me just because I didn't belong.

"You have to let me open this," I said.

Deirdra's growl of warning echoed in the small space and made me wish I'd worn a pantyliner. "You've split apart my family and didn't even wait around to see who walked away."

"That's not true. I wrenched myself away. I don't want anyone to get hurt." It was a small lie, and I sold it well. There wasn't even an inflexion in my voice.

Deirdra launched herself forward, suddenly more Danger Mouse than field mouse. She grabbed my arm and twisted it behind me as her were-teeth came out to play.

I had no intention of being imprisoned or a dog chew, but I didn't want to hurt her either. With my spare hand, I fashioned a channel of wind between us, holding her at bay long enough to break free and throw open the freezer.

I recoiled from its contents and spun away to vomit on the floor. I wiped the back of my hand across my mouth as Deirdra looked at me in horror.

Then we both peered into the freezer together.

"Holy mother of—" said Deirdra.

"Uh-huh."

The freezer was jammed full. Not of frozen bags of vegetables, casserole portions, Yorkshire puddings or turkey left over from Christmas. It held three dead male wolves, packed tightly like a game of Tetris. Their glazed eyes stared up at us, their fur gouged and iced white. At one edge, underneath a leg protruding at an unthinkable angle, I spotted a blubbery seal skin.

My stomach heaved.

Deirdra closed the freezer. "This room is Gunnolf's. The padlocks went on a few months ago. We never questioned why. No one ever questions the alpha."

"Ezra did. I don't suppose you have a carrier bag?"

She stepped over the splash of vomit and disappeared in the direction of the kitchen, returning with a Tesco's bag.

I opened the freezer again, carefully plucked out the selkie skin, silently grossed out by its weight and slick texture, and put it in the bag. "My job here is done."

Deirdra turned her head in the direction of the warring wolves. "Ezra's job isn't."

We took one look at each other and rushed outside. The selkie skin slopped in the carrier bag at my side. My stomach went rock hard with fear, and my knees locked as I took in the carnage outside.

The lawn had been shredded by their claws, and the pack watched on, grim-faced, jerking with every blow. They loved both of these men.

They must have been fighting for a quarter of an hour already, and still, they hadn't eased their pace. Gunnolf's black wolf lunged time and again, tearing strips off Ezra. Ezra had taken a deep cut to his snout. It oozed blood. His tail hung limp, but there was a resolve to his body. He stood tall as he rounded on Gunnolf, sinking his teeth into the black wolf's flank before circling again.

Gunnolf reeled around, powering off his muscly legs and pinned Ezra to the floor. He sank his yellow teeth into Ezra's neck, just above his charm necklace. Ezra yelped, and the sound drove a stake into my heart.

I clapped my hand to my mouth to stop myself from crying out. Ezra couldn't afford for me to disturb his focus.

Why didn't he teleport? Why didn't he fight dirty? He was holding back; I knew it.

Then it happened. His head flopped in my direction.

I flinched, thinking it was all over. A wail ripped itself from me, an avalanche of sorrow.

Ezra's beautiful copper-grey eyes focussed on my face, and suddenly he rolled over, his ears upright and no longer flat against his head. He flipped the position so that he was the dominant force, pressing down on the black wolf.

The black wolf frothed at the mouth, raging at Ezra.

Ezra lunged, clamped his jaw around the black wolf's foreleg and twisted. The bone snapped, clear for all to see, its ivory-white fragment poking through the black wolf's flesh wound.

The copper-grey wolf leapt aside and sat, watching with narrowed eyes, waiting for the black wolf to make another move.

The black wolf righted himself and bared his teeth. But his body could no longer match the attack in his eyes. He fell into the dirt, curled up into a ball and licked his foreleg, growling a warning at Rashida when she ran to help him.

"It's over," said Deirdra. "We have a new alpha."

As Ezra's wolf surveyed the farmhouse, the land and the peculiars on it, I realised she was right.

19

Marina tended to Ezra in her surgery, supervised by Echo. Fae Yen and Faeza were there, too, applying healing ointments from Chinese herbology they insisted would complement Marina's traditional methods. Although, from what I could tell, it was Ezra's thistle charm that had done the most work, supercharging his innate werewolf healing powers. His wounds had already started to knit together.

Marina tutted. "This really would be much easier if you had stayed in wolf form, Ezra. I'm not sure how I'm supposed to sanitise all your wounds and keep you free of infection, with you presenting yourself here in another form."

Ezra was pale and shivering in his boxers on the stainless-steel examination table. "Teleporting as a wolf is tricky, especially in this state. I have to make sure my mind is wholly centred to emerge in the right place."

I brought him a blanket. "Why didn't you teleport when you fought Gunnolf? You could have finished him off easily before he'd even left a mark on you."

"I wanted to give you enough time to get inside the house and get what you needed. I held on until I saw you get back."

His voice was monotone, his eyes empty. He didn't take any joy in displaying his power over his uncle. "And it wouldn't have been fair to fight him with an advantage. This way, the pack knows I won a fair fight, and they'll accept me as their alpha."

I bit my lip. It was hard to see him like this. "You knew that if we returned to the farmhouse, it would result in an alpha challenge, didn't you?"

Ezra scrubbed a hand over his face, his eyes dull. "I owed it to my uncle to give him a chance to explain."

"I have caught the whiffs of your scent-marking, wolf." Echo curled his lip. "You do not seem like an alpha to me. More a beta or omega. But not an alpha."

"You're right. The pack system sometimes suffocates me. I prefer to roam, much like you, leopard." Ezra's eyes found mine. "But sometimes life forces us to be things we might not have chosen. I have to trust that it will all work out okay in the end."

"We did your tarot card reading, wolf. Your path is not easy." Fei Yen closed one pungent bottle of ointment and gave me another. "Put this on this pillow when he sleeps. It will help him recover his strength."

Faeza winked. "In more ways than one."

"I'm proud of you both. Let's celebrate this weekend. I have to get on now. My next patient is in twenty minutes." Marina gave Ezra a stern look. "I know you heal quickly, but alpha or no alpha, I'm prescribing rest and relaxation."

He gave her a weak smile. "Aye, aye, captain."

"We can drop them at Alisha's flat," said Fei Yen. "It wouldn't be any trouble."

"We can check our grammar homework with you on the way there," said Faeza.

Ezra sat up with help from me. He shook his head. "I can take Alisha home."

My brow furrowed. "Are you sure?"

"You don't need to worry. I'm fine." His voice rasped, and I couldn't help my mothering instinct respond, despite his protestations.

I turned to the foxes. "In that case, I have another favour to ask. I've been worried about Flinar and wondered if you might track him down for me. If anyone can find him on the streets, it's you two."

They nodded, entirely in sync with one another. "It would be our pleasure."

"We will call you as soon as we know more," said Fei Yen.

"Marina, can you keep this Tesco's bag in your freezer for now?"

She wrinkled her nose. "To be honest, I'm not that keen."

I grinned. "The time will come when we'll need it as a bargaining chip. I'll be back for it as soon as I can."

I tucked away the ointment in my satchel. Ezra stood shakily and wrapped his arms around me, and we melted between the worlds.

Echo's growl rang in our ears. "Clearly, there's no space for a leopard between those lovebirds."

Moments later, I stepped out of the circle of Ezra's arms and surveyed my surroundings in awe. We stood in a beautiful, landscaped garden with hedged enclosures and a sunken lawn. At the end of a pathway was a small thatched cottage. Wisteria climbed up its walls and draped over the front door.

"Will you excuse me for just one moment?" said Ezra. "I need to call the Prime Sorcerer."

I nodded, and he stepped away, whispering furiously. But when he returned, all his angst fell away, and his expression became open and happy.

"Where are we?" I asked. "I thought you were taking me home."

"This is home, Alisha. It was my parents' once. You're the only woman I've ever brought here."

I swallowed hard and allowed him to tug me down the winding path.

At the front door, Ezra crouched down in his bare feet and boxers and reached under the mat for a key. Mottled bruises covered his body. "I rarely come here but used it as a base the night the Ravenmaster attacked us. I have a few clothes here and bought a few supplies to keep going."

I pursed my lips. "Why didn't Gunnolf look for you here?"

"He might well have if you'd not distracted him. But the truth is Gunnolf is singular-minded. The pack house is everything to him, and he never understood why I kept this place." His grey eyes lit up. "Come. I have a surprise for you."

"What surprise?"

He led me through the cottage, looking back now and then to gauge my expression. Though the sun shone outside, the cottage itself was dark, with heavy curtains drawn across its windows and dust sheets covering the furniture. The house smelled abandoned, as if no soul had lived there for a hundred years. As if a coldness had crept into the walls that could never be clawed out. There were no books, family pictures, or children's drawings. The floorboards creaked as we reached the back bedroom.

His grey eyes darkened. "There are two bedrooms upstairs. My parents' bedroom and my childhood one. But I prepared a room downstairs for us."

Lights flickered from under the door. My heart rate spiked as he pushed the door open.

This room took my breath away, from the textures to the ambience and scent. Fairy lights lined a four-poster bed that had been made up with white linen. A vase of burnt orange roses, a bowl of Maltesers and a tray of essential oils sat on a side table alongside a burning amber-and-vanilla blossom candle.

I soaked up every detail and then turned to him. "This is beautiful."

He stood in his boxers and charm necklace, his hands gently clasped around mine. "I promised to make our first time special. I want to feel close to you before the coming storm. You can feel it, too, can't you? I don't know if we'll be the same."

My breath hitched in my chest. It meant so much that he'd brought me here, to the place of his family's happiness before it was all torn apart. But the sense of dread in me was all-encompassing.

I didn't understand it. We had come out on top, hadn't we? But I could feel it too. We were being pulled apart, despite our attempts to edge closer together.

The past few days had shown me that we weren't perfect, but give me a relationship that was, and I'd show you a lie.

I loved him. I could feel the truth of it beating in my chest. My reaction to him being in danger proved it. We had earned this moment of peace together, and I was going to take it.

A fluttering in my chest. "Are you well enough?"

"Oh, I'm well enough."

I traced my finger over the scar on his neck, where Gunnolf's teeth had met his soft flesh. "You need to heal."

The alpha's eyes on mine. A low growl in his throat. "I need you."

My breath quickened, and my tongue tied as he edged towards me.

There was an inch between us, and still, he didn't touch me. "I'm at a disadvantage here, hellfire. Take off your clothes."

I held his gaze as I shrugged off my bag and kicked off my shoes. My fingers fumbled with the button of my jeans. I sucked my tummy in, suddenly conscious of how I wasn't perfect. How I hadn't done enough sit-ups or had time for running and had eaten too many spoonfuls of Nutella when I should have eaten a carrot. Without hummus.

His fingers brushed mine, featherlight, as if he was holding back.

I quivered as he unfastened the button and slid my jeans over my hips. I stood, vulnerable and aching, as he pulled my rose-coloured T-shirt over my head.

He stepped back, his eyes roaming over me.

I stood there in my huge tummy-sucking knickers and a bra that had been designed for scaffolding rather than sexiness, and he hadn't run in the other direction. In fact, the fire in his eyes told a different story. I stuttered, my words a whisper of uncertainty. "I bought new underwear to make it special, but I don't have it here."

"I can't wait to see it, but you couldn't be any more perfect than right now."

With infinite gentleness, he traced his fingers over the scar on my arm, the circle of raised dots that the birds had drilled into my skin as a child. He leaned in to kiss me, the pressure of his lips gentle on mine.

I needed more, but he had other ideas. I giggled as he scooped me up as if I weighed nothing, forgetting his wounds for a second. He buried his face in my hair as I lay against his chest. I wanted him to dump me onto the bed so we could lose ourselves in each other. So we could forget about the world, and everything would slow to just us in this little cottage, a pinpoint on the map that he had brought no one to but me.

Disappointment swelled in me as he used his back to open a door I hadn't noticed. Inside was a small en suite bathroom with a simple shower, fresh towels and a bar of soap. He let me down on my feet wordlessly as I held my breath, my lips parting with my need for him.

A moment later, he'd turned on the shower and spun to me with an invitation in his smouldering eyes. I swallowed hard and stepped out of the remainder of my clothing, just as he did, then followed him into the shower. Hot jets of water ran in rivulets down our bodies, and finally—mercifully—the distance closed between us as he pulled me to him, and our bodies merged. Every nerve ending in my body tingled as his hands found my hips and his mouth met mine. The hot water, his touch, and the desire that pulsed between us made me lightheaded. I arched against him, urging him on.

He shook his head. "Slower."

I trembled as he picked up the bar of soap and washed every inch of me. Then I returned the favour, taking care to avoid the parts of him that were still red and raw.

He took the soap from my hand and turned off the water before wrapping me in a towel and carrying me back to the fairy-lit four-poster bed.

My inhibitions had long fled. My nails clawed his back as he explored me with his hands and tongue. I shivered with pleasure, my head empty of all cogent thoughts. There were only Ezra and me, and our bodies damp from the shower and lust. We forgot the world and its machinations, forgot his enemies and mine, and forgot everything except the tender sparks between us. The way our hearts raced in proximity to each other and our pupils dilated.

He pulled me so that I straddled him. I didn't feel self-conscious about being on top, the extra inches I carried on my stomach, or the fact my breasts weren't as pert as they once had been. I bit my lip as he cupped them, turned on by his arousal, and lost myself in the feeling of being desired just as I was. I bent my head to trail featherlight kisses down from his collarbone to his pecs and lower still to where he was hard. He moaned and pulled me up for a kiss that left me dizzy with need. I rocked against him, begging him with the motion of my body to give me what I wanted, but he wasn't in a hurry.

He wanted me to beg.

All it took was one word. "Please."

Ezra smiled and flipped me over onto my back, and entered me. I gasped and clung onto the bed post as we found a sweet dance all our own. His hands clasped mine, but I needed him to go faster. I freed my hands to clutch his tight buttocks and urge him on. His eyes darkened, and my name was on his lips. When we reached our apex, we collapsed against each other, spent.

After a while, Ezra pulled the duvet over us and kissed my forehead, a satisfied growl in his throat. "Don't sleep too long, Alisha. I bought those essential oils knowing *exactly* what I am going to do to you."

I flushed and raised my head from the crook of his arm. "I love you, Ezra."

His smile made my heart do a backflip. "And I love you, hellfire."

I didn't ever want to leave this cocoon.

20

———

As the moon rose in the night sky, I received a cryptic message from Fei Yen and Faeza about my ginger tea being ready for pick up. Given that they knew I hated ginger tea, I took it as a klaxon to rush to their shop, despite the post-coital delight of sleeping entwined with my wolf.

I set aside my glowing mobile phone and kissed Ezra awake—the alpha.

"Just one more minute of this bliss," he grumbled and pulled me closer. I melted into him, revelling in the feel of my skin against his, but not fully relaxing. He opened one eye. "I can hear your brain churning from here. You are a naughty druid."

I nipped his lip with my teeth. "Will you take me to Shanghai Moon?"

He sighed. "I guess the party is over."

The cloud of dread, which I had pushed aside, bubbled to the surface. "For now."

"What time is it?"

I checked my phone. "Ten p.m.. We've been asleep for hours."

He sat bolt upright. "Shit. That only leaves me two hours."

"For what?"

"To get to the Court of the Wolves."

We dressed quickly, with a shyness that belied what had gone on the night before. Ezra's body had almost completely healed, and I said a silent word of thanks to his aunts, whose charms had saved him—and me—from sticky situations more than once. However, there could be no friendship between us if they had supercharged Sahil's powers, as I suspected.

We switched off the fairy lights and left the cosy ambience of the bedroom with regret in our hearts, then teleported to the tea shop. Two houses down, a couple screamed at each other, their argument playing out in silhouettes across their beige curtains while the cries of their baby drifted out of the open window.

"We closed down the bot basement. Shouldn't there be peace and harmony on these isles?" I said.

Ezra shrugged. "It's just a one-off lovers tiff. They happen without meddling gods."

In Shanghai Moon, a night light shone, and an incense stick burned on the counter. The foxes, wearing matching kimonos, huddled together with the intimacy only lovers shared. Echo was in there, too, with his nose buried in a pile of dried mushrooms.

I knocked on the window, where a display of teapots took precedence.

A worried expression marred Fei Yen's smooth visage as she detangled herself from Faeza's embrace to open the door. "Come in, come in. After you told us about the bot room full of dark elves, we were worried our message would not arrive without interference. But then I remembered how much you dislike ginger tea, and I knew you'd understand to come here."

She closed the door and locked it behind us.

Echo bounded over, purring with delight. "I have been

trying to advise the foxes about how to achieve more custom."

I kissed his head. "I am sure they are very grateful for your advice."

He sniffed the air. "This shop smells of herbs. Herbs are a curse on all of mankind, ruining the pure taste of meat. If the foxes wish to appeal to leopards, it is imperative they rid themselves of half of these jars."

"It is a shame that you dislike herbs, Chanakya Gunbir Hredhaan of Maharashtra," said Fei Yen. "Since the land of your ancestors is rich with them. We will not change the shop since leopards aren't the clientele we wish to appeal to."

"How rude," said Echo. "But you are only foxes. What could you know of business?"

Faeza rolled her eyes at him and embraced us. "You look better, wolf. Our tonic has worked wonders."

I shot Ezra a teasing glance. We both knew it wasn't the tonic that had cured him.

The look between us didn't go unnoticed.

Fei Yen and Faeza exchanged glances and then giggled.

Echo's emerald eyes narrowed, and then he, too, grinned. "Has somebody been up to hanky panky?"

I spluttered. "We're not in kindergarten."

Dark shadows lurked under Faeza's eyes. She took pity on me. "Quite right. Let's get on, shall we? We looked for Flinar in all his usual haunts. At his home, on Streatham Common, under Blackfriars Bridge, in the alley behind the Vicarage and even as far as the woods where he hid with Tielbu and the runaway dark elves. We followed graffiti tags and dust trails and couldn't find him anywhere. We checked the elves' new drinking spot in the secret garden in Regent's Park. At first, we thought that, too, had been a wasted trip, but just as we were in the pergola tunnel leading to the cast-iron exit, one of Flinar's friends appeared out of nowhere. Fei Yen let out a squeal because he was a particularly ugly specimen of dark elf—"

"To cut a long story short, we found him," said Fei Yen. "Or at least, we know where he is."

Faeza trembled. "The rumour is that the Ravenmaster took him as revenge for him helping you. The elf should have known better than to meddle with the gods, but I suppose his love for you overrode all common sense."

Ezra cursed. "So he's in the Tower?"

Faeza nodded. "We think so."

Tremors coursed through my body. I thought we'd beaten Hermes. I couldn't bear the thought of my friend all alone in that cold place and the fact that my big mouth might have led the Ravenmaster straight to him.

"Do you think my brother was behind his capture?" How else would the god have known to target Flinar? It was his friendship with me that had put him in danger.

"It could be," said Echo. "Stinky werepigeon."

My eyes filled with tears. "We have to rescue Flinar. Right now."

A weighted look passed between the foxes, and then Faeza spoke for them. "We will come too. We love the elf."

Ezra's gaze ping-ponged between me and the rest of the group, and his lips pressed together in a slight grimace. "Dammit. What am I being roped into again?"

I glared at him. "I know. But I have to go, with or without you."

"Always so stubborn." He brushed his calloused thumb across my cheek and sighed. "Okay, for you as much as the elf. But I have to make it to Wildwoods by midnight, come what may."

Echo growled. "I go where the druid goes. And I like that weird little fellow. Is there time for a snack before we go?"

"No," we said in unison.

Echo grinned. "It is good we are on the same page. I did that."

"Ezra teleports us in. We get Flinar, and we get out. We watch each other's backs. No chit-chat. No heroics." I gulped. "If Sahil is there, we'll have to be careful. He's not trustworthy."

"The stinky werepigeon will pay," said Echo.

I bit my lip. I couldn't hurt my brother. I put a hand on my satchel. Feeling the edges of the catalogue of creatures in there comforted me. "Ezra, I need my sword. It's in my knicker drawer at home. Would you mind?"

The corners of his mouth lifted in a wry smile. "Not the kind of invitation I expected, but I'll take it."

He disappeared and came back in twenty seconds and handed me my weapon.

I wriggled into the baldric, and we stood in a circle.

"Ready?" said Ezra.

I didn't feel ready, but I nodded all the same. The five of us spiralled between the worlds through the monochrome layer beneath all colour and logic. We emerged in the vast, damp, moonlit room where the raven enclosures loomed. We scanned the room, alert to a small whimpering sound, but the cages were empty.

I frowned. "I don't understand. Where is Flinar? The Ravenmaster has him here. He can't bear to leave behind all the remnants of prestige, even though the ravens have flown. He has no intention of leaving. Which means Flinar is here too."

Worry painted frown lines on Fei Yen's face. "I have caught the elf's scent, but that doesn't mean he is in this room. There are endless miles of secret tunnels in and under this city, and many of them are in this very building."

Another muffled sound met my ears, a shaking and a scratching.

Echo prowled beside the central raven enclosure. "I can

smell the werepigeon and the elf. They are here. Hidden by magic.

"The leopard is right. I can smell them too." Ezra touched the moon charm on his necklace, and the lights in the room blazed to life.

I gave a startled gasp as the light revealed my brother skulking in the corner.

He grinned. "Well, isn't this a party? How clever you are, my little sister."

In his hand, he swung the same key on an iron ring I had seen in the Ravenmaster's manicured hands.

A chill ran up my spine.

Echo hissed. "You're not a werepigeon. You're a weasel."

"I'm many things." Sahil shrugged. "But carry on underestimating me. It seems that is all anyone has done since this new life of ours unfolded."

"So it's true," I said. To think, all this time I had thought Lavinia to be the one who had led him astray after the coven dinner. "You're working for the Ravenmaster."

"I like to think I'm working *with* him, sis. But don't get your knickers in a twist. We each make our choices, isn't that right? Speaking of choices, why did you bring two old Chinese women with you?"

"He means it as an insult," said Fei Yen to Faeza. "But ageing is the greatest privilege in life."

"Is that from a fortune cookie? Never mind. I'll show you your little friend if it makes you happier, Alisha." He strode to the raven enclosures, whistling a merry tune, then waved the key over the lock of the middle one.

A growl laced Ezra's voice. "Stay together."

My breath caught in my throat. It was as if a curtain had lifted. Flinar slumped on his knees in the central enclosure. His parched lips hung open, and a handful of his wispy hair lay at his feet like he had twisted it out in anguish or someone had torn it from his scalp. His milky eyes were slow to register our arrival. They grew large and fearful.

"I knew you would come, Alisha. The Ravenmaster said his birds would peck my eyes out. That he wouldn't even give me the coins for my passage to the afterlife. That I deserved it for creating the black holes." He lifted his chin, and there was a ligature mark around his neck, a red rim of pain on his dull grey skin. His voice quivered. "For helping you."

"You're my brother," I said to Sahil. "We're a family. Give me the key. Let him out. You wouldn't have shown me he was here unless you wanted to help."

"Nah, Alisha, I just wanted to show you I won," said Sahil. "He's staying right where he is. It's more than my life is worth to defy the Ravenmaster, but at least I got to brag a little. He will be back any minute, and you can speak to him yourself."

Flinar gripped the bars of the enclosure. His eyes darted to the shadows behind us. "Save yourself, Alisha. Please leave. If I die here, you should know that the red-haired woman in the elf drinking hole wasn't Rashida."

"Quiet, elf," hissed Sahil.

Flinar cowered and stuttered on his words. "It was Margola. I got them confused. I'm not good at non-elvish features. When I found out, I was bundled into a postbag and brought here. There's a roomful of elves intercepting messages in her basement."

"It's okay," I said. "We found it. We just need to get you out of here."

Then Ezra would do his thing at the Court of the Wolves, and we could get back to enjoying each other. I drew my sword and eyeballed my brother as only a little sister knew how. "What would Mum and Dad think? One way or another, I will take those keys off you."

A sly smile lifted his lips. "They'd tell us to sort it out

between ourselves like grown-ups. But I know you, Alisha. You don't have the killer instinct. You would never cross that line. You wouldn't hurt a fly."

Wasn't I supposed to get into adulthood supporting and supported by my sibling? Now wasn't the time to tell him about the vampire I had turned to dust or the wolf I had slashed.

"I would cross that line," said Echo. "And sing a song while I mauled you."

Faeza held Fei Yen's. "My wife and I feel the same way. We strongly believe in karma."

"Sorry, mate, if I weren't technically your mentor, I would too." Every cell in Ezra's body looked active. He didn't seem ready to attack my brother, but he'd defend us to his dying breath.

My sword whispered to me. I replaced it in its sheath like I'd been burned, ignoring Ezra's look of concern.

"He's right about one thing. A sword's not the way to deal with my brother." I adopted a kickboxing stance, widening my feet, bending my knees and raising my fists. "I don't need metal to kick your arse. Now give me that key."

Sahil's lips twisted into a sneer. He put the key in his pocket. "Come and get it."

"Keep an eye out for any sign of the Ravenmaster. And hands off. He's mine." I ran at my brother and landed two punches to his jaw, an uppercut and a hook.

He clutched his face, shocked that I'd actually had the guts to do it.

I didn't give him time to recover. I delivered a right hook kick to his legs. I was smaller, but he hadn't taken the self-defence classes I had. His legs buckled, and his self-assured swagger disappeared quicker than water down a drain. He curled into a ball on the stone floor, and I almost felt sorry for him. He'd always gotten by on his good looks and deviousness. But I knew he had a soft side too. I didn't want to hurt him. I just wanted that bloody key.

"Would it be bullying if we all jumped on him?" Ezra drawled.

Faeza sounded eager. "I have seen WWE. We could try."

I could not believe how undignified this was getting. I took a deep breath, ready to pin my brother down and stick my hands down his jeans to fight for Flinar's freedom.

"Oh. My. God," said Fei Yen.

Sahil shrivelled before our eyes, warping, shrinking and cooing, and out popped a jubilant werepigeon with the key gripped in its orange beak. I leapt on him, but he evaded me, flying up. The beginnings of a blue glow emanated from him.

"He's engaging his shield," I cried.

Echo had a hunter's instincts. He sprang up on his powerful hind legs and caught the grunting werepigeon in his mouth. If Sahil's mouth had been free, maybe he would have chomped down on Echo in a bid to escape, but his beady eyes swivelled in his head in terror, his shield fizzled out, and the iron key clattered to the floor.

I tossed it to the foxes, my gut wrenching at seeing the hope flooding Flinar's face.

Then I returned my attention to Echo and Sahil, terrified that Echo's powerful jaw would maim Sahil forever.

Not that he didn't deserve it.

I needn't have worried. The werepigeon shrank in size again, transforming into the bulbous spider that was my brother's other form. He slipped from Echo's grasp and fell to our feet, scuttling away.

Ezra's urgent voice. "I hear the knocking of a staff. We have to leave."

Echo surged into the shadows and dipped his head, sucking my brother off the floor and into his mouth.

I squealed. The knocking grew louder. "Echo, spit my brother out."

His emerald eyes begged me to change my mind, his words hard to decipher, given the creepy crawly in his mouth.

"Spit him out!"

Echo spat. "He tasted disgusting anyway."

Out came my brother in all his spidery glory, wet with Echo's gloopy saliva.

The foxes scooped up a weak Flinar between them just as a flash of red and navy of the Beefeater's uniform came into my peripheral vision.

Blood rushed to my head as Ezra grabbed us all and teleported us to safety.

Glee bubbled up inside me as we escaped. Take that, heathen god. He deserved neither respect nor fear. I would refer to him forever more as Herpes, not Hermes.

The Ravenmaster's bellow of fury chased us into the unknown.

21

Flinar was dehydrated and could not walk unsupported. His thin legs buckled repeatedly on the way up the stairs to Fei Yen and Faeza's flat. In the end, Ezra cradled him against his chest and laid him in the foxes' bedroom, a room of sumptuous red and brown velvets and silks. The elf closed his eyes against the plump pillows with a painful grimace, and we tiptoed out. He seemed to have survived his ordeal intact, but his psychological state scared me. He must have felt so alone.

My stomach clenched, thinking of my brother being in cahoots with the Ravenmaster.

"We will let him sleep and patch him up and feed him broth to build up his strength," said Faeza. "And he can sleep in our bed, even if he smells like a rotting corpse. I suppose there is truth to the rumours about elf hygiene."

Fei Yen scolded her. "Darling, this is one of those moments we were talking about. The poor elf has been held captive amongst raven mess. You mustn't always believe what you read."

Ezra looked at his watch. "I need a quick change of clothes. Then we must go. The Court of the Wolves awaits."

"What kind of justice happens this quickly anyway?" I said.

"Justice in the Otherworld is always swift, Alisha," said Echo. "Or else it doesn't happen at all. Tonight, the whole senate will be in attendance to see what happens to one of their own."

"We will stay and look after the elf," said Fei Yen. "Wildwoods is no place for us."

I nodded and hugged them before placing a kiss on Flinar's grizzled cheek. "Then we will see you on the other side."

———

TRADITIONALLY, the Court of the Wolves took place under the moonlight. It needed neither a building nor an audience. In fact, justice in the Otherworld happened so quickly that it was down and dirty. A few hastily gathered facts, a drink of truth tonic, a witness or two, a majority verdict of peers, an assembled pack of the ruling wolves, a sentence decided and carried out by the Justice Minister. A draining of magic, imprisonment for the ages, the wiping of fortunes or rehabilitation under the tutelage of gentle giants.

Except, rules had to be hastily rewritten when the peculiar in charge of proceedings happened to be in the dock himself. It was unconscionable and unprecedented that the Justice Minister himself could be on trial.

But there we were.

For the purpose of Gunnolf's trial, it fell to Phinnaeous Shine—as the Prime Sorcerer and the most senior member of the senate—to step into the role of presiding judge. It was a task he was born to perform—a man who loved the drama, flourishes and oratory that came with a grand stage.

We met Marina at the Yew Tree, and she handed me a cool bag.

I hugged her. "This is it?"

"As you asked. You know, Robert says there hasn't been a change in civic relations since you destroyed the bot room, but it takes time for human relationships to heal after they have fractured." She turned to Ezra. "Neuhoff, you look hot."

Echo purred plaintively. "Why does no one ever say things like that about me?"

I ignored him. "What will happen to Gunnolf if the senate decides against him?"

"Who knows? Gunnolf called the shots, with Senate approval. There was always a grey area. I wasn't comfortable with the Prime Sorcerer as the presiding judge. His instincts are more sadistic than some." There was a tightness in Ezra's face. Seeing his uncle like this, his role in putting Gunnolf in the dock wasn't easy for him. He cleared his throat. "When we're in there, I'll be presenting the case. I may have to call one or all of you as witnesses. Even in small doses, the truth tonic is potent. Just remember, only answer the questions I ask."

Marina grimaced. "I didn't much like it the first time when the witches spiked our drinks. Green juice is awful enough without taking it up another notch."

"There are many people who are outed as fools when they take truth tonic. I look forward to evaluating the inner monologues of my enemies. It gives me a wonderful sense of superiority," said Echo. "But since we are on the same side and most peculiars are too unintelligent to pay attention to the subtle body language of a leopard, I will swish my tail like a flag as a signal for you to stop talking."

"Much appreciated." I hoisted the cool bag onto my shoulder.

Ezra's voice made my skin tingle. "It's nearly midnight. Ready?"

I squeezed his hand. "You'll be fine."

The corners of his lips lifted in a sad smile.

We followed him through the trees. Goosebumps ran up my bare arms as we arrived in the arena, where quiet reigned. The senate, with Phinnaeous Shine at their centre, sat on a long bench, whispering amongst themselves. Globes of light floated above them, untethered to any electricity. Only Gunnolf sat apart, alone on a stark, straight-backed chair, as if all the vestiges of comfort afforded the senate and the support of his pack had already been stripped from him. His beard had grown unkempt, and his eyes stared straight ahead as if he refused to acknowledge or partake in the grave proceedings. Ezra's pack had gathered on the right of the senate. Five wolves waited, anxious and alert to every movement, and incomplete without their alpha and beta to lead them.

Ezra wore a white, open-collared shirt and black trousers, with his hair slicked back in a more formal style. He strode towards the Prime Sorcerer with more confidence than he felt. They exchanged brief words as Marina, Echo and I filed into wooden pews that seemed to have dropped from the sky into the sawdust.

Orpheus's dark eyes smouldered as we took our seats. *Trust you to escape from the pack farmhouse and not take your punishment like a good girl. Although perhaps congratulations are in order? Robert Jameson told me what a busy girl you've been.*

I grinned at him and didn't fight his voice in my head. It was no longer an intrusion. Somewhere along the way, we had become friends.

Not so much with Gunnolf, however, whose eyes seared with hatred at the sight of me, even though it had been his own decisions that had led him to this point, not mine. Calypso, whose blade runners shimmered dangerously in the moonlight, was deep in conversation with Lavinia. The witch's pink-tipped fingers curled around a decanter of truth tonic.

But it was Margola's reaction that stood out to me. She stood up, her eyes fixed on the cool bag as if her skin called to her like a beacon.

We were no longer enemies. At least, I didn't think so.

Sometimes the way of the world pitted women against each other. I understood now that her hand had been forced, and there were many things that would cause me to act in a way others might judge harshly. Hadn't I struck my own brother?

I met Margola's eyes and softened my gaze, willing her to understand that the selkie skin was hers and always had been and that I wouldn't keep it from her, whatever came next.

She stared at me, and only when Orpheus laid a hand on her arm and whispered in her ear did she sit down, her eyes never moving from the cool bag.

I gave the minister your message. You continue to surprise me, druid. Most other peculiars would have used the skin you hold as a weapon against their enemy. Or at least strung out the pain as revenge for the thoughtlessness with which she has treated you, said Orpheus. *Although I would do well not to run to your rescue so often, given what happened last time.*

I'd started to like our private moments. *Yeah, sorry about that. My instincts are always more important than rules or traditions. I hope I didn't leave you in a bad spot when you vouched for me.*

Orpheus rolled his eyes, but the rest of his body remained still. *Given how things have worked out for the werewolf, I dare say it doesn't matter—this time. But if we are to remain friends, I'd like to think that sometimes you could follow my advice.*

Marina nudged me and broke our connection. "Are you making eyes at Orpheus Might?"

I flushed. "Err, no. Of course not."

"Shh," said a fallen angel in the pew behind us. "It's about to start."

The Prime Sorcerer rose to his feet. His robes swept the floor, and the shape of his silver-tinged afro mirrored the moon above, giving him a celestial aura. By now, I was pretty sure he'd carefully dressed to create that impact. His keen eyes scanned the arena and lingered on my face.

A piece of paper and quill shot up in the air from the presiding bench and documented the proceedings.

"We have convened here tonight at the Court of the Wolves to address a most grave matter." The Prime Sorcerer cast Gunnolf a haughty glance. "Those who serve on the senate do not do so for their own advancement. We are here to serve the Wildwoods community. To shape it in a way that benefits peculiars for generations to come. To betray this duty is almost as grievous a sin as the murder charges. We are here to decide whether Gunnolf Zev is guilty of the charges of murder and if he has betrayed the post of Justice Minister by behaving in a manner unbefitting his post. Stand, werewolf."

Gunnolf stood, keeping his eyes lowered.

"Do you understand why you are here and the charges which have been filed against you?" said the Prime Sorcerer coldly.

The response rang out across the arena, amplified by magic. "I do."

"You understand that the decision we reach tonight will reflect our mutual wisdom and is non-reversible. It will be binding."

This time Gunnolf lifted his head, and his eyes blazed with barely restrained anger. "I do."

"Then let us proceed." Phinnaeous Shine paused to gather his breath, and a pin drop could have been heard. "Who is presenting this case?"

Ezra, who had waited silently amongst the wolfpack, stepped forward. "I am, Prime Sorcerer."

There were no defence or prosecution lawyers at the Court of the Wolves. Those functions had been rendered obsolete by the truth tonic. There was only the truth, the testimonies, the evidence and the verdict.

"It is very unusual to be presenting at your own alpha's trial," said Phinnaeous Shine. "Do you promise before the court that you will drink the truth tonic so that neither pack nor familial bonds will compromise your presentation?"

"Forgive me, Prime Sorcerer, but my uncle is no longer the alpha. I am," said Ezra. "I'll take the tonic."

"Then let us drink the tonic brewed by the naked witch Ravynne," said the Prime Sorcerer.

Marina giggled. "She's sitting behind us, sheathed only in a pashmina. The sort of woman who gives you an eyeful in the sauna when you're least expecting it."

"Shh," I said. "Gunnolf will only get what's coming to him if Ezra doesn't lose his nerve, but he's got to drink that stuff too."

The Prime Sorcerer waved his hand, and the crystal decanter in front of Lavinia uncorked itself and bobbed along to the end of the bench, stopping before each senator to pour a shot's worth of viscous amber liquid into the glasses before them. Each senator drank their portion in turn, grimacing as they gulped down the noxious fluid. When all had finished, the decanter poured out another two glasses.

Ezra picked them up and offered one to Gunnolf, who clenched the glass so hard I thought it would break. The two men exchanged a long glance, and it was Gunnolf who dropped his eyes first. They chinked glasses and poured the liquid down their throats.

"Begin, Mr. Neuhoff," commanded Phinnaeous Shine.

Ezra grimaced, put the glass down and addressed his uncle. "Gunnolf Zev, you have been an upstanding member of this community for many years. That is not in question. Yet you stand before us accused of murder. Let us establish first, are you a killer?"

Gunnolf's lips curved into a hard smile. "We all are here.

You. The pack. The senate members pretending to be holier than thou."

Ezra nodded. "How many have you killed unjustly?"

The older wolf gulped, but it was impossible to lie with the truth tonic coursing through his veins. He spat the words out. "Six wolves that did not belong to our pack. I did what was necessary in the name of harmony."

"Whose harmony, Gunnolf?" said Ezra.

Gunnolf made a jittery movement with his fingers. "The harmony of our pack."

"It is time, Prime Sorcerer, for the vault of evidence," said Ezra.

Phinnaeous Shine lifted his arms and brought them down with force.

I gasped as the freezer from Gunnolf's padlocked storeroom landed in the arena. The senate remained stoic, neither moved nor surprised by the theatrics or the horror that lay within.

"I see the meat has landed," said Echo.

Ezra walked over to the freezer and opened it. "Here lie the remains of three wolves. What did you do to the other bodies?"

"I instructed the pack to build pyres to burn them," said Gunnolf.

"Why did the wolves come to our land?"

The words flew out of his mouth, but his clenched fists showed how he fought to resist. "Because there are forces gathering that no one understands. The wolves wanted to join a stronger pack."

Ezra suppressed a shudder. "How did you kill them?"

"I know the woods like the back of my hand. They didn't expect me to strike. Even if they had, a black wolf seems like a shadow in your peripheral vision until it is upon you. I bit them cleanly."

"You could have just turned them away," said Ezra.

He glowered. "I turned away many more. After taking you in, many made the mistake of thinking the pack would take in stray wolves. But had I accepted them, I could not be certain I had the strength to rule over a larger pack with unknown parts within it. I am old. I thought I would not survive an alpha challenge. Indeed, I was right. I just didn't think it would be my own nephew who usurped me."

A shadow passed over Ezra's face. "An alpha's job is to protect the pack. Not to endanger it. If times are darkening, then a larger pack would have been in our best interests."

"I had already investigated another way to save us, boy, but you refused to see sense. We would have grown our pack with pups who were loyal to us." A bitter laugh erupted from him. "Even our own kin can be a disappointment. Isn't that right, nephew?"

Ezra bit the inside of his cheek. For a private man, playing out this family drama in public must cost him. He swivelled to face the Prime Sorcerer. "I ask permission to call a witness before the court."

"Who is this witness?" Phinnaeous Shine leaned forward.

Ezra took a deep breath. "The druid Alisha Verma."

Phinnaeous Shine sighed. "Why is it that the druid is always at the centre of all our troubles?"

Ezra's expression shuttered. "I cannot say, Prime Sorcerer."

"Then you are not very candid, Mr Neuhoff," said the Prime Sorcerer. "Step forward, druid."

I left the cool bag with Marina and tripped over my feet in my hurry to reach the bench.

The Prime Sorcerer glowered. "You dare come armed to the Court of Wolves?"

Orpheus rolled his eyes. *You need to come back to my classroom, druid, so I can teach you some manners.*

I mumbled an apology, ripped off Transcender and my satchel and handed them to Calypso for safekeeping. The decanter of truth tonic poured a fresh glass under Lavinia's watchful eye.

"Drink it," said the Prime Sorcerer.

I swallowed it in one go and wiped a hand across my mouth.

Nice work, said Orpheus. *Talk slowly so you don't say more than you intend. The tonic is a tricky thing, even for me.*

Ezra rubbed the back of his neck. "Alisha Verma, can you tell the court what else you discovered in the freezer at the farmhouse?"

I nodded. "A slimy selkie skin."

"Who did the skin belong to?"

Margola Silver leaned forward, her expression pained.

"To the very beautiful, very manipulative Information Minister Margola Silver, who has absolutely no qualms about frolicking naked in the Thames. At like six o'clock in the morning when most people are grouching over their cup of coffee."

You have as much restraint as a leaky faucet. Orpheus's face was red with suppressed laughter.

I frowned at him.

"A one-word answer will suffice." Ezra blinked. "And where is that selkie skin now?"

"Wrapped in a Tesco's bag, stashed in a cool bag, on my friend Marina Ambrose's lap, here in the arena. We'll be glad to return it to its owner, actually. A bit odd having that next to a packet of fish fingers in the freezer. Worse than those weirdos who freeze their placentas and then chop them up into little bits to eat. What goes out should stay out. You know?" I clapped my hand over my mouth.

Echo's tail swished furiously.

Ezra sighed. "You may return to your seat."

I clasped my hands together in apology, retrieved my

belongings from Calypso and gave wolf Deirdra a thumbs-up before returning to my seat.

"You are an embarrassment," said Echo. "But you are our embarrassment."

"Gunnolf, did you steal Margola Silver's selkie skin?" said Ezra.

The ex-alpha spoke in a flat voice. "I did."

Ezra neared him, hackles rising. "Can you enlighten the court as to why?"

Half-lidded eyes regarded Ezra. "I needed her to distract you and the druid. I knew my only chance of getting away with the murders was if your mind was otherwise occupied. And I hoped bad publicity for her would drive you into Rashida's arms, and my plan for the pups would come to fruition."

Ezra's posture went rigid. Chords twanged in his neck. For a moment, I thought he would give in to the urge and become his wolf. His desire to hurt Gunnolf warred with his duty to complete the proceedings as per convention. He wasn't the executioner here. He was merely the person who brought the facts to light.

He closed his eyes and exhaled, and when he opened them, his veneer of control was back, although I could only imagine what raged underneath. "Margola Silver, do you corroborate this information?"

Margola held her chin up, though her eyes filled with tears. "I do. Gunnolf stole my skin and threatened to set it alight. We were friends and colleagues for years, but he thought nothing of taking the most precious part of me, even though every shifter at this court knows how callous a crime it is to steal the very thing that allows us to be our true selves."

That was it—the turning point.

The moment when every person in the arena turned against Gunnolf Zev.

It didn't matter that Gunnolf was a murderer. Nobody knew those dead wolves. But they recognised the truth in Margola's words. That Gunnolf had betrayed the very people he should have understood the most. That even as Justice Minister, he had shown no sense of fairness and justice to even those he knew.

The wolves howled. And Ezra, too, threw back his head and howled.

A mournful howl that sent shivers up my spine.

The Prime Sorcerer stood and smoothed out his robes. "The wolves have spoken. They have deemed this the point at which we decide. What say you, senate?"

They each spoke in turn, the ones who had been Gunnolf's allies and others who didn't care a jot about his fate, such as Erelim, the fallen angel, looking bored but oh so hot.

Will you concentrate? said Orpheus.

The verdict was unanimous.

"Guilty," boomed the Prime Sorcerer.

Lavinia smiled.

I couldn't help but think that, without Gunnolf there, her witchy manicure would sink deeper into Ezra.

"As presiding judge," boomed the Prime Sorcerer, "it falls to me to pass the sentence. We live in a world where shadows vie with the light. Where those in power, in the halls of Westminster and the palaces of this country, too often have feet of clay. It falls upon this senate to be exemplary in discharging our powers. Gunnolf Zev has sadly fallen short of this expectation. He has murdered in cold blood and stolen from one of our own to protect his power. I ,therefore, sentence him to fifty years in confinement in the dungeons under the Ritz Hotel and for him to be indefinitely stripped of his powers by a witches' binding potion."

Gunnolf's body sagged. "Phinnaeous, please—"

The Prime Sorcerer raised a hand. "Count yourself lucky not to have been sentenced to death."

Gunnolf jumped up and glanced about in frantic desperation, then looked up at the moon.

"Uh oh," said Marina. "That's a cornered animal if I ever saw one."

My mouth fell open as Gunnolf transformed into his wolf, his back arching and limbs cracking, clothes tearing and teeth growing.

But Ezra was there too, and he didn't hesitate. His shirt ripped and his trousers too as muscles bulged and his wolf emerged, snapping and snarling at his uncle, tossing him to the ground with skill and ease.

We fled the pews, and the senate scattered as the rest of the pack joined Ezra, circling the black wolf who had once been their alpha. A disgraced wolf who soon wouldn't even be a wolf anymore. They showed no mercy in subduing him, tearing flesh and fur from his graceful frame until he was a pitiful, cowering wreck.

Lavinia took her chance. She whipped out her dull but remarkable umbrella. I knew better than to underestimate her. A spike emerged from its end. The wolves parted to allow her access, and she stabbed the black one quickly, then tore a strip from Gunnolf's clothing that lay in scraps in the sawdust. Her eyes gleamed.

"This will do. Sorry, brother-in-law." Then she ejected the blood onto the clothing from the point of her umbrella, chanting all the while. With a swish of her umbrella wand, the blood-soaked ribbon burst into flames. The witch blew out the flames with a satisfied smile and dusted the ashes off her hands.

When I looked to Gunnolf, the black wolf had gone, and instead, his human body lay curled and panting between the paws of the pack. They circled him, howling. He wept at their centre.

I didn't care. I'd save my sympathy for his victims.

As we watched, Ezra accompanied Lavinia to the ranks of the senate.

"Do you know what this means?" said Marina.

"I do," said Echo.

I had no idea what it meant. But I had a feeling I was about to find out.

22

The wolf pack left first, ushering a broken Gunnolf through the trees, presumably to his fate in the basement of the Ritz. Next, the freezer of wolf bodies sank into the sawdust, but the metaphysics of magic meant I couldn't be sure whether the bodies had been buried beneath the arena, whisked to another place to be studied and prodded or returned to the families for funeral ceremonies.

Then, the Prime Sorcerer plucked the notes and quill from the air and shook the page. It multiplied into two, and he offered Margola a copy.

She folded it and slid it into her handbag, then hurried over to me to collect the cool bag. "All I could think of while sitting up there was ripping this from your hands. I am grateful for you retrieving it but furious that my home is missing. Still, I didn't earn your friendship."

"Lady, we're not friends," I wrinkled my nose. "And if I'm honest, I couldn't wait to get rid of this thing."

Margola's eyebrows snapped together.

I realised the truth serum was still doing the talking. I wasn't the only one still impacted, either. Marina tugged me over to Orpheus and Ezra, still in wolf form. My ears burned red.

Orpheus's eyes were hard as flint as he stared down at Ezra. "I played poker with that wolf for years. You're no replacement for him. You don't deserve the druid either."

My eyebrows shot up. *Now who's letting the truth serum do the talking?*

Hardly. Those were intentional insults now that Mr Neuhoff has gone up in rank, just so both of us realise who the superior is.

I gave him a death stare, then crouched down next to Ezra and buried my face in his soft neck. "Shall we go home?"

Every sinew in Ezra's body tensed as he let out a warning growl.

Echo bounded over to my other side with a hiss.

I looked up. The trees shifted, and a nightmarish vision approached. I blinked to check my sight didn't deceive me. Anxiety curled its fingers into my vision and swirled in my stomach.

The Ravenmaster stalked towards us in his red-and-navy tunic. The red of blood and the black of the ravens and night, just as Marina had warned me. His strawberry blond curls and clean-shaven face reminded me of heavenly cherubs, but I knew by now that his heart was charred black. As we gawped, he walked clean through us with the slow gait and supreme confidence of a ceremonial procession. His staff swung in the air, and golden wings fluttered on his hat and boots. When he reached the bench, he occupied the central seat that had only just been vacated by the Prime Sorcerer.

As if he owned the world.

This could never end well.

My breath hitched in my chest as my eyes darted to the Prime Sorcerer. He was the leader here. Surely he'd do something? But all I saw was his retreating back, taking half the senate with him. What on earth was he playing at?

Calypso sighed. "And so the faithful remain, and the lily-livered leave. It was always so."

Rayna grimaced at her departing colleagues, then addressed the Ravenmaster, putting on her best headmistress voice. "Leave this place. You are not welcome here."

The Ravenmaster jerked his head towards her. "Are all druids this tiresome?"

"Keep Marina safe," I said to Echo. Ezra's throat reverberated with a growl as I stood and faced the Ravenmaster. "You lost, Hermes. Everything is going back to normal. It's only a matter of time."

The Ravenmaster smirked at me as if no one else in the arena existed. "No, druid, you might think you have won, but look around and see how divided you are. The leader of the Otherworld has fled, leaving just a handful of you to defend this great emblem of peculiars."

Orpheus stepped forward. His voice betrayed no hint of fear, even though vampires tended to have a healthy fear of gods, what with stakes and crosses and holy water. I worried for a moment that he might take this chance to die at the hands of a god if he still willed it.

In the name of literature, forget about my emotional health and concentrate on the immortal being in our midst, druid. Aloud, he said to Hermes, "You stand on protected ground. Why did the yew tree allow you entry?"

"Such tepid barriers can't keep me out, vampire. The gods have walked this earth for millennia. And look at your compatriots. Not even a truth serum helped you find common ground. That's the thing about communications. I didn't need to take a jackhammer to cause divisions between you. A little spark, and you are perfectly capable of it yourselves."

I frowned. "We destroyed your room of elf bots, Hermes. It's over."

"You think I have one bot room? How small you think. I

have any number of rooms dotted across this measly island. With every keystroke, a seed of harm is sewn. Take your Wildwoods performance, for example. A flurry of messages to those in this arena and you were pressured into an attempt to animate a fox. Imagine that—a wind druid thinking that her animation powers would stretch to foxes. You mortals are very stupid sometimes. Anyway, a little prompt from my hackers and you ended up with egg on your face and didn't even connect it back to me."

Lavinia smirked. "Wonderfully devious when you think about it. Perhaps we could learn a thing or two from him."

"I learned long ago not to fall for sycophancy, witch. Save your compliments for someone else. I am well aware of my brilliance. And soon, my reputation will spread. When I'm finished here, wait and see what havoc I'll wreak in Silicon Valley." His glacial eyes nullified his jaunty tone. "Elves are wonderful little fellows. What they lack in digits, they make up for in nimbleness and perseverance. Very hard working and quite wasted as street cleaners. They remind me of myself in some ways. All I have to do is offer them a few trivial powers, a tiny Faustian contract in exchange for what I want."

So that was why the elves hadn't escaped of their own accord from Margola's basement.

"Extraordinary how many are tempted by the offer of flight," said the Ravenmaster. "It tends to be a top five superpower wish list. It was only a matter of time before you found out. You are so meddlesome that I decided to pip you to the post. I didn't want you coming to my home again. So you and the wolf aren't going to make it out of here tonight."

Ezra lunged forward. I held him back with the slightest touch. He bared his teeth at the god, every sinew in his body alert.

Leave, said Orpheus. *Take the wolf and go. It is too dangerous for you here.*

You leave, I said, although my knees were so wobbly I needed a lie down. *I started this. I'm going to finish it.*

We couldn't run this time. How could we run from Wildwoods when it was the emblem of our country's Otherworld? Abandoning it would mean the god had won. And I wouldn't let him win, not without putting up a fight.

I addressed Hermes, "Wildwoods will adapt to destroy you. Or we will."

I looked at the motley crew left in the arena. Seven remained, who lined up with me against our foe, our backs to the cabins in the trees that made up Wildwoods: Ezra, Marina, Echo, Orpheus, Rayna, Calypso and inexplicably, Lavinia, wielding her umbrella like a cricket bat. Calypso removed her suit jacket like she meant business. Would eight against a god be enough? I closed my eyes and said a silent prayer for Gaia to hear us. Although, hadn't she said she was a cheerleader only?

"You won't turf me out of this place so easily. You came to my home uninvited. The Tower of London has been my sanctuary for decades. It has kept me safe, even while others were mutilated there. It is where I lay my head to rest at night. Where I weathered crises of faith. Where I have met dignitaries and tended to souls entrusted to me. And yet, you violated my home by breaking into it. Even then, I respected the rules of hospitality. I gave you a chance to run. But then you destroyed the temporary home of my ravens. You returned to my sanctuary when I was not there." He toyed with his staff. "So I came to yours."

"I dislike the druid as much as anyone. But the fact remains, you are not welcome here, Hermes." Lavinia pointed her umbrella at him with her right hand and raised her left arm in an *en-garde* position. "And you will not harm a hair on the wolf's body."

"Settle down, witch. I remember Salem," retorted the god.

Orpheus was as still as a cobra about to strike. I had yet to see him in action as a warrior. I had no idea if he was a biter, a strongman or a martial artist. Did he fight open-handed or with closed fists? Did he hold a weapon or ride a stallion? Was he a damsel who would need rescuing or a scrappy fighter who could hold his own?

For the love of life, druid, stop distracting me. "This is your last chance," said Orpheus. "You heard the druid. Leave."

The Ravenmaster stood up. "I am a god. You would do well to remember that. Not all of you have to die." He raised his hat, and a spider scuttled down his face and onto the bench. "In fact, our brother would prefer you lived, but mortal lives don't always play out according to plan."

With a pop, Sahil transformed from the bulbous spider into his werepigeon form.

A bitter taste filled my mouth. Just when I thought this couldn't get any worse.

Marina groaned. "I'm starting to think I should have stayed in to play doctors and nurses with Robert."

"The werepigeon does it again. He is incapable of making an entrance to cheers," said Echo.

Hermes chuckled. "The beef-obsessed leopard is amusing. He may remain at my side once this is all over."

I turned my eyes away from my brother, whose beady yellow eyes were fixated on me, and focused on the god. "All this to alleviate your boredom. All this because you wish to return to the old ways of pigeon carriers. All this because you can't bear not to be the one with your hand on the tiller. The one in control."

"A bored mind is an idle mind. How can a god not see the possibilities of this world?" said Calypso.

"So what if the world is a little chaotic and disjointed?" I said. "When did you lose faith in beauty?"

"The day we fell from the heavens," said the Ravenmaster. "How can there be beauty when He is dead? How can our Father expect us to continue acting in God's image when he is not here to provide an example? The world is not what it was. Humans no longer pray to us in gratitude. They pray only in fear and need."

"Yes, I know. And those diminished prayers are why the strength of the gods has diminished over the centuries. Gaia told me."

His blue eyes narrowed. "But she didn't tell you everything, druid, did she? Gaia is a master at chess. She only reveals one piece at a time. Haven't you wondered why, after years of living beneath the radar, the gods are coming out to play?"

Lavinia cleared her throat. "I am the Defence Minister. You should be having this conversation with me, Ravenmaster."

"I have never seen a Defence Minister dressed head to toe in pink." The Ravenmaster gave a bark of laughter. "I will continue to speak to the person in the room with power." He turned to me.

If Lavinia didn't hate you before, she does now, said Orpheus.

The winds around us rose. I didn't know if it was nature or if my emotions were bringing about the change.

"She told me as much as I need to know." I believed it to be true. Gaia was infuriating, but she had never let me down when I needed her. She had always told me enough to survive. "I know the gods are toying with humankind just for fun. That you have lost your faith to such an extent that you have become a nihilist when once you were an inventor. A creator."

Marina spoke up in a small voice. "And I know that you are raging against your slide into irrelevance. I know that the reason you wear that uniform is that you like pomp and pageantry. But the fact is that change happens to everyone, even gods. And you take yourself too seriously. Lighten up, dude. In the olden days, I heard you fashioned an instrument from a tortoise shell. But have you ever been in a mosh pit? Go to a gig and tell me there's no joy left in the world."

Echo nodded. "I can share the Beatles back catalogue with you."

"You dare speak to me like I am your equal?" He punctuated his words with the slamming of his staff on the bench. "I no longer hear my Father's voice in my head nor sense his divine presence. It has been centuries. And you think this can be solved with a little revelry in a mosh pit?"

I nodded. "Yes, Herpes. I think it can."

Oops, that was the truth serum speaking.

Orpheus guffawed. *Did you just liken the god to a sexually transmitted disease? I thank you, Alisha, for giving me cause for laughter before we meet our ends.*

The Ravenmaster glared at me, and his cherubic face turned red. As if the moon above wasn't a shimmering yellow orb but a blood moon that tinged his skin. The wings on his round-brimmed Beefeater's hat and his boots quivered to life and soon became a golden blur mortal eyes could not discern. His slim blue-and-red-booted body shot into the air, and I knew the talk was over. My werepigeon brother fluttered into the air next to him and pooed a big white splotch on the judge's bench as if he were making a promise to defecate on us all.

Fear seared through me, and I drew my sword. My back twinged, a sure sign I was in severe need of yoga. We had to stop Herpes. "Leave my brother out of this."

"Why?" said the Ravenmaster. "I wasn't lying when I said I escorted your mother to the afterlife. She asked Gaia to look after you. And she asked me to look after your brother."

Whispers rushed into my ears as the hilt of my sword grew hot in my hand. I held on and raised it aloft, convinced we were on the side of right, even if we stood no chance. I cast a look at those standing beside me, left and right. "Without prayer, his power is not an infinite well. We can weaken him. Avoid his staff. He has the power to send people to sleep."

Battle cries sounded around me. Ezra's growl, Echo's roar, Lavinia's cackle of glee, a scraping of blades as badass Calypso whipped out two knives from leg holders. Orpheus flung off his long, dark coat and limbered up like a boxer. Rayna set aside her potions belt, but not before retrieving the knife from it.

Only Marina looked like she was about to wet her pants.

"Get to that treeline and stay away from the action," I said.

She hugged me and headed for the treeline. Sahil's beady eyes watched her go, but I knew him well enough to know he'd not harm her. Whether he'd harm me was another matter entirely.

Then there were seven of us left. Seven left to take on a winged god and a werepigeon.

"There is no time to call the coven. He is a formidable enemy, despite those boyish curls. We will need to make every blow count," said Lavinia.

The Ravenmaster didn't wait another second hovering in the air. He flew at us, cherubic face mottled with fury. His staff transformed. The entwined snakes around the staff woke and turned a searing red, with tongues that darted in and out, their eyes hypnotic. He set me in his sights, weaving with ease to avoid pellets shooting from Lavinia's umbrella.

"It is Alisha he wants." Echo roared and leapt into the air to disturb the god's trajectory as he tore towards me.

The god didn't slow. A casual flick of his staff sent Echo sprawling.

The leopard cried out, his hind leg burned by the staff, and Sahil fell upon him, werepigeon teeth sinking into Echo's exquisite fur. Ezra was my brother's next victim, and feathers flew, Ezra's experience in battle giving him an advantage over Sahil's untrained attempts to cause havoc. A spell from Lavinia stuck Sahil headfirst in the sawdust, with his pigeon toes wiggling in vain above ground.

The god kept coming for me.

I raised my sword, slashing.

Ezra arced into the air with radar-like precision, matched by Calypso on the other side, whose strong thighs and blade runners gave her soaring height. They grabbed the god's heels and brought him down hard to the ground, winding him. In came Orpheus and Rayna in a dance of knives and fangs. Orpheus's speed and boxing gave him the grace of Muhammad Ali, except with the additional advantage of his fangs. Rayna's vines grew from the arena to bind the god, roping around his limbs. He broke free easily as if the vines were paper chains.

It wasn't enough. An immortal couldn't be killed.

He flung them off as if they were flies and reared up into the air again, clearly locating me despite the chaos, his gaze confirming he wanted Ezra too.

I sent a whirlwind to destabilise him, but he evaded the current and the trees that grasped him at Rayna's behest. He rushed at the headmistress first, touching her with his staff, and she slumped to the ground in a deep sleep.

He'd keep coming for us. How long could I expect this motley crew of peculiars to protect us? I knew the ones who had stayed were partly driven by the audacity of the Ravenmaster in desecrating Wildwoods, but they couldn't be expected to lay down their lives to protect us.

You underestimate how much the witch loves her nephew. And how you have moved me to act in ways I haven't for centuries, said Orpheus.

Echo and Ezra bounded over to my side as the Ravenmaster came flying towards us, slowed by Calypso, whose whizz of knives threatened to separate the wings from his hat and boots. Orpheus, too, had the grim look of a man careless about his own safety. A man willing to sacrifice himself in pursuit of his enemy. Fists and fangs and jumps took him as high as the god, and he didn't flinch from the burning staff, didn't hesitate to touch a being that had once been so holy.

I remembered Gaia's words. *I have a right mind to cut Hermes apart and bury the pieces of him in pits so far apart that it takes him millennia to reform.*

I had to bring this to an end.

I dragged in a breath and reached for my catalogue of creatures. "Echo, take Marina to the sphinxes. They are touchy fellows, but the two of you may be able to convince them to help. They are guardians of Wildwoods, after all, and this place is in danger. We need more people. He is too strong."

No sooner had I spoken than he raced away, legs pounding hard against the earth.

Lavinia came towards Ezra and me in a tumble of umbrella and Lycra.

"I have a plan," I said, "but I will be vulnerable for a few minutes, so you'll all need to keep him busy."

What do you think we're doing, druid? said Orpheus.

Lavinia jutted out her hip like she was on a catwalk and not in a battle. "Who died and put you in charge?"

Ezra nudged his auntie, warning her with bared teeth and a low grumble that rolled through his throat.

She relented. "Very well. Being an alpha suits you, nephew."

Orpheus and Calypso fought on. The Custodian's eyes narrowed in conversation, dreadlocks flying as she danced with her knives. But she tired, and Orpheus noticed. He tried to use his speed to wear down the god, running circles around him and throwing jabs and hooks, but Hermes was just as fast. The staff blocked each punch, and though the vampire didn't fall asleep, his skin sizzled.

Ezra and his aunt ran into the fray together as I sank to my knees in the sawdust, ignoring Sahil's wriggling legs nearby.

The imbecile.

I knew the catalogue back to front by now. I had studied it during waking hours and in my dreams. When one creature was animated and the page disintegrated, the catalogue rearranged itself in my consciousness as if it were a secret language that would always be mine. As if fate had determined, my hands would hold it.

The ravens. Dad's ravens.

I found them in an instant and ran my hand over the page, getting a sense of their dimensions, width and depth.

The page spoke to me. These weren't happy creatures. They were always craving, always unsatisfied, a black hole of nothing where their soul was, waiting to be filled by the purpose I assigned them.

My command would have to be foolproof, my concentration unwavering.

Calypso, Orpheus, Ezra and Lavinia advanced on the Ravenmaster time and again, in a relay, as a team, the witch riding her umbrella, the others from the ground. They grew weary, bloody and bruised, welts appearing on their skin as the god barely took a hit. When Calypso collapsed into a dead slumber, the arena itself finally came to life to protect its own. It threw sand in the god's eyes, sending arrows of glass at his head and body, trapping him in a cube he shattered with one touch of his poker-hot staff.

In rushed the two sphinxes, Mammatas and Rhokon, with their lion bodies and human heads, bellowing with the joy of movement in their stone bodies, permitted only when Wildwoods came under threat.

Marina rode Rhokon with the gusto of a cowgirl. She slid off and ran back to her position of safety, leaving Echo to follow the sphinxes into the fray.

Orpheus, I said. *Tell the sphinxes to hold Hermes down. They should take his arms. He can't harm their stone bodies to put them to sleep, given their very purpose is to be vigilant. Echo and Ezra should take his feet, the safer end. Stretch him taut as if he were on a rack in the Tower of London torture chamber. The rest of you should strip him of his boots, hat and staff.*

I hope you know what you are doing, said Orpheus.

I blocked out the sounds of the battle and found the breath of the universe. The winds swirled around me as my fingers found the threads of the ravens. Sweat broke out on my upper lip, and my hands grew clammy. The ravens' cells and veins and feathers crept towards the surface, and they broke through, pecking at my hands, ten black, mischievous, clever birds. I told them their purpose, and they made gurgling croaks that would always haunt me.

They were my creations—and Dad's—but I feared them.

I turned, lightheaded, and staggered to the god, who lay writhing and stretched between the sphinxes, their stone mouths clamped around his limp wrists. Stripped of his wares, without his staff, with orange-peel feet and a bald spot, he looked pathetic.

But even pathetic gods inspire fear in mere mortals.

Fear was writ large on the faces of my allies. Only the impenetrable sphinxes knew no fear. They needed me to lead them.

I stood astride the god.

No amount of face cream was going to make up for the stress lines I gained at that moment.

"You shrew." The Ravenmaster's glacial eyes bulged, and he lobbed great globules of spit at me.

"You know what to do," I said to the ravens.

The Ravenmaster looked confused. He clicked his tongue, trying to find a common language and rapport with the birds he had trained for decades.

But these weren't any ravens. They weren't his ravens.

They were mine.

And I had told them to dismember him. I had told them to bury the pieces of his body in every corner of the British Isles.

And they listened to their purpose.

I stood above Hermes as he was pulled taut by my friends. I stood and directed the black ravens like a conductor at a symphony. I clenched my jaw as I worked, flinging out my arms this way and that to indicate which pieces the birds should assail first.

The sphinxes roared, Ezra howled, and Echo clutched the foot for which he was responsible until it became dislodged from the whole. The raven's sharp beaks broke Hermes apart with such voracious hunger that even Lavinia looked away. Orpheus stood vigilant over the fallen staff, unblinking in the face of the horrors.

Blood and flesh fell like nightmarish confetti over me as the ravens did my bidding.

I left the god's heart and head for the very last moments.

His head, separated from the rest of him, rolled on the ground. It didn't lose its venom. "Those who attack immortals never survive long, druid. You may win tonight, but I have an infinite life to exact my revenge on you."

There was no way I was picking up his head, so I asked two ravens to pick it up by the curly blond hair and dangle it in front of me. I looked the Ravenmaster in the eye, and the teacher in me came out. "One day," I said, "you will re-form and rise again, and when you do, maybe you'll have learned to be a better person. A lack of faith is one thing, but you don't have to be an utter arsehole."

His hovering head opened its mouth. "I am a—"

I lifted my hands, and the ravens flew at his head and heart. Hermes looked surprised, like no one had ever interrupted one of his rants before. The ravens carried off chunks of meat, their battle cry punctuating the tearing of flesh. I closed my eyes to the slaughter.

One day, he would live again. Just not today.

When the sounds stopped, and the cries and cursing of the god fell to nothing, the beating of wings filled the air around me. I kept my eyes squeezed shut, lifted my hands and sent a burst of wind 360 degrees to speed the ravens on to their destinations with the flesh bundles. Then I sank to the ground and rolled onto my side as a black cloud crept into my vision. I tried to slow my heartbeat, but I couldn't. My whole body quivered, and even though I told myself to get up, my brain wouldn't respond.

"Get Alisha to the infirmary," said Orpheus. "Who knows what damage she has done to herself by animating nearly a dozen of those hideous things at once. Did anyone know she could do that?"

Marina's voice, panting and full of worry, "Let me help."

"What are you waiting for?" Orpheus snapped. "Sphinxes, back to your position. A stretcher for Rayna and Calypso. And where the hell did the Prime Sorcerer go?"

Someone scooped me up into their arms—someone naked, who smelt familiar, like mountain air and roll-up cigarettes. I laid my head against his chest as voices muttered around me, my body ragdoll limp.

"There's something rotten at the heart of this place. She won't survive another encounter like this," said that someone.

"Our new Minister for Justice is right. The ground has shifted. We can dilly dally no longer. We have to find the eternal girl," said Lavinia.

"Yes. Yes, we do," said Orpheus. "I am afraid a dark age is upon us. Without her and the disintegrating tome in the prophecy, we don't stand a chance if Death does open the door between the worlds."

My last thought was of my brother, upside down still in the sawdust. Then I drifted into unconsciousness.

23

———

Alma woke at the crack of dawn to cook us a feast in my mother's kitchen. She was of Spanish origin. Given Mum had been French, I had the sneaking suspicion that Dad had a penchant for European babes. Despite her obvious disapproval of our—Echo notwithstanding—meat-free household, Alma had cooked up a mouth-watering array of dishes befitting her heritage. It was an obvious but much-appreciated attempt to woo us for our first meal together since the romantic development between her and Dad. There was vegetarian paella, fig tapas, Catalan grilled vegetables, croquetas, white herb and bean salad and churros with salted chocolate sauce.

Mum had been a feeder too. The thought drifted through my mind, and for the first time, the memory of what she had been brought comfort rather than pain.

Animating the ravens had drained me, and I still hadn't recovered my entire strength. But at least there were no wounds for Dad to worry about. It did me good to see him happy at last, and I wasn't going to spoil that.

In their excitement, Dad and Alma had laid the table in

the dining room with a frilly tablecloth and an extraordinary number of doilies handmade by Alma herself, an award-winning hobbyist. I couldn't think of why anyone would award prizes for doilies, but Dad was quite adamant about that point.

Alma fussed over the table while Dad and I nattered over a cup of tea in the living room.

He checked the coast was clear, then lifted a sofa cushion to slide out a copy of *The Otherworld News*. "Alma's very tidy. An absolute dab hand with the duster, but she'd never think to look under here. Have you seen it yet?"

Druid Heir Does It Again in Wildwoods Showdown

"Damn it. I quite liked the attention dropping away from me when everyone thought I was a failure. I wish Margola would move on to a new subject of interest," I said. "I don't know where she gets her information. Half of it is wrong, and the other half is embellished, so it bears no relation to the truth. Not to mention all the omissions."

Dad grinned. "But your legend lives on, eh, Alisha? Quite a recovery after what happened at your animation performance. You make me so proud."

Alma popped her head around the door. "Lunch is ready."

Dad froze like a rabbit in the headlights.

"What's wrong, Joshi? Keep that paper for me, will you?" said Alma. "I quite fancy a crossword later."

"Yes, love," said Dad.

Alma scurried away.

Dad pushed the paper at me. "Bin it. Burn it. Feed it to the leopard."

I laughed. "He's too busy traumatising the koi in your pond. Come on. Everyone's waiting."

We went arm in arm into the dining room.

Dad and Alma sat opposite each other at the heads of the table. They smiled at us.

"I'm so glad you could join us, Gaia," said Alma. "It's a wonder we haven't met before. Joshi has been telling me all about what an upstanding member of the community you are."

Gaia beamed. She wore a turquoise-and-green Punjabi suit with a sequinned border. Her black hair cascaded down her back. It had been freshly died with henna, giving it an orange tinge. "That's so kind of Joshi to say."

Alma offered the white bean and herb salad around the table. "How long have you been living in South London?"

"About two hundred years, give or take," said Gaia.

Alma gave Dad a sympathetic frown, assuming that Gaia had Alzheimer's.

He shrugged and turned to Sahil. "You're quiet today, son. Something on your mind?"

A nerve twitched in Sahil's jaw, and he hitched his neck back and forth like the pigeon he was. I suspected Sahil was traumatised enough by the sawdust he kept coughing up after all that time with his head buried in the arena. It served him right.

I scowled at him. It was killing me not to vault over the table and slap him silly. I had decided not to be open with Dad about the fact his son was a villainous prick. A further fracturing of our family unit would steal any last remnant of joy he had, and I couldn't do that to him. Playing the happy family sucked, but I had to trust that karma wouldn't let Sahil get off scot-free. And who knew, maybe I'd get to give it a little nudge.

Sahil spluttered into a tissue and balled it up for the umpteenth time.

Alma frowned. "You really should see a doctor about that cough."

"He's quite all right, dear. Another two hacks, and he'll have cleared it all. Then there'll be space for your churros." Gaia smiled at Dad. "Has he always been a problem child?"

Sahil glared at her, but when he opened his mouth, an unintelligible series of coos burst forth that scared the bejeezus out of Alma.

Gaia winked at me and gave me a self-satisfied smile.

Dad frowned. "All children have their ups and downs."

"Pigeons have a more wayward trajectory than most. They seem to defecate from spite rather than need," said Gaia.

Alma looked at her like she was a lunatic. "Please, everyone, eat. I want us to be one big happy family."

I sighed and shovelled food onto my plate.

After lunch, Gaia and I walked in my parents' garden under tangerine ribbons of sun threading the sky.

The goddess picked her way across the lawn in her sandals, like a ballerina crossing a minefield. "I like to give the worms a fighting chance. Poor things always end up squashed before they even get to live. Their ability to regenerate was one of my better ideas." Her lips curved in amusement as she watched Echo play in the koi pond. "Only a few minutes more, Chanakya, or those poor fish will leave this earthly realm."

Echo landed on the lawn in a spray of water before launching himself back in. "Of course, goddess. I would not dare to defy you."

Gaia slipped her arm through mine. "Your heart is heavy. Speak your mind."

I grimaced. "I prayed to you on the night the Ravenmaster attacked Wildwoods, but you didn't come to our aid."

"I am sorry, druid." She pouted. "I didn't abandon you, although it might feel that way. I was there in spirit. I put that idea in your head about dismembering him."

My eyebrows shot up. "That was you?"

"Of course it was." She sighed. "It really is very unfortunate. His wasn't a dignified end. Not an end at all, really. He'll probably be furious by the time he is resurrected, but with any luck, you'll be dead by then, so you won't have to deal with it."

I stared at her before sinking onto a bench. Sometimes I couldn't wrap my head around how much my life had changed.

"Do you forgive me?" said the goddess.

"Of course I do." I smiled at her turn of phrase. As if a goddess would need to ask me for forgiveness. "I think you made quite an impression on Alma."

Gaia sat. "It is not my job to consider what impression I make on others. I can only be myself. I like Alma. Her croquetas were some of the finest I have tasted, and she has one of the qualities I admire most in mortals."

"What is that?"

"The ability to make a home. Not many can do it well, but to have the ability to create a space that others can feel at ease in takes a special kind of person," said Gaia. "Many people underestimate how important that feeling of belonging is. The dragon has a home, but he misses you. You have a home, but you have found many more these past weeks. Hermes had a home, but now he is in the dirt. The disgraced alpha was ripped from the home he loved and now resides in a dungeon. The pigeon has many homes, and still, he defecates in the wrong place." She looked into the distance, entranced. Her pupils expanded, and in them, I saw mountains rise, and cities burn. "Then there is duty and desire. You set aside your desires to do your duty. Hermes set aside his duty to fulfil his desires. The new alpha is torn between his desires and his duty. The pigeon knows only desire. One day, he may choose duty. Or better yet, his duties will align with his desires."

She sounded like a garbled tape.

I frowned. "Are you okay?"

"Oh yes, dear. I'm just a little tired. Nothing that a hot water bottle and my desire for a cup of chai won't fix. I am afraid the offering here falls beneath my expectations, so I give you my thanks, druid, and my praise, and now I must go." She pressed a kiss to my forehead.

It healed the aching parts of me, body and spirit.

I bit my lip. "Gaia, when I held Transcender, I thought I heard Mum's voice."

"Of course, you did, Alisha. Why did you think your sword is called Transcender? I did say that you'd be able to channel your ancestors if you mastered it."

"It was just a whisper. I couldn't catch it all."

The Earth turned in her eyes. "Well, it's not a walkie-talkie. It's just a spark of essence."

I looked away in case I couldn't process the truths there. "I think she wanted me to go easy on Sahil."

"Well, mothers know best. How lovely of her to reach out to you with something positive rather than the usual haunting malarkey." Melancholy filled her voice. "You must gather your strength, for this is not yet over."

I gulped. "Will you always be in the shadows rather than at my side?"

She blew out her soft velvet cheeks with their sprinkling of rouge. "This game the gods are playing is one I refused. For that, I pay a heavy price. But I have plotted a path for us, and it is still possible we might win, Alisha, if you just hold on."

"Do you know what might happen next?"

"Might is such a powerful word, don't you think? Such potential. I think it's just perfect leaving the future open. I'm not being deliberately tiresome. I am bound by an ancient oath to neither reveal nor thwart my Father's children." She grinned. "At least, not directly. You do understand, don't you?"

I nodded, but how could a mere mortal possibly

understand the choices of a goddess? Instead, I remembered the MC Hammer rucksack I'd stashed for her in the wardrobe of my childhood bedroom. "I have something for you. Wait here."

I brought it downstairs, frightened Alma would catch me on the stairs with it glowing in my arms. As an afterthought, I popped Dad's copy of *The Otherworld News* into it, too, to save Dad a spate of tricky questions from Alma. She was an Otherworld virgin, after all.

Then I returned to Gaia. "These are yours for safekeeping. Calypso thought them too dangerous to keep in the Celestial Library."

Shrewd eyes fell upon the rucksack, and Gaia took it from me. "The Custodian is wise not to keep items that would imperil her." She stood. "Before you go home, talk to the pigeon. Even anger can be wrapped in love."

I chewed my lip. "I can't forgive him."

"Then you hurt only yourself, Alisha." She gave a little hiccup of recognition. "Speak of the devil. Thank your father and Alma for me, will you?" She put on the MC Hammer rucksack as if she were a school child and not a centuries-old goddess, walked a few steps and went to say her goodbyes to Echo, who by now was sunning himself on the grass.

Sahil skulked over, his mouth in a frown. "You can tell me to bugger off if you like."

"Why would I do that? This is your home as much as mine." I scowled at him. "I don't have to like you, though."

"Touché," he said. "Have you ever liked me?"

"Of course," I said. "But you are a prize wanker far too often. I mean, what were you thinking? Why did you let me think you had those powers from Lavinia?"

He shrugged. "I've always played a good hand at poker."

I punched his arm. "Hermes could have killed me. Would you have let that happen?"

His brown eyes met mine. "You're speaking like it's an option to say no when a god wants something."

My frustration was nuclear. "It is," I said through gritted teeth. "Wouldn't you have tried? For me? It's like you don't care one iota about who you hurt. Even if it's your own sister."

He puffed out his chest, and it showed the pigeon in him. "I know my limits, Alisha. I'm not the one who stands up to playground bullies. I *am* the bully. It's who I am. It's how I've been so successful at work. You can't expect me to change my colours."

"How did you even meet him?"

Sahil frowned. "The Ravenmaster? He made Mum a promise to look out for me. Then he found me. Turns out Mum leaving her car to me in her will wasn't so bad after all. It's been touched by the gods. It's like a beacon from them."

My head jerked up in surprise. "Bloody hell, Sahil. Where is it now?"

"Keep your knickers on," he said. "It's hardly roadworthy. It's in my garage."

I eyeballed him. "You should destroy it."

His face tightened. "What is it with you always trying to tell me what to do? You should stay out of my business, little sis."

I let out a huff of breath. "Grow up, Sahil, or I'll…"

He smirked. "What? You'll run to Dad? We're in our forties, Alisha."

I rolled my eyes. "No, I was going to say you don't get kid gloves from me just because you're my big brother."

"Do your worst, little sis." He crossed his arms, making his biceps bulge. "I'm not scared of you."

I wanted to scream. I didn't want him to be scared of me. I wanted us to be on the same page. To be close.

A hand on each of our shoulders made us jump.

"It's so good to see you two spending time together." Dad shimmied around to the front of the bench, squeezed into the middle of us and put his arms around us. "That's right, make space for your old man. How long has it been since we enjoyed a day like this?"

24

———————

I lay back against the fluffy silk pillows with a contented sigh. On the bedside table, a cup of English breakfast tea —just the right colour—and a good book waited for my attention. Not that I had spent the morning reading.

I'd been otherwise occupied.

The receiver pressed to my ear as I stretched my toes. "I can't believe that while I was resting up, you took my cat to a karaoke booth."

Marina's warm laugh reverberated down the line. "Robert literally couldn't believe his ears. He was a very reluctant ally. I had to make him mouth the words every time someone popped their head into the room to cover up the fact Echo was my duet partner. And the foxes were wild. They have lungs on them. You should have heard their rendition of 'I Wanna Dance with Somebody.' Whitney Houston, eat your heart out."

It was so good to be able to use our mobile phones again without fear of manipulation. "So, is Robert happy with how everything is panning out? Ezra and I thought Flinar could be in charge of the rehabilitation of the errant elves."

Ezra had refused to let me get involved, but in the past

three days, he, Robert and Lavinia had teleported to locations across the United Kingdom to dismantle all of the Ravenmaster's bot rooms. Without the Ravenmaster, the assorted powers he had given his elf bots no longer worked, stripping the errant elves of their fear of and motivation to help him.

"That's a brilliant idea," said Marina. "Robert's ecstatic. The bot rooms fell like a house of cards. He said he's not been part of such a satisfying operation since the time he headed up a team in the drugs squad."

The current front bench in Her Majesty's Government had lasted a week. The Prime Minister was very pleased his personal life was running smoothly again after he bribed his wife to forget the affair with the promise of posh new wallpaper at Number 10. The Royal family turned up en masse at the Chelsea Flower Show without a cross word between them. There was a reported drop in divorce petitions and domestic incidents. Not to mention an incremental decrease over the last few days in rough sleepers. And my programmed ravens were doing a stellar job at the Tower of London. The new Ravenmaster was very impressed. He even had more spares than usual.

Still, a frisson of apprehension tempered the lightness in my chest. "Wonderful. It was all worth it then."

Marina immediately caught my mood. "Alisha, I don't want to go through that again. I thought you were a goner when you went limp like that. Whatever wins we have from being part of the Otherworld, it's not worth losing you over. I would rather be ordinary with you than extraordinary without you."

She made me feel safe even through a phone line. My throat scratched with tears, and I swallowed the lump there. "Marina, you are always extraordinary. Even when you're hungover with your rainbow head over a toilet bowl."

"Oh, you say the nicest things. But I've decided. I always

feel like you're the one doing the protecting when I want to protect you." A note of uncertainty flooded her voice, the crack before she asked me something big. "Do you remember when Calypso told us about the necklace your Mum left with her for safekeeping and that Rose of Jericho book she loaned from the Celestial Library?"

I braced myself. "Uh-huh."

"I've been looking into it, and it turns out that flower has healing properties. I think that's what your Mum was doing in the lab. That's why she didn't share her work with Melissa, even though they shared everything. Because that project was about you and keeping you safe. And I want to finish what she started if you'll let me."

"What did I do to deserve you?"

"I'm glad it's a yes. I had a whole speech planned."

I smiled. The buzz of the electric toothbrush in the other room stopped. I said to Marina, "See you tomorrow?"

"Why, are you busy?" she teased.

"Bye. Love you." I put the phone down.

Ezra came in from the en suite, his teeth tingly fresh. We'd started to fill his parents' cottage with our things and opening up all the rooms that had been unlived in for so long.

He sprang onto the bed, bent his head to nuzzle my neck, and peered at the bedroom floor, where my new underwear lay in a heap. "Where were we again?"

I giggled. "Round one was a stellar performance."

The copper specks in his eyes danced. "I aim to please."

I kissed him, breathing in his scent, revelling in the feel of his stubble against my skin, his strong hand threaded through the hair at my nape.

"Ezra?" I murmured against his lips.

He raised his head. "Uh oh. That tone tells me you're thinking. My job is to chase all the thoughts out of your head."

I pressed a lingering kiss to his cheek and then pulled away. "I thought you'd be all serious now you're a senator."

With Gunnolf gone, Ezra had become not only alpha but Minister for Justice. It had been stupid of me not to realise it the night at the Court of Wolves when his ascendancy onto the senate had been clear as day to Marina and Echo.

I knew he could do it, but I had always thought of him as a warrior rather than a paper pusher—a renegade rather than a committee member. I couldn't help it, but a part of me didn't want him to have conflicting interests in his life. I always wanted to be the one at the centre of his universe.

"Do the rest of the senate know Gaia told me I'm the eternal girl?" I asked.

Ezra sighed and lay back against the pillow.

My skin immediately craved his touch, so I reached for his hand.

He traced a slow pattern on my palm and shook his head. "I didn't tell them. I made a promise to you. But, Alisha, if I doubted it before, I don't doubt it now. And my aunt suspects. The vampire too."

"Orpheus isn't the problem." I bit my lip. "And maybe Lavinia isn't either. I respect her for fighting alongside us."

Ezra nodded. "I do too. But we have to be wary of her. She is unpredictable. I think, however, that between me, her and the vampire, we have enough votes to force the rewriting of the Pragmatist's Law."

"Never meddle in the affairs of the gods."

He grimaced. "Quite. Because if the gods meddle with us, how can we stay neutral? There are more links between the gods and the senate than we realised. If nothing else, the past few weeks have proved that."

"They proved that I love you too."

A sad smile tugged at the corners of his mouth. "Things have changed now that I'm a senator. I'll need to keep things from you even when I don't want to. I can't always be on your side. I need to show impartiality."

I frowned. How could you be impartial about love? How could we be so close one moment and on different paths the next?

Ezra pulled me into a bear hug with a tenderness that made me ache. "I don't want to lose what we have. I'll fight to keep it."

I had the distinct impression that the ground was falling beneath me. I clung to him, and his lips chased away all my worries, like the sun chases the clouds.

ACKNOWLEDGMENTS

To my readers, thank you for taking a chance on this story. Your enthusiasm spurs me on. I'm so grateful for every message and review, and yes, I always want to know if you are #TeamEzra or #TeamOrpheus.

A big thank you to my book team, particularly my editors Jeni and Toni, whose skill and instincts I have come to rely on. To my cover artist Maria, your work brings me so much joy. To Debbie and Sherry, my beta readers, what would I do without your encouragement and steers? A thousand thanks and an extra hot bedroom scene are yours.

To Nafu Aunty, who loves words and crafts her own. Thank you for always understanding the joy of creativity and encouraging mine. I wish I could bring to life a protective, teleporting werewolf-wizard just for you.

To our three beautiful children, each one of you is a gift. I hope you know that even if sometimes I stick my headphones in and tell you I'm busy. I promise once this book has been submitted, we'll bake, kitchen dance, and take the dog for long walks in the woods where you can find the Rabbit Kingdom again.

To my husband Jan, my first reader. Sometimes life is such a whirlwind that I forget to tell you, so here it is in black and white: I am the luckiest woman alive to have you at my side. Thank you for being you. For being constant, funny and kind and for being a magnet for my cold feet at night.

FREE SHORT STORY

If you enjoyed this book, please leave a review online to help other readers find this story.

The Druid Heir novels are written in Alisha's perspective, a 40-year-old teacher living in London. The short stories explore the world from an alternate character's viewpoint.

You can get the Druid Heir short stories for free by signing up for my fantasy newsletter at www.nillunasser.com.

MIDLIFE DRIFT: DRUID HEIR BOOK 4

By now, my hopes of a quiet life in the Otherworld are dead and buried. I've accepted that I'm the prophesied eternal girl, but Ezra wants me to keep it under wraps. We can't be certain unless I step into a tank with the magical octopus, and I've had quite enough of batty Wildwoods rituals, thank you very much.

When I receive an offer to turbo charge my druid training, I jump into the deep end and don't flinch. A new threat is rising. I can feel it in my waters, even before Dad is kidnapped and I'm forced into working with my wayward brother. To make matters worse, a rogue goddess emerges to take Londoners to their watery grave.

With Ezra now a senator and Marina knee-deep in researching how to keep me safe, my allies are few and far between, but I still have my trusty leopard. A visit to an otherworldly chiropractor to fend off the midlife aches and I'm ready to live up to my true potential. I'll be damned if Dad and countless others succumb to dark undercurrents on my watch.

If you're a fan of Paranormal Women's Fiction and magic-wielding heroines over forty, continue this journey with Druid Heir Book 4.

ALSO BY N. Z. NASSER

DRUID HEIR

Midlife Dawn, Book 1

Midlife Tremors, Book 2

Midlife News, Book 3

Midlife Drift, Book 4

Midlife Portals, Book 5

Midlife Eclipse, Book 6

Midlife Battle, Book 7

Druid Heir Collections

MAJESTIC MIDLIFE WITCH

To Save a Sister, Book 1

To Curse a Rival, Book 2

To Trick a Raja, Book 3

To Hunt a Foe, Book 4

NEWSLETTER EXCLUSIVES

The Magical Grandmother, Druid Heir Short Story 0.5

A First Date in Paris, Druid Heir Short Story 1.5

Midlife Battle, Druid Heir 7 Bonus Epilogue

To Become a Witch, Majestic Midlife Short Story 0.5

Biryani Junction, a Majestic Midlife Witch Cookbook

ABOUT THE AUTHOR

N. Z. Nasser is a writer of paranormal women's fiction. Her stories are about women who change the world, filled with magic and rooted in friendship.

A lover of barefoot walks along the beach, she is glad to have left behind her career in the civil service and to never wear heels again. Whether she is writing in her garden office or wrangling laundry, she is happiest with a cup of tea at her side.

She lives in London with her husband, three children, two cats and a fox-mad dog.

For new release alerts, you can follow her at Bookbub or Goodreads. For a more personal touch, join her Facebook reader group Nasser's Book Nymphs, say hi on social media, or visit her online store at www.nillunasser.com.

facebook.com/nillunasser

instagram.com/nillunasser